BLOODLINES

To Ed,
Welcome to the Afterlife.
Gordon Bean

Also by Gordon Anthony Bean:

Dawn of Broken Glass
Down the Dark Path, a short story collection

BLOODLINES

Gordon
Anthony
Bean

guardianforeverpub.ca

BLOODLINES
by
Gordon Anthony Bean

Guardian of Forever Publishing
Website: guardianforeverpub.ca
Contact: publisher@guardianforeverpub.ca

Cover design by Pam Marin-Kingsley, Website: pammarin-kingsley.com

Editor: Rosalie Bean

Paperback ISBN: 978-0-9918275-5-8
Ebook ISBN Kindle: 978-0-9918275-6-5

Printed in the United States of America

Library and Archives Canada Cataloguing in Publication

Bean, Gordon Anthony, 1967-, author
Bloodlines / Gordon Anthony Bean.

ISBN 978-0-9918275-5-8 (paperback)

I. Title.

PS8603.E35234B56 2015 C813'.6 C2015-907442-8

This book is dedicated to Al, Doris, Bill, Mollie and Shelley, members of my bloodline who have since moved on. One day we'll meet again in the House.

Also dedicated to Greer, Alexa and Midnight (RIP).

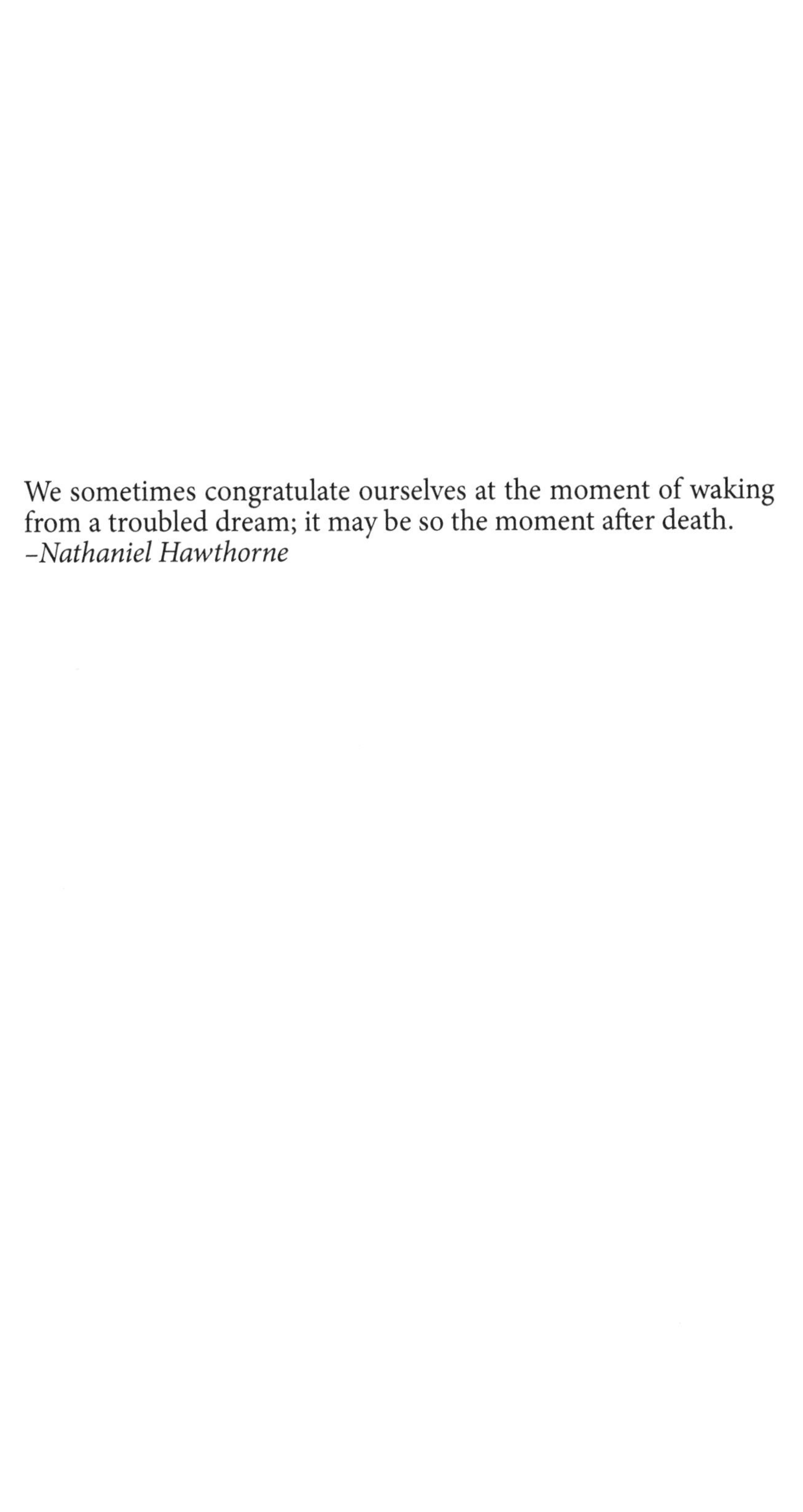

We sometimes congratulate ourselves at the moment of waking from a troubled dream; it may be so the moment after death.
–Nathaniel Hawthorne

PROLOGUE

November 13, 1956

The Packer skidded to the side of the road, and came to a shuddering stop. The wind was blowing a frosty wintry mix in gusting torrents and the wipers were barely able to clear it fast enough. The road was already thickly covered with snow which swirled and spiraled above the ground, making it impossible to tell where the hard packed- clay ended and the soggy, muddy edge of the woods began.

The man stepped out of the car and walked around the front, crouching down to inspect the tire. Cursing loudly, he pounded his gloved fist repeatedly against the hood of the car. He stood up slowly, his head bowed forward as he knew there was no good way to break the news to his wife. Walking over to the passenger side of the car, he motioned for her to roll down the window.

The woman saw the look in her husband's eyes and quickly did as he asked, causing a frigid blast of blowing snow to sting her face. She cried out as the freezing wind blew icy knives across her cheeks and brought tears to her eyes.

"Is it bad?"

He simply nodded.

"Please tell me that you can fix it."

He pulled his scarf down and spit a steaming wad of phlegm into the snow. Within seconds, it was covered by fresh powder. "The front axle is bent. That pothole we hit must have done it. The car isn't going anywhere."

Her eyes widened in horror. "Oh, Tim, we'll freeze out here. I haven't seen another car on this road for at least two hours. What are we going to do?"

Tim let out a long, exasperated sigh. "Better bundle up, dear. It looks like we don't have any choice in the matter. We can stay by the car and hope someone comes by who can give us a lift. The problem is, if no one is foolish enough to venture out in this storm we risk freezing to death in the process. Our other option is to be proactive and try and find someone who can take us in and provide some shelter until this storm ends."

"Tim, we're in the middle of nowhere. We might not find anyone around here who can help us. I don't even remember when we last saw a house"

"Damn it, Marie. We don't have any choice. It's getting dark and cold as Hell out here. I don't want to just sit here and wait to die. Do you?"

Marie wiped her mittened hand across her eyes in a vain attempt to stop the tears. "I guess not."

Tim put his arms around his wife and held her close. After fifteen years of marriage he *thought* he knew her better than he did himself. She was a strong woman who bore him two strong boys who were safe with their aunt in Portsmouth.

He suddenly wished he were back there right now. Instead, he had volunteered to drive up to Quebec to collect whatever personal effects he might want from his father's home before they were sold at an estate auction in two days. It killed him to think of his father, working hard his entire life, only to die from a sudden heart attack while sitting alone watching a hockey game on television. For three days his corpse had lain undisturbed on the couch. When he hadn't shown up to work for two days without any notice, his boss suspected something was wrong and called the police. With Tim being an only child, it was his duty to go up to that miserable little town in Quebec near the US border, settle his affairs and take whatever keepsake from a life he had managed to escape from close to two decades ago. He was grateful to Marie who helped him get through the entire miserable ordeal. Of course, he never dared tell her about the abuse. That was a secret he would carry to the grave. He considered himself lucky to have her in his life.

"Come on, honey," Tim said, desperately trying to keep the fear from his voice, "let's get out of this storm."

They walked along the edge of the road for close to a half hour, bent low to shield their faces from the stinging snow and freezing rain. Even though they both wore hats and gloves, the effects of the storm began to take its toll. Their faces were numb and Marie could barely feel her fingers. She suspected that Tim was in the same boat but was simply too stoic to admit it.

The road took a sharp turn and they found themselves staring at a sign announcing that they were entering Ashland, with the tagline 'Formerly Township No. 11, 5th Range' stenciled in beneath. Tim and Marie looked at each other and smiled. A town meant people and, while they knew they still had to conserve their strength, their chances of getting out of this mess alive were looking considerably better.

They followed the road for roughly a half mile when they saw a paved driveway branch off the main route. The drive was framed by high stone walls, with a large wrought iron gate attached to each wall and joined in the middle of the road. Beyond the gate, the drive wound out of sight behind some trees.

Tim looked at the wall and saw there was no way they could climb it. The walls were simply too high and, with the driving snow and freezing rain beating down on them, they'd never manage to get a handhold on the slick and frozen stones. The gate itself, upon closer inspection, was not actually closed, but held slightly ajar and bound together by a heavy padlocked chain.

Marie looked at her husband. "I think if we take off our coats, we can squeeze through the opening of the gate. What do you think? Want to try?"

Tim was too cold to return to the car a few miles back on the main road and while the idea of taking his coat off in this nor'easter certainly did not appeal to him, at least there was likely shelter beyond the gate on the grounds somewhere. "Okay, let's do it. I don't think we have much choice."

Tim shrugged out of his coat and handed it to Marie. The bitter cold and unyielding elements hit him immediately. He knew he needed to do it quickly. He squeezed halfway through and was about to call to Marie to hand him his coat when his shirt caught on the clasp of the gate. It tore through the thin material and dug sharply into his skin. He howled in pain and pulled himself through the rest of the way.

Marie ran over to the gate and quickly handed Tim his coat. "Tim, are you okay?"

He looked down at the bleeding gash on his chest and then quickly put his coat back on. "I cut myself, but it looks worse than it is. I'll live. Okay, honey, your turn. Just watch for the clasp, okay?"

Marie handed Tim her coat and easily squeezed through the opening. Doing up her coat, she smiled at her husband. "Let's find the house, okay Tim?"

Tim nodded and together they walked down the winding road. The air seemed to thicken and a cold mist slowly blew in. Soon, it was impossible to see more than a few feet in either direction. Tim didn't wish to alarm his wife but he felt sure that they were being followed by something that chose to remain hidden in the mist. A half mile in they came to a clearing. Set back on a huge expanse of ground was the biggest house either of them had ever seen. The front had huge marble steps leading up to a massive door. Large Grecian columns framed the porch on each side. The house was made entirely of grey stone and blended in with a rocky outcrop of the mountain behind it. From their angle, the house seemed to have been built out of the face of the rock.

The house appeared to stretch outward on each side further than they could see, becoming one with the storm and disappearing in the swirling white mists. The home stood two floors high and, while there were many windows, they were all dark and no activity could be seen inside.

They ran across the lawn and up the steps to the door. Up close, they were taken aback at the sheer beauty and elegance of the house. The porch was covered by a small roof and framed by four Grecian columns, two on either side. The porch and the stairs leading up to it were carved from a rich, white marble with grey veins throughout the stone, perfectly complementing the pale grey stones of the walls. The door was a rich mahogany with a gold knocker set in the middle.

Tim looked for a doorbell and, finding none, used the knocker. They heard the sound reverberating from within, but nobody came to answer. Tim knocked again, this time a bit louder. He then tried the door handle and found it unlocked. He gave a gentle push and the door swung open a crack.

"Tim!" Marie cried out, "What are you doing?"

"We can't stay outside because, if we do, we'll freeze to death. Look, if no one is home, we'll at least be warmer than outside. If we find someone inside, I'll explain to them our circumstances. Surely they'll understand."

Marie looked at him and pursed her lip the way she always did when she was stuck making a decision. "Fine," she replied, "but I don't feel right about this."

Tim pushed the door open a bit wider and they both stepped in. Gusts of wind blew snow and ice into the foyer so Tim quickly shut the door behind them. Several oil lamps were already lit so, although the house was still a bit dark, the lamps cast a warm and reassuring glow, causing shadows to dance and flicker against the walls.

"Hello," Tim called out, venturing deeper into the house, "is anyone home?"

His voice echoed quietly off in the distance but elicited no response.

Marie took her husband's hand. "We shouldn't be here."

"Nonsense," Tim replied, trying to ease his wife's peace of mind. "Clearly no one is home. Look, if it were our home, would you fault someone for trying to stay alive by seeking shelter?"

Marie looked down at the ground, unwilling to meet his eyes. "I suppose not. Still…"

A thundering crash came from deep within the house, followed by a scream.

"Someone *is* here, Tim."

"Apparently," he said with the smallest hint of sarcasm.

"Let's leave. Please."

"Damn it, Marie. It sounds like someone is in trouble. The least we can do is check if they're okay."

"Tim. This place gives me the creeps. I mean, a home like this must have cost millions, yet who would live in a place like this in the middle of nowhere? Anybody with that kind of money would be in New York or Los Angeles or at the very least in one of the fancier suburbs of Boston. Also, there were lit candles in the foyer, but the rest of the place is dark. Why would someone do something like that? And did you see any cars in the driveway? People with this kind of money usually have more than one car."

"I see you've been reading the pulps again, Marie. Jesus, do you think this is something out of a Lovecraft or Machen story? Do you think some slithering abomination that should not be will suddenly turn the corner and suck the lives from us? This is real life, dear. Our car broke down in the middle of east butt-plug in the middle of one of the worst nor'easters in recent memory. And we got lucky enough to find somewhere we could ride out the storm. Now it sounds like someone may be in trouble. I'm going to take a look around and see if I can be of help. It's the Christian thing to do, Marie. It's probably best if you wait here, though, just in case there is a problem."

Tim turned back to look at his wife to see if she was okay. Marie looked really scared and vulnerable and Tim felt he really should return to his wife and wait by her side. Just as he had made the decision to return, he heard a small, plaintive cry off in the distance. He was sure it sounded like someone crying for help. He realized he could never live with himself if he simply ignored it and did nothing. His father had been a war hero and raised him to be a man with honor, and that was how he chose to live his life. Tim picked up one of the candleholders and, without another word, started off in the direction of the noise.

"Tim....," Marie pleaded as she watched her husband walk away. She thought of going with him and nearly hurried off after her husband. Marie knew that Tim wasn't a hero like his father, but when push came to shove, Tim was a good man and was always willing to go that extra mile for another human being. She loved that in him. Sure, he would never be president of a company, nor would they ever own a huge home, but he was stable and honest and one of the most caring men she had ever met.

Marie found an overstuffed chair near the entryway and sat down. Tim was already out of sight and Marie was beginning to regret her decision to not go with him. The house was far too quiet and Marie was feeling very alone and vulnerable. She kept seeing movement on the periphery of her vision and, while she knew that it was nothing more than the flickering images from the candles, it made her even more aware of how alone she truly was here. She knew that sitting there all alone, in one of the expensive wing chairs, only made her more paranoid of her surroundings. After careful consideration, she decided to go look for Tim.

Marie stood and took one of the candleholders and began walking in the same direction Tim had gone. The house was far bigger than she could have imagined. The main hallway stretched as far as she could see and, every so often, hallways branched off the main corridor. Down each of the halls were countless identical doors. She tried a few of the doors and found each one to be locked. Marie turned and realized that she had walked further than she thought. The front door was off in the distance but, in the darkened house, she certainly couldn't see it.

"Tim?" Marie called out. Her voice echoed down the hall and seemed to get swallowed up by the thick darkness. She waited for Tim's response but none came. Marie kept walking and called her husband's name again. She paused and waited, straining to hear his voice, waiting for him to call out to tell her that he was fine. As much as she hoped to hear her husband, to reassure her that he was fine, he did not call out to her. She had never felt so alone in her entire life. At this point, Marie knew that she would welcome anyone as company. Anything was better than the sense of utter isolation she was feeling.

She came to the end of the hall and found herself at the bottom of a large spiral staircase that rose up into the darkness. Marie looked up but couldn't see the top of the stairs as they were swallowed up by the gloom. She raised her candlestick, hoping it would shed some light, but it didn't help. She was about to turn back when she heard Tim's voice faintly calling down to her. It seemed to come from somewhere at the top of the stairs. She couldn't make out the words but something about his tone of voice made the hairs on the back of her neck stand on end. After fifteen years, she was well-attuned to her husband. And while she couldn't make out the words, she knew one thing; he was terrified.

Marie ran up the stairs, taking them two at a time. Every instinct was screaming at her to go up slowly, and with caution, but Tim was her life. She reached the top landing and then hurried down a darkened hallway with the flickering glow from the candle as her only source of light. She passed door after door, each one a carbon copy of the one before it.

"Tim?" Marie pleaded, "Are you there?"

Off in the distance, she heard her husband's voice. It was shrill and seemed to come from everywhere at once. "Marie? Oh God, Marie. You need to get the Hell out. Run. Run while you still can."

"Tim, where are you?"

Tim's voice now rang out from behind her. "Marie. I'm so cold and it's so dark. Hold on. Let me see if I can make my way to you. Wait...Someone is here with me. Who's there? Oh my God...Roger, is that you?"

Marie froze. *Did Tim just say Roger?* "What did you just say?" she whispered.

From off to the side, Tim's voice was growing fainter. "Roger. It's me. It's dad. Oh God, is it really you?"

"Tim", Marie shrieked. "What's going on? Where are you? Who's with you?" But Marie already knew. Roger was their first son who had died of leukemia at the age of six. His passing had left a horrible void in their lives. The grief almost tore their marriage apart and it had taken them years to finally heal and claw their way out of the darkness his passing had left them in. As much as she did not want to know what Tim was seeing, she had to see it for herself. She knew one thing. Whatever her husband was seeing, it wasn't their son and she would make him see that too. "Please, honey. Where are you? Please tell me."

Marie waited, but Tim did not say another word. She became very conscious of the fact that she now heard whispering from all around her. The sounds seemed to come from hundreds of voices in many languages. Unable to take any more, she turned to run. From the shadows, a figure seemed to bleed out of the darkness. He was tall and gaunt with pale skin with a hint of grey to it which almost seemed to shine in the dim light. His silver hair was slicked straight back, exposing a lean face with thin lips, an aquiline nose and piercing grey eyes. He wore a black suit that blended in with the darkness and he clutched a mahogany cane with a silver wolf's head at the top. "Hello, Marie," the man said. His deep, baritone voice was so clear, so mellifluous, she felt almost mesmerized. "Welcome to my home."

"Who are you?"

"My name is...Anthony," he replied. He extended his arm and held his hand out for Marie. Against her will, she took his hand. His skin was cool and dry, almost papery, to the touch.

"Anthony," Marie managed to ask weakly, "have you seen my husband?"

Anthony smiled, "Of course, Marie. Tim and I just had the most incredible conversation. He's made himself at home here in the house. He's accepted his journey and is waiting for the next part. Would you like to see him?"

Marie nodded, tears welling in her eyes. "Please, Anthony. Where is my husband? Has something happened to him?"

"Come with me, Marie. I wouldn't want to keep you from your husband. He's been peacefully waiting for you to come join him. But don't worry, Marie. I've got such sights to show you and, once we're done, you can be reunited with Tim." As he led her off into the inky darkness, it just occurred to her that she never told him their names. *How could he possibly know our names?* Anthony opened a door and led Marie inside the room. It took her a moment for her eyes to adjust to her surroundings. She looked off in the distance and saw a shape coming towards her. It was tall and covered with coarse dark fur. It shook and undulated as it moved, almost needing to fold in on itself to gain traction to propel itself forward. She let out a blood curdling scream and closed her eyes as the amorphous terror approached her and seemed to draw her into itself. As she felt her world spiraling away from her, she saw a light off in the distance and her son waving to her. She closed her eyes and embraced the cold darkness.

PART 1

Pulling back the Veil

CHAPTER 1

Windham, New Hampshire. November, 2006. 9 years earlier.

They stood before the huge, sprawling home under a gunmetal grey sky. The crisp air blew cold, odorless gusts around the two men. Aside from a light howl of wind, everything else was as still and quiet as a grave.

Greg Burgess turned back and peered down the road behind him which wound between the tall trees. He assumed it was late fall due to the sharp chill in the air and the fact that the trees were nothing more than large skeletons, bleached of color and reaching their claws upwards as if trying to tear the sky from its moorings. He was about to say something to his brother, Paul, and then he paused. *How did they get here,* he wondered? *Where was their car?* He doubted they had arrived at the old house on foot. Something did not make any sense.

With a quizzical look on his face, Paul turned to his brother. "Greg," Paul asked, taking a moment to pause for his thoughts, "where are we? And, this may sound really stupid, but how did we get here?"

Greg turned to his brother and readied his reply. He had been here before, yet he could not place where or when. He studied his brother, so much like him, yet so different. Paul stood at six feet even with his once dark hair greying and thinning just enough to be noticeable. He had an aquiline nose and a thin mouth that usually held a smirk, as if he were contemplating a secret joke. He had dark bags under his blue eyes and looked weary. He was of medium build and was wearing jeans and a black Italian leather jacket over an Izod

T-shirt. While generally even- keeled, external stressors made him quick to anger, something Paul was working hard to control.

"I was wondering the same thing, Paul. What bothers me is this house seems familiar. I feel like I've been here before but, for some reason, I can't place when. It's more than a sense of déjà vu, though. I feel strangely drawn towards the place, yet it terrifies me."

Paul scratched at the stubble on his chin. He looked at his older brother who seemed lost in thought. Greg also stood at six feet tall, with a light brown hair cut short and slicked back on his head. He wore glasses, a recent change, Paul noted, which made his hazel eyes seem somehow partially hidden and seemed to give his brother a more pensive look. Like his brother, he was also of medium build and wore jeans and an old denim shirt.

"You know, Greg. I feel like I've been here before, too. I can't put my finger on it, but I seem to remember this place, too. Maybe we were here as kids. This might sound strange to you, but somehow I get the sense that something terrible happened in this house."

"That's it," Greg exclaimed. "After our parents were killed in that car crash, and we were sent to our Aunt's house, I dreamt I was here with them."

Paul frowned. "You know something? I did as well. If we both dreamed it, how can we be here right now?"

"Maybe we're both dreaming?"

"The same dream at the same time?"

"I don't know, Paul. Instead of standing here wondering, let's just go in and try and figure out why we're here."

Paul nodded and reached into his pocket. He looked frustrated as he tried all the pockets on his pants, followed by his jacket.

"Did you lose something?"

"Greg, do you have your cell phone? I always carry mine with me but somehow I don't seem to have it."

Greg tried all his pockets and looked at his brother with concern. "No. Not only do I not have my cell phone, but I don't have my keys or my wallet. I never leave home without my keys. I can't imagine why I would now."

Paul glanced at his watch. "My watch is frozen as well. Ten thirty-seven. The second hand is not moving. Want to bet that your watch is stopped at the same time?"

Greg checked his watch and nodded. He glanced back over his shoulder and his eyes grew wide. "I think we need to go inside... now"

"What's the hurry?"

Greg pointed behind them to the two shapes that were coming up the drive. They were roughly man sized, and covered entirely with a thick and glossy fur which glistened in the low light as if wet. They had no arms or legs, with only vestigial stumps instead. They didn't walk, but rather seemed to hurl themselves forward, undulating and shaking. The wind seemed to pick up, whipping itself into a frenzied maelstrom as the creatures approached.

"What the Hell are those things?" Paul shouted over the wind.

"I don't know. I feel like I've seen them before, but it's a thought that is clawing at the edge of my memory and seems to be just beyond reach. One thing is for sure, my instincts are telling me that we better be long gone when they get here. Whatever the Hell they are, they scare the shit out of me." Greg ran up the steps to the large wooden door. Paul quickly followed. The front door stood ten feet high and several feet wide. A large golden handle was directly in the center of the mahogany door. The porch was covered by a large overhang with Doric columns to each side.

Paul looked back and saw that the two shapes were rapidly approaching. "Open the door, Greg!" Paul yelled.

Greg grabbed the brass handle and pulled. The door didn't budge.

"It won't open," Greg screamed. He looked behind them and saw the two shapes were getting closer. He felt a sense of complete dread and, though nothing indicated that these creatures were there to do them harm, his instincts told him to get as far away as possible.

Paul ran up and grabbed the handle. He pulled with all his strength and yet the door remained shut. "What are we going to do? There's nowhere to go. If we go back, those *things* will get us."

"I don't know," Greg said. "I just need some time to think." The wind was blowing with storm-like ferocity. The stench of rotting meat seemed to be carried on the wind and grew stronger as the two shapes approached.

As the brothers were trying to figure out their options, the front door silently opened. Paul noticed it and grabbed his brother by the arm. "Come on, Greg. The door just opened."

"How could the door just open, Paul," Greg screamed over the howling wind.

"Do you care? We can either go inside or face those things and see what they want. Somehow I suspect it isn't an invitation to a barbecue."

Paul and Greg ran into the house and the door slammed shut behind them. "That was close," Greg said. He checked the door and seemed satisfied that it was locked. He heard the creatures pounding on the other side of the door. While he suspected the door would hold, at least for a while, he did not wish to stick around and find out.

"So, now what do we do?" Paul asked.

Greg shrugged. He looked around and saw that they were in a large vestibule that led to a spacious sitting area. The furniture in the sitting area was old and expensive and was centered in front of a fireplace where a hearty fire crackled and blazed, spreading a comfortable warmth across the room. A long hallway led off from the sitting room. Paul tried to see where it went, but it was swallowed up by darkness.

"Should we explore?" Greg asked. He really did not wish to go any deeper into the house than where they were. It was bad enough things felt so familiar to him, but even more chilling was the feeling that he was somehow bound to this house.

Paul looked up at his brother. His eyes appeared to be glazed over and he seemed to be looking through Greg. "I need to leave."

"Where are you going to go?"

Paul started walking down the hallway. "I need to leave," he repeated. "We each have a role to play in the house." He then turned back to look at his brother, his features slack, and walked away, blending into the shadows."

"Wait," Greg called out. He ran down the hallway but his brother was nowhere to be found.

From behind him, he heard the sound of the front door breaking. He knew that those things outside would be in any minute now. If he didn't move quickly, they would soon be upon him and he knew that he wouldn't survive the encounter.

He turned and ran down what seemed like an endless array of hallways. Before long, he was clearly lost. On more than one occasion, Greg stopped in front of one of the countless identical doors that lined each hallway. He considered trying the doors but, at each one, he was struck with a sense of dread. He somehow knew that the doors were not to be opened, so he decided to follow his instinct. Even though there was no sign of his brother and, while Greg was concerned, he somehow sensed that this all had happened before and that they would meet later on.

He came to a curved staircase that led upstairs. Unlike the ground floor, the floor was shrouded in darkness. Greg started climbing, although he had no idea why. He tried to stop himself from going upstairs, but he kept climbing, as if his will were no longer his own.

At the top of the staircase a large hallway extended off into the murky darkness. Greg noticed a small pinpoint of light. He started walking down the dark corridor towards it as the light grew larger. He soon came to a small sitting room where a fire was blazing in a hearth set in the middle of the room. Chairs were positioned around the fireplace which was open to all sides of the room. The fire from the hearth cast warm tendrils of light, pushing back the darkness in flickering waves.

Greg sat down by the fire, enjoying the feeling of warmth and the sense of safety the light provided. He was starting to feel drowsy, and felt himself slumping back in his chair. He was nearly asleep when he felt a strong hand on his shoulder.

"Paul?" Greg asked, while turning. He looked up to see a very tall man with pale skin looking down at him.

"No, Greg," the man said, his voice raspy like wind rustling through tall grass. "My name is Anthony, and I'd like to welcome you to my home." The man smiled, showing a mouthful of very white teeth. His smile appeared forced and looked out of place on his features. "I think you'll like it here. I have such sights to show you." He pulled Greg to his feet and dragged him by the collar into the waiting darkness.

Greg woke up screaming.

CHAPTER 2

In the House. October, 2014. One year ago.

The gaunt man sat and brooded in the darkened hall. The seemingly endless throng of the dead had left and, with the last of them gone to judgment, he had to admit, he was glad to be rid of them. He didn't think it possible, but the very thought of performing his duty left him with a very foul taste in his mouth. He wasn't sure if it was simply a matter of ennui, or whether he had been performing his assigned tasks for so long that they had left him completely and utterly numb.

Just one more year, he thought grimly. One more year and I won't have to listen to any more of their pathetic lies. As if they believed he was so naïve to be unable to see through their pitiful attempts to dissuade him from pronouncing their final judgments. He was a being who was all knowing and all seeing. Time did not exist in the same manner here in the Great Hall. It expanded to include past, present and future. There were simply no secrets that could be hidden from him for long. He sighed. He could do a year easily enough and, compared to how long he had been at his task, what really was a year in the grand scheme of things anyways? He had performed these odious duties for far longer than that and always managed to execute them flawlessly. While he grew tired of the endless parade of souls before him, he took enough pride to ensure they were all dispatched properly. Of course, during his reign there had been one exception. He looked over to the still figure in the corner of the Hall. It had been millennia since he was placed there as punishment, and yet he could not bring himself to release him. He supposed that it was the man's upcoming role in the drama that would soon play out that stayed his hand. Still, while the future was more or less written, time was not entirely immutable and though he had near perfect clarity when it came to his prescience, he was by no means infallible. For some reason, the near future was clouded in enough uncertainty to concern him.

He stood and felt the weariness in his joints. It had been far too long since he was allowed to run free in the tall grass under the welcoming warmth of the sun. It was amazing that after so long, images from his mortal existence still sprung to mind. He smiled wryly and acknowledged that, even after all this time, he still bore some small shard of humanity. His life and very existence was now relegated to a never-ending supply of work in the gloom of this cold and sterile hall. The day when he could leave his work to another and move on was but a year away. Thankfully, at least now there was something to look forward to. Change was imminent and, while he pondered what lay beyond, he found he was actually excited about facing the unknown after such a long and banal existence. Again he smiled, thinking that his grim and somber mood actually made him seem almost...human.

The gaunt man slowly walked down the stairs and stepped onto the polished stone floor. He felt the coldness of the stone through his shoes and welcomed the biting sensation. He walked slowly to the edge of the room and gently ran his fingertips over the smooth surface of the stone wall. He noted the sharp contrast between his pale, alabaster skin and the cold liquid obsidian of the stone. He walked to the nearest brazier and lit the torch that hung next to it. The room filled with a warm, flickering glow. He didn't need the fire for either warmth or light, yet somehow, its presence was comforting to him when his spirit was low.

The man walked the length of the room, and gently stroked the uneven stone wall as he walked. The tactile sensation of his fingertips to the cold stone always made him feel alive and helped him think and put into clarifying perspective things that might be troubling him.

He furrowed his brow and his thin, pale lips twisted into a frown. Things were coming to an end and he still hadn't been shown who was to be appointed his successor. It made no sense. There was only a year left and there were so many details to iron out. It would not be fair to leave his successor with no instructions but, if that was how things were going to be, then so be it. He tried to reach out and see who it might be, but whenever he got close, something blocked him from seeing. There was an order to things and he knew that the next year would prove to be very taxing. Still, he had time to think and plan. Let things fall where they may. As always, he thought, I will be ready.

A rustling noise from above tore him from his thoughts. He didn't see anything up in the shadows but felt a presence that was both familiar and yet entirely repulsive to his very being. It had been a long time since he felt the other's presence, and its taint had not lessened with time. He raised the torch and saw the bird perched on a stone shelf up near the ceiling. It was a large bird with a wing-span that easily measured six feet across. Its head was that of a falcon which was made up of bright red feathers that stood out from the obsidian darkness of the body. Small, black eyes twinkled with hidden malevolence. From its beak sprouted two long fangs which curved somewhat back toward the bird's chest. He had never seen such an abomination, but then he assumed the shock value alone was worth creating such a mismatched creature. Seeing that it was now discovered watching from its hidden perch, the bird-thing threw itself into the air and hurled itself upwards, blending into the shadows.

With a screech that filled the Great Hall, the bird-thing appeared out of the shadows and came at the gaunt man with blinding speed. Its talons raked across his cheek, tearing at the pale skin and muscle beneath as if it were nothing more than parchment. Pools of dark blood welled up in the furrows caused by the creature's talons. With another shriek, the bird-thing took off towards the ceiling, heading for the safety of the long shadows.

The gaunt man saw the bird try to escape. His face contorted in rage, furious at the indignity of being attacked in his own hall. He took the lit torch and hurled it like a javelin at the bird-thing with frightening speed. The creature was struck cleanly in the middle and it let out a horrific shriek as it burst into flames and plummeted to the cold stone below.

The bird-thing landed with a sickening crunch, still partially smoldering from the flames of the torch. The gaunt man walked over to it and kneeled down before the dying creature. He leaned forward so he could look into the creature's eyes and, for a brief moment, he saw something else was there.

Brother, he hissed between clenched teeth, *how dare you send an emissary to spy on me? In my own home no less. This affront will not be tolerated.* He stood and spat on the bird-thing before he reached down and snapped its neck. He held it in his pale hands as he surveyed the Great Hall. While there were no other apparent uninvited guests, the fact that he was being watched was very disconcerting. His brother always had some twisted plot in play which for the most part it was mere posturing, yet this little incident might now spur him on to action. If his brother felt any weakness, he would be quick to take advantage. If he did, the gaunt man felt quite sure that he would handle it as he always had. Sending a creature like the bird-thing could almost be considered as a call to war. Brother would certainly like that, but the gaunt man was far too wily to be lured into a conflict this close to his last days. Still, he knew he must be careful. His brother was very dangerous and would stop at nothing to change how things happened a year down the road.

The gaunt man gazed at the bird-thing's corpse. He knew enough of what was coming and, while his brother was prepared to take chances in order to stir up conflict, he was not. The next year was murky in its predictability and he would do whatever it took to stay the course. Thankfully, he thought, things are now well under way to counter any such measures and ensure that things progress to where they were always fated to go.

CHAPTER 3

Windham, New Hampshire. Two days ago.

Greg awoke with a start. His heart was hammering in his chest and his tee shirt was soaked with a cold sweat and clung to his skin. He looked around his spacious bedroom and noticed that that it was only 3:54 in the morning. His wife Grace lay on the bed next to him, fast asleep, contorted in some odd shape that only she could manage. She stirred slightly, and muttered something incoherent. After all these years of marriage, his wife's little idiosyncrasies still managed to make him smile. He kissed her on the forehead and padded over to the bathroom at the far end of the master suite.

As he relieved himself, his dream came crashing back to him. As he had dreamed so many times over the last decade, he had been in a strange house with his brother Paul, yet in some bizarre way the dream versions of him and his brother seemed different, as if they were them from some other reality. He shuddered at the crystal clarity of the dream. Like all of his dreams which involved the house, he had been there with Paul. He knew that he had never been in that house before yet, somehow, the two of them felt very much at ease in the sprawling gothic mansion. It was as if they had been there many times previously. In all dreams, his brother had left him early in the dream and Greg had simply wandered the halls of the mansion as he felt his unease growing. Something was very wrong and he needed to get away from the home before he lost his very soul, but he was compelled to stay and keep searching. What he was looking for was vague and indistinct, but he knew that if he stopped looking, his life would be forfeit. What was worse than the pervading sense of loss and isolation which echoed through his dream, was the very notion that if he stopped searching he would be at the mercy of the soul eaters. The soul eaters were loose within the confines of the mansion's grounds and Greg knew that if they caught up with him, it would be the end. He knew this with the same fuzzy logic that always accompanied his dreams and, yet, it chilled him to his very core because he sensed it to be true. After losing Paul, Greg had wandered through the mansion alone, experiencing one horror after another. He saw atrocities that he seemed to remember committing in his life, yet it wasn't his life. He was a dreamer in someone else's dream and seemed to be experiencing the other's horror firsthand. He'd eventually come to the end of a long and terrifying search when a familiar man in a black suit appeared. He was tall and very gaunt, with pale skin with hints of grey and Greg felt more afraid of this man than he'd ever been of anyone else at any point in his life. Somehow he felt this man was the harbinger of his Death.

The man took Greg by the shirt collar and dragged him deeper into the house. The older sections were dark and gloomy with cobwebs adorning the walls. Peeling paint and a general state of disrepair only highlighted the dark and oppressive feeling of loneliness given off by the house. This part of the house felt older and neglected. The sense of malaise in the air was palpable.

The tall man stopped before a rotting door and swung it open. Greg stopped at the threshold, refusing to step inside. With barely any effort, the man in the black suit picked Greg up as if he were a child and physically hurled him into the room. Greg landed in a painful heap on the floor and heard the door slam behind him.

Greg stood and surveyed where he was. It was gloomy and long shadows hung over the room, casting fingers of inky darkness that seemed to beckon to him. In the center of the room sat an orange Naugahyde couch facing an old black and white television which showed nothing but hissing static. Sitting motionless on the couch were two figures staring at the set. The rest of the room was bare except for the grimy tan-colored shag rug which covered the floor. The door behind him, he noticed, was firmly shut.

One of the figures turned its head towards him and rasped, "Andrew? Is that you, dear?"

Greg froze in terror. It suddenly hit him that the figure on the couch was his mother. But that couldn't be. *Ma is dead,* he thought to himself. *Ma and pa died in a car accident over ten years ago. This couldn't be them.*

"Ma, is that you?" Greg whispered and slowly advanced towards the couch.

"Andrew?" she whispered, her voice rough like scraping nails over glass, "Come here and sit with your father and me."

Greg paused. He shouldn't be here. He was in someone else's dream and needed to wake up. He pinched himself but could not force himself awake. "Ma, it's me. It's Greg."

She hissed, "Andrew, stop your games and come sit with us... now!" Her voice took on a sharp edge, bordering on a growl.

Greg paused. No fucking way was he going anywhere near that chair. Something was very wrong here. Every fiber of his being was screaming at him to turn and run. But he knew in the pit of his stomach that if he turned around, the thing on the couch pretending to be his mother would get him. He started backing up, slowly and cautiously, not wanting to make any noise and alert the thing masquerading as his mother.

"Andrew," the couch-thing roared, "where the fuck do you think you're going? Your father and I have waited over ten years for you to come home. Now get over here and sit with us." She stood slowly and turned to face Greg. Following her lead, the other shape on the couch, the one belonging to his father, also stood and turned towards him.

Greg screamed and felt his bladder loosen. The couch-thing was indeed some manifestation of his mother, but not the woman he remembered. Her face was a mess, the left side being completely caved in. Her skin was grey and hung in tatters around the ruined left side, hiding the gaping hole where her cheekbone and eye socket used to be. Greg saw the grey, jellied mass of her brain through the cracks in the back of her skull. She grinned, a lopsided and twisted smile, and her one remaining eye twinkled malevolently. "We've missed you, Andrew," she gurgled. "Come and give us a kiss."

Greg backed up even faster. His father stood and walked over to stand next to his wife. He was missing the top half of his skull, his head ending just above the nose, and Greg wondered how the thing that was his father could see without any eyes. It coughed and gurgled and a thick, black ichor drooled from its broken mouth.

"Your father is really happy to see you, Andrew," his mother said, still grinning. "But we can't wait any longer. We need you to join us. We're so very cold, Andrew. We're so lost. We need your warmth and the bright light that shines from your core. Only you can take away all this pain. Come sit with us, son. Be with us forever."

Greg felt his sanity begin to slip. He turned and ran for the door. He tried the handle only to find it locked. He screamed and began pounding on the door, pulling and twisting the handle in desperation to get the door open. He sensed the two things making their way across the room towards him.

Just as Greg managed to wrench the door open, he felt a sharp searing pain in his left shoulder. He turned to see his mother standing right behind him, his father a step behind her. He smelled the fetid stench of her breath and was close enough to see the maggots writhing beneath what was left of her skin. Her bony hand held him securely by the shoulder and dug into the soft skin beneath his shirt.

"I've got you, son," she hissed, "now we can all spend eternity together, as a proper family should."

Without thinking, Greg leaped through the open door and slammed it shut behind him. He heard the screams and obscenities that his mother yelled from behind the door. No matter what vile curses she yelled, neither the mother-thing nor the father-thing made any attempts to open the door. Greg sat down hard on the floor outside the room, closed his eyes and drifted off. It was at that point that he had woken up.

Greg splashed some cold water on his face. His hands still shook. He dreamt of the house off and on for the last decade. Things accelerated recently, as every night for the last month, he had dreamed of being in the house. And each night, his dream took him deeper and deeper into the house, the story unfolding before him in frightening clarity. Tonight's dream was the worst. He had never experienced anything in the dream that had felt so real before. What worried him most of all was the way the dreams were getting stronger and more corporeal with each subsequent night. Dreaming of his dead parents brought back feelings he never wanted to revisit. He had locked them away in his vault, sealed forever. He thought to himself that the government would release the files on JFK's death sooner than he would deal with that mess. Their dying had screwed him and his brother up in a big way. With no relatives willing to take them in, they had bounced around from foster home to the next until Greg turned eighteen and was afforded guardianship of his younger brother. From there, they tirelessly worked until they had managed to turn their lives around and achieve a modicum of success.

"Greg, what happened?"

Greg turned to see his wife standing behind him, her eyes wide with horror.

"What do you mean, Grace? I just got up to go to the bathroom."

"Your back," Grace replied slowly, an expression of pure terror etched on her features. "What happened to your back?"

Greg turned and looked over his shoulder to the bathroom mirror. He froze and stared at the mirror in utter shock. There were five deep and bloody furrows in his left shoulder where the thing that had been his mother had grabbed him in the dream. He wanted to reassure his wife, to tell her everything was okay. But the words wouldn't come. Whatever it was, the threats that lived in his dream had suddenly become all too real.

CHAPTER 4

Seattle, Washington. Two weeks ago.

Megan finished typing the last few words and sat back in her chair, feeling pretty damn proud. She took a long drink from her large, no-fat double mocha café-au-lait and sighed contentedly. Looking around the coffee shop, Megan took stock of the crowd of people all lost in their own worlds. She wanted to jump up and hug the nearest person. After a rough year, she had just finished her first novel and wanted to scream the news from the rooftops. Sure, she knew that she was a long way from having her book see print, but the first step was done. She had written an actual story with a start, middle and end. And damn it if it wasn't an awesome book. Her best friend Josh was a writer and he always said that writing the damn thing was the easy part. What followed next was the painful part: the endless hours working with editors, cover artists, layout professionals and the publisher. After that came the promotion, the public appearances, the interviews and the constant push to sell books.

It took so much work and dedication that Megan wondered why she had bothered. Heck, why *anyone* even bothered was more apropos. People barely read anything these days outside of random blogs. Publishing houses really had no interest in unknown authors and, frankly, the money wasn't there. When you factor in all the time it takes to write a decent novel, your return isn't even minimum wage. She had heard about more than her share of well-known writers who couldn't afford health care, or who had lost their homes or even died penniless. But she knew the truth. Most writers would be thrilled with success, but they were realists and were aware that they might be able to eke out a living but wealth was something that only happened to the lucky few. Most wrote for the sheer love of it.

Megan had to stop herself. She knew she had a tendency to get mired in negativity and this was one time where she wouldn't allow it to take over. She had just written a book, dammit, and this was a happy occasion and cause to celebrate. She forced a sly grin and thought of the pint of rocky road ice cream she had in the freezer. Perhaps a little indulgence, she thought. Maybe she'd call Josh and see if he'd like to grab drinks to celebrate. She always found Josh to be kind of cute and, even though they were only friends, both were single. Megan wondered what Josh would say if she proposed a friendship with benefits. Megan was so lost in thought she barely registered the shadow that had crossed over her table.

"Excuse me, miss."

Megan looked up to see him standing there. He was about forty, six foot two, and, while fairly slim, he had a soft, almost doughy look to his body. His hair was jet black and loaded with enough pomade to keep every hair in place all day. He had a somewhat lopsided face, with a mouth that leaned a bit too much towards the right side of his face. His nose was bulbous and, like his forehead, shiny with oils. He wore tan khakis and a striped red and white Ralph Lauren dress shirt that gave him the look of a giant candy cane. He had on a yellow tie that glaringly clashed with the outfit and Megan forced herself to suppress the chuckle she felt building in her throat.

"Can I help you?" Megan asked cautiously. Although he was dressed somewhat like a circus performer, there was something about the stranger that made the fine hairs stand up on the back of her neck.

The stranger swallowed hard and his Adam's apple bobbed up noticeably. "I saw you," the stranger stammered and tried to regain his composure. He wiped his brow with his red and white sleeve. *His candy cane arms*, Megan thought and stifled a laugh. *He's the candy cane man and he's come to take me away to Candy Land because I'm such a bad girl.* He continued, oblivious to her reaction, "I saw you sitting there and I thought to myself that you are simply the most beautiful woman I have ever seen."

Megan smiled shyly and looked up at the stranger. While he

sounded sincere, she knew his words rang hollow. She was no great beauty. Every morning, standing in front of the mirror she tended to look at herself, sometimes a little too critically. Her face was fine, but nothing that men tended to remember. Her eyes were brown and certainly not the color one tended to get lost in. Her mouth was a little too full and her nose a little too angular. Her long brown hair seemed to have a life of its own and never seemed to style the way she wanted. Her biggest criticisms were reserved for her body which tended towards the thicker side. Her legs, waist and rear were stout and not something that guys looked at in an era where actresses tended to look as if they starved themselves to look like malnourished teenage boys. Her heavier lower half made her small, pert breasts appear almost non-existent. And while she often thought about surgery to augment what little God had given her, His one actual gift, an allergy to silicone, had pretty much made the decision for her. She could always exercise, but she knew that was unrealistic. Between her day job, and writing on the side, she barely had any time for other pursuits.

"Miss," the stranger asked softly, "Are you okay?"

Megan looked over the stranger. He certainly wasn't her type. She knew she shouldn't be choosy. After all, it had been many months since she was last asked on a date and over three years since she last had sex, not counting the little friend she kept hidden in the top drawer of her nightstand. Still, there was no reason to settle. Her life, while certainly not one of a busy socialite, was not bad either. She had several good friends and was rarely alone. Even when she was, her pets and books always kept her company. Besides, she was in her late twenties and the guy was clearly a good decade older than she was.

"I'm really flattered, sir," Megan replied as sweetly as she could, "but I'm just here trying to get some work done. I'm honestly not looking to meet anyone."

The stranger smiled, which looked very inappropriate on his face. It reminded her of the old Mr. Potato Head toy where a plastic mouth was affixed to the plastic potato. Sure, it fit, but it also looked off and out of place. "Of course you are. I'm sorry if I bothered you."

Megan felt a pang of regret. Maybe he was just a nice, lonely guy. Maybe he wasn't so bad after all. "Honestly, you didn't. Thank you for being so understanding."

The man smiled again. "My name is Perry. " He handed her a card. "I often come to local coffee shops looking for fresh new talent. These are the best places to find writers and I'm always on the lookout for the next big thing. I saw you writing and thought I'd see if you were indeed an author. If you change your mind, please give me a call." Perry turned and walked out of the coffee shop and didn't look back.

Megan looked at the card. It read:

PERRY CHRISTOPHER
PUBLISHER/LITERARY AGENT
DARKWORDS PUBLISHING

On the card was a phone number. Megan wondered if she hadn't been too hasty. An agent was exactly what she needed now that the first draft of her novel was done. She was an avid believer in fate and wondered if she was meant to meet him the day she happened to finish her book. She slipped the card in her purse. Perhaps she'd call him tomorrow. After all, what did she have to lose?

Megan finished her coffee and packed up her laptop. She had to get home and feed Ralph and Ed, her two cats. One was an American bobtail, the other an American shorthair, although Megan suspected neither was a purebred. She walked the two blocks to the garage where she had parked her car and rode the elevator in silence. She stopped at her car and absently fished through her purse for her keys.

"Excuse me, miss?"

Megan whirled around and saw Perry Christopher standing there. However, this time, he didn't look shy or uncomfortable. Instead he looked angry, and his eyes seemed hooded and dark. His odd mouth was now twisted into a frown and while his smile looked out of place, the frown looked right at home among his other features.

"Can I help you, Perry?" Megan asked. She tried to keep her tone even, but something in his eyes made her want to run.

"I'm sorry to have bothered you again," he replied, "but you dropped this."

Megan relaxed somewhat. She looked at his closed fist, trying to see what it held. "What did I drop?"

"Your guard," he hissed through clenched teeth and grabbed her by the hair with one hand and shoved a wet cloth over her mouth and nose with the other. Megan struggled, swinging her arms around as wildly as she could, but Perry held on tightly. For someone that looked as soft and weak as he did, he had remarkable upper body strength. She tried not to breathe in the slightly sweet smelling mixture, but trying to shake him free was forcing her to exert too much energy. She took a huge breath of the heady mixture and instantly regretted it. She felt a bit disoriented and less focused. With each breath, her resolve weakened until there was nothing left but the bittersweet oblivion of nothingness.

Megan woke with a splitting headache. Her arms were numb and it took Megan a few disorienting moments to realize that they were shackled to a pipe above her head. She felt a chill and realized she was naked. She tried in vain to cover herself, but she was held too securely.

Megan noticed that her ankles were bound by shackles that were chained to steel stakes driven into the concrete floor, causing her legs to be partly splayed. She pulled one leg back, testing the amount of give. She managed to get her leg back enough so that her knees were fully bent. In doing so, she felt a sharp stabbing pain between her legs. She looked down as best she could and saw with horror that her genitals had been fully shaved. Even worse was the sticky pool of blood that was coagulating on the concrete floor beneath her. *What has he done to me*? She shuddered as a series or horrible images flashed through her mind.

Looking around the room, Megan saw she was in a dark basement, with the only source of light coming from the single bulb hanging from the center of the ceiling. The light given off was low, making the corners of the room seem dark and menacing. The basement was fairly nondescript. It was mostly empty except for a work table at the other side of the room. From her vantage point on the floor, she couldn't see what was on the top of the table. To her left were a row of cages, but, due to the dimness of the light, she couldn't make out what, if anything, was kept in them. *Or anyone*, she thought grimly. Straight ahead was a set of old wooden stairs that presumably led up to the house. Perry's house, she thought. And if the number on the card had been valid, the area code indicated that it was in the Seattle area.

Megan struggled but quickly realized she wasn't going to get loose. She was all too aware that no one knew where she was and that she was likely going to die alone in this basement. She felt the tears starting and hated herself for being so weak. She couldn't stop herself and cried until she fell asleep.

Megan was awakened by a cold hand caressing her body. She looked up to see Perry Christopher on his knees between her legs running his hands over her shoulders and over her breasts. He was breathing very hard and had a thin film of sweat on his oily brow. His eyes were glazed and he looked drugged.

"Get off me," Megan screamed. She tried to jerk her body away from him but the chains were too tight. Perry ignored her and began licking her neck. Megan cringed as she felt his hot breath on her, rank and fetid, leaving behind a greasy wetness on her skin. She tried changing positions, but Perry kept at her. After a while he stopped and looked up at her and smiled. Megan spit into his face, the only act of defiance left to her. Perry's grin dropped and a dark cloud crossed over his features. He stood and then kicked her in the ribs over and over again until she lay there whimpering in pain, barely able to breathe, let alone move. He then grabbed her by the hair and punched her in the face.

Perry unbuckled his belt and slid his trousers to the ground. He took himself in his hand and spit on his already engorged member. The last thing Megan heard before she blacked out was Perry's growl that he was going to tear her apart.

CHAPTER 5

In the House. Present day.

Jason sat up and took stock of his surroundings. He was naked in bed in a sparsely furnished room that looked washed of color, as if he were viewing the world through a sepia-tinted lens. He recognized his surroundings as his old bedroom back when he had been married. But that was long ago and something felt very wrong with his being here again. His wife, Rachel, was fast asleep next to him. *As she had been the last time he saw her alive.* Jason shook his head as if trying to shake the cobwebs. *Where had that thought come from?* He stood up and crossed the room to the window. He looked out on the early morning streets of the Haifa district he called home. The sun cast a warm golden glow over the rooftops of the houses across the street from him. Despite being a little arid, the air was pleasant and warm, and carried with it the familiar smell of suburbia. *The smells of home*, Jason thought. There wasn't a soul in sight, but Jason knew better. Even though there was peace yesterday, there was always the chance of unrest. Such was life in Israel. He had wanted to leave and emigrate to the United States, but Rachel had refused. She had adamantly told Jason that she had been born in Israel, and that she would die there. *In a vicious terrorist attack that would leave her and their unborn child a bloody mess in the street,* he thought grimly.

Jason walked to the kitchen and poured himself a glass of water. He felt good being home with Rachel, but somehow knew that he no longer belonged there. He had the fleeting image of an old man in a large home in the United States, which struck him as odd because, to date, Jason had never been out of the country. Jason was a young agent in the Mossad with an upward career trajectory that made him one of the agency's most promising recruits of the last decade.

Jason looked around the kitchen and glanced at the calendar. It read 18 Kislev 5754. He froze. How could that be? That was the day Rachel had *died*. He paused. How could he possibly know that? Even worse was the fact that he thought of himself as Jason. That wasn't his name. Even in his assignments he had never taken that name yet, somehow, it felt very familiar and comforting as if he were as accustomed to the name as he was to his own. He had been born Ari Friedman in Tel Aviv on 28 Nisan in the year 5731. His father was Chaim and his mother was Hanna. Both were former Americans who had decided to move back to the Holy Land and become citizens of Israel. His father had been a teacher and his mother a homemaker. The lived a simple life free of excess and extravagance, but it didn't matter because they were happy. They knew that they were each other's soul mates and there wasn't a day that went by when they didn't feel an affirmation of that. Their happy existence had been brutally cut short one afternoon close to a decade ago when a bomb strapped to a six year old Palestinian girl exploded in the café where they were having lunch. They were killed instantly. It was that day that young Ari made the decision to join the Mossad. He strongly identified with everything that the Institute for Intelligence and Special Operations stood for. He was tired of living in fear and wanted his homeland to be safer for his people. It seemed as if the threat to Israel grew daily. No matter what the Israelis did, their enemies always seemed to come up with new ways to try and kill them. Sometimes he wished his life had taken a different route

"Ari," Rachel called from the bedroom, "are you home?"

"I'm in the kitchen."

Rachel came into the kitchen as naked as Ari and put her arms around him. She stood at five foot three with shoulder-length brown hair. Her skin was a light olive color which made the bright green of her eyes look even more striking. She had a lean face with high cheekbones and a full mouth. Ari always believed she could have modeled had she been so inclined. Each day that he was able to gaze into her eyes confirmed the fact that marrying her had been the best decision of his life. And, with the news that Rachel was pregnant, life couldn't have gotten any better. She gently kissed him and held him tight. She eventually broke their embrace. “I had the oddest dream last night. I was in this dark maze and something was following me. Every time I turned around, it always managed to be just out of reach. I looked for you but you were nowhere to be found. I was so scared, Ari.”

“Shhhhh,” Ari said softly, gently stroking his wife’s hair. “It was just a dream.” Yet, despite reassuring his wife, his thoughts suddenly clouded over. He dimly remembered something of a maze, and the very thought of it filled him with mortal dread. He seemed to recall someone in a maze, someone large and menacing, but obscured by shadows. No matter how hard he tried, the memory was fleeting and danced there on the periphery of thought, just out of grasp.

Rachel stood on her tip toes and kissed Ari. “I know. I’m just glad you’ll always be here by my side. It makes me feel safe and secure.”

Ari frowned. If today was the day that Rachel was supposed to die, and that he had some knowledge towards that end, then he would do whatever he could, no matter what it took to ensure that his wife lived. He wondered if saving Rachel would alter his future and whether the pieces of memory he seemed to have from future events would disappear completely.

Ari took Rachel by the hands and led her to the couch. “What do you have planned for today?” he asked.

Rachel smiled. “I really don’t have too much planned. I have some errands to run. After that, I thought I’d visit with my mother. Why do you ask?”

“Because I thought I’d spend the day with you today.”

Rachel frowned. “Is everything okay at work? Is there anything you can talk about with me that is not a matter of national security?”

“National security?” Ari laughed. “You know I’m just a junior agent. Trust me, Rachel. I don’t think I’ll be privy to any dark secrets anytime soon.”

Rachel smiled and her eyes twinkled. “In a few years, my dear Ari, you will be running the Mossad.”

“That will be the day.”

“I have faith in you, my husband, even if you don’t have the same faith in yourself.” Rachel stood and turned towards the bedroom. She gave him a coy smile, winked and said, “Well, if you are to be home today, perhaps you can help me out in here.” She then flounced into the bedroom. Ari quickly got to his feet and followed. He would stay by her side and make sure whatever memories he had of her death were wiped clean and replaced with others of their long and happy lives together.

Ari kept by Rachel's side as she ran her errands. Every person who approached them fell under Ari's scrutiny. After a while, he began to wonder if he was being foolish. He had nothing to go on but a gut instinct that Rachel would die. For all he knew, it was a remnant of a past dream.

They had lunch at a quiet outdoor café. The streets were busy, but nothing more than normal. Ari wished he could relax and simply sit back and enjoy his wife's company, but he trusted his instincts. They had gotten him through life and managed to get him into the Mossad where he was regarded as an up and coming agent. He would trust these instincts now as well.

Lunch was uneventful, and they had a wonderful meal of *schnitzel* at their favorite restaurant. After their coffees, they walked through the downtown core taking in the sights. They still had some time before she was due at the obstetrician's to discuss her upcoming delivery. As it was such a beautiful day, they decided to walk around the town.

They walked to a park and sat on one of the benches. Ari marveled at how close they were to the senseless violence that raged through the Middle East, yet here they sat in such an idyllic setting. He held Rachel's hand and they sat in a comfortable silence while watching some children run and play. Across the park a woman in a black hijab walked with a young girl in each hand. Ari glared her way, but she did not notice him. She seemed a lot more preoccupied in controlling her children. The girls then broke away from their mother and ran to play with the other kids.

The woman in the black hijab walked over to the bench next to Rachel and sat down. She looked over at Rachel and nodded a silent greeting. Rachel smiled back. Ari leaned back, letting the sun warm his face. So far, his day had been perfect. He checked his watch and turned to Rachel. "We have to go. We're due at the clinic in ten minutes."

They crossed the park and walked to the clinic. It was fairly modern and staffed by doctors from the US who had decided to make Israel their home. Their obstetrician ran his series of tests and told them that, barring anything surprising in the test results, the baby was doing fine and appeared to be perfectly healthy.

They walked out of the doctor's office and started down the stairs to the ground floor lobby. Ari noticed the woman from the park walk in the front doors, followed by her two girls. Her hands were shaking and she seemed a bit unsteady on her feet.

"Ari," Rachel asked, pointing to the woman in the black hijab, "isn't that the woman from the park? Something looks wrong with her. She looks sick or something."

Ari's guard immediately went up. "I think we should get out of here."

Rachel started down the stairs calling back after her. "I'm sorry, Ari but that's nonsense. She needs help and there doesn't seem to be anyone around to help her."

Things unfolded all at once. Ari screamed at Rachel to stop, and started to follow her down the stairs. Meanwhile, the woman dropped her hijab and dress, revealing dozens of sticks of explosives taped all around her. Her children did the same.

Rachel froze and turned back to Ari who was desperately trying to reach her. Everything seemed to happen in slow motion. The woman and her children exploded in a blinding sonic blast, destroying everything around them. Rachel stood there, a tableau frozen in time. Ari watched in horror as the blinding light rose up and shredded his beautiful wife before his very eyes. He felt the concussive blast and was lifted violently backwards. Ari felt a numbing pain before everything went dark.

CHAPTER 6

Windham, New Hampshire. Yesterday.

Greg woke up screaming. He had the dream again, but this time it was even more disturbing. In tonight's dream he was in the house with his daughter, Amy, following the same path that he had in each of his previous nightmares. They ran into Paul in the same upstairs room as always. Only this time, his children were with him as well. He sat there in a semi-lucid state alongside his son Mike and daughter Beth. As Greg and Amy entered the room, Paul and his kids turned slowly together to stare at them. Their eyes were a glossy liquid black.

"Hello, Greg," they all said in unison, "why don't you and Amy come sit with us while we wait?"

"Wait for what?" Greg asked nervously. He looked over at his brother and saw that they were all smiling.

"Why the Soul Eaters, of course," they replied in a sing-song kind of way. "They are almost here and they are coming to eat your souls". They all started to giggle and tears of a thick dark, black blood began to flow down their cheeks.

Paul and his kids stared expectantly at Greg. "The Soul Eaters have come from far away. Our souls are drawing them to this house. Let's all sit and wait together, brother. There's no use resisting them."

Greg was horrified. He turned to Amy and saw that her lips and eyes were sewn shut. *When had that happened?* She clawed at her face and struggled in vain to rip open the stitches. She tried to scream but only managed a low muffled cry. Greg picked her up and threw her over his shoulder in a fireman's carry as he prepared to run. He turned back to his brother and saw that he and his kids had assumed the same trance-like state as before and that their eyes and mouths were also sewn shut. Greg and Amy left the room and they ran down hallway after hallway looking for the way out. He didn't understand how he could have gotten lost. The house didn't appear to be that big. No house was endless yet, somehow, in the dream, *and all his instincts were screaming at him that he was indeed dreaming*, he knew for a fact that the house was truly endless. He was helplessly lost. He ran past rooms that looked eerily familiar. From other rooms he heard voices long forgotten. He didn't dare stop or open any of the doors. The memory of the room with his dead parents was still fresh in his mind. Amy began to cry and Greg felt helpless as he watched black tears squeeze past the sewn eyelids. He heard a primal roar and he knew, somehow, that the Soul Eaters were in the house and looking for them. He felt a twinge of shame when he realized that he hoped the Soul Eaters took their time with his brother's family so he and Amy could have some time to escape.

Greg ran down a hallway that wound up at a dead end. He turned and saw a tall, gaunt man with pale skin with grey highlights and angular features that seemed to extend from the shadows. He froze as he recognized the stranger from his previous dreams. The stranger seemed to glide towards him and came to a stop just in front of him and Amy.

"Your destiny is here, Greg," the pale man said, his voice rough and grating like crushed glass. "I have been waiting a long time for you and Paul...and especially the children. The time of the Ascension is here. It's time for you to come to the house and fulfil your destiny."

"Who are you?" Greg asked, looking around the hallway for something he could either use as a weapon or as a means to get free of this man.

"My time draws to a close and yours is drawing near. Hear me, Greg Burgess. The Key from your past will unlock the way to the House. Though the Key is needed to enter, it takes the mighty Oak to get you here. Remember my words, Greg, for all eternity depends on it."

"Ok. That's great. Now let me pass." Greg pushed his way forward and was surprised to see the man step aside. With a fluid motion, the man grabbed Amy and melted back into the shadows. Amy howled in terror and, even though her lips were tightly sewn shut, she still managed the most mournful wail Greg had ever heard. Greg turned and saw the man disappear with his daughter into the liquid darkness. He ran after them and smashed straight into a wall. The stranger and his daughter were gone. Only her screams still lingered.

Greg awoke once again soaked in sweat. He looked at the clock radio on the table next to his bed and saw that, like all the other times he had awakened from one of his nightmares, it was 3:54 in the morning. Something felt very wrong, though. There was a different feel in the house than before. His home felt unclean as if his space had been personally violated.

Greg threw on a robe and ran to his daughter's room. He saw her covers piled up on her bed but he didn't see her, even though she usually slept on top of the covers. He touched the elephant pillow pet she used to sleep on and found it warm to the touch, as if she had just gotten up from the bed. He felt an icy twinge of fear grip his chest. He began frantically looking around her room. He checked under her bed, in her closets, and then raced about the house, from room to room, calling his daughter's name. Amy was nowhere to be found.

Greg heard his wife call from their bedroom. "Greg, is everything okay with Amy?"

He swallowed and called to his wife. "Grace. You better come here. I'm downstairs in the den"

"What's wrong?" she called back, the nervousness apparent in her tone.

"Just come here," he snapped, as the rage began exploding from him. "It's urgent."

Grace ran downstairs, taking the stairs two at a time. She looked around, her eyes wide with panic. "What's wrong? Did something happen to Amy?"

"It's about Amy," Greg said softly, trying to keep himself from completely losing it. "She's gone."

"What are you talking about? Where is Amy?" She grabbed his

arm. "Where the Hell is our daughter?"

Greg looked down at his feet. "I'm not sure about this, but I think she was taken by the man in my dreams?"

"What? Greg, are you insane?" Grace screamed. "I'm calling the police."

"Dammit, Grace. Sit down and I'll tell you what I know first."

"Our daughter is missing and you're asking me to be calm? Are you out of your fucking mind?"

"Sit down, Grace," Greg screamed. Grace saw the look in her husband's eyes and reluctantly sat down.

Greg began slowly. He told Grace about the nightmares he had been having every evening. He told her that tonight's dream had been different and that instead of being threatened by his dead parents, the mysterious figure in the dream had babbled something incomprehensible about keys and oaks and then snatched their daughter away.

"I don't understand this, Greg. Dreams are just dreams. They're not real. And they certainly don't have some creepy guy crossing over into our reality just to steal our child."

Greg gave his wife a reassuring hug. He felt her tremble. He always counted on her to be his rock, but tonight she was on the verge of a complete breakdown. "I don't think he wants to hurt her. He said it was my destiny to be in the house. I think he's using her as a lure to get me there."

Grace started crying. "This is insane. This makes no fucking sense. I just don't buy it. Someone must have broken in and taken her."

"Damn it, Grace, look around the house. All the doors and windows are locked. The alarm is still on. There is no way anyone could get in and out without setting off the alarm and waking us."

They went back upstairs and looked around Amy's room hoping to find something that would serve as a clue to their daughter's disappearance. Grace sat on Amy's bed, picked up her pillow pet and buried her face in it as she broke down in a torrent of grief. "I don't care what you think, Greg. Somehow she got out. Just call the damn police, okay?"

Greg sighed and did as told. Even though the police said they'd be right over, he knew they could not possibly help. Unless the cops could patrol his dreamscapes they would only be wasting everyone's time. It was time that Greg could be using to find his daughter and the pale man who abducted her.

The police arrived fifteen minutes later and spent the next hour asking questions and taking notes, looking at the house, and checking for any sign that would indicate that she was abducted. They eventually left, but not before making Greg feel very uncomfortable, as if he were the one the police considered a suspect. The very thought repulsed him. He loved his little girl and would never harm her. He'd sooner take his own life.

Greg decided that his best bet would be to find the house of his dreams and the gaunt, tall man. He knew this would be much easier said than done. Somehow, his dreams held the clue as to the whereabouts of the house. He was heading to the computer to start his web search when the telephone rang. Grace picked it up and after a few minutes came over to Greg, handing him the phone.

"Who is it?"

Grace paused. Her features were drawn and pale. "It's your brother, Paul. It seems as if he also dreamt about that damned house. According to Paul, you were in the dream as well."

"Why is he calling then at this hour of the morning?"

Grace wiped the tears from her eyes. "He said there was this tall, skinny pale guy with dead eyes who took his kids during the dream and that when he awoke they were gone."

Greg took the phone and, after a few minutes, confirmed that his brother's kids were gone as well. Greg told him that he didn't have a clue as to where the house could be. All he knew is he had been there before. He didn't have anything concrete on which to base this hunch. It was at best, a residual memory. Paul didn't have any other ideas so he agreed with Greg that they would get together in the morning, after they had a chance to think about things and to plan their next steps. Then they would find the kids and then make the bastard who took them pay.

CHAPTER 7

Egypt. 2,566 BC, 4th Dynasty.

The men lined the shadowy hall of the great pyramid. They stood patiently and silently until they were able to shuffle another step forward. Each man held a small Canopic jar in his hands. The men did not speak. Their mouths were sewn shut as were their eyes. The men each had ragged gouges in their chests leaving a gaping, empty hole where their hearts used to be. The hearts were safely held in the jars, ready to be weighed in judgment by the Lord of the Dead.

At the front of the line, Khufu waited to be admitted to the Great Hall. Eventually, the stone doors swung open and he shuffled in. Great braziers lined the stone walls of the Great Hall, casting flickering and dancing shadows over the walls. Set back against the far wall was a large golden throne which sat atop a stone dais. Four stone steps led up to the throne. The floor of the Great Hall was a polished black marble and reflected the light cast from the flames in the braziers.

Sitting on the throne was a tall bronze man. He was naked except for a diaphanous linen robe thrown loosely over his shoulders and had a belted and pleated leather Shendyt that he wore about his waist. He was long and lean and his musculature was perfectly defined. The air in the Great Hall was humid, almost moist, and the man's skin glistened with a light perspiration. His head was that of a large black jackal and his yellow eyes, with vertical black pupils, glared at Khufu as he approached the throne.

Khufu kneeled in supplication at the base of the dais and waited for his God. The tall jackal-headed man stood and stepped down to stand before the kneeling man. He spoke in Coptic, in a deep resonant voice that seemed to come from everywhere at once. He held out his hand and beckoned to the kneeling man. "*The jar, Khufu, give it to me.*"

The kneeling man kept his head bowed and reverently raised the Canopic jar. The man with the jackal's head took the jar and carried it over to a large table which stood next to the throne's dais. On the table was a golden two-sided scale. Also visible on the table were several ostrich feathers.

The tall jackal-headed man lifted a feather and held it up before the kneeling supplicant. "*Ma'at!*" he cried out. "*Let your judgment begin, Khufu. And let the feather reveal the truth.*"

Khufu dared lift his head and angled it towards the tall man. He spoke slowly and with difficulty through his sewn mouth. "Wise Anubis, I am a good man. Please don't let a few harsh years while I was Pharaoh be all there is to judge my soul."

Anubis' yellow eyes seemed to flare for a second. "*Know your place, mortal, or without ceremony I will call Ammit.*" He then reverently placed the feather on one side of the scale.

Even in the low light, it was obvious that Khufu grew very pale. He lowered his head and returned to his bowed state. Ammit was the worst possible outcome. The feared Devourer, who would come to our world to eat the souls deemed too far gone to be either offered redemption or moved on to a higher plane. Ammit would then create a new soul from the shards of the old, leaving nothing behind of the former soul's spirit. It was a final death and one feared by all.

Anubis walked over to the stone table and took the lid off the Canopic jar. He grabbed the still-beating heart from the jar and placed it on the scale on the other side of the feather. The scale stood still for a moment and then the side with the heart came heavily downward.

Anubis' yellow eyes flared. "*Judgment has been made. Khufu, stand to receive sentence.*"

Khufu stood on trembling legs. He didn't beg or plead. He would go into the afterlife with his dignity intact.

Anubis raised his hands above his head. "*Ammit…devourer… soul-eater, you are called. Come and claim your soul.*" The air behind him seemed to get thick and started to shimmer. An almost imperceptible tear appeared in the fabric of the air and slowly expanded downward until the rip was several feet long. Khufu gasped as a long, almost shapeless stump covered in a glossy black fur reached through the rift, followed by another. The Soul Eater was coming.

CHAPTER 8

Toronto, Ontario. Yesterday.

David sat up in bed and wiped his eyes. His hands felt wrong, somehow. In fact, everything felt off. He felt more energy than he had in years. He jumped out of bed and headed to the mirror above the dresser. His ten year old face stared back at him. *That's not me*, David thought. He ran his small hands through his chestnut brown hair. *Did I really keep it this long*, he wondered. He absently ran a finger over the line of freckles across his nose. *These will fade as I grow up*, he mused. He saw posters hung crookedly on the walls and books and sports cards casually tossed on the dresser. He was back in his childhood bedroom. He hadn't thought about his youth in years, and now he was back. David wondered if he was dreaming. It seemed too vivid, too real, yet he knew he wasn't ten. He was a grown man staring down the barrel of fifty.

He threw on a tee shirt and a pair of jeans and walked to the bedroom door. He tried the light switch but the room stayed dark. He flicked the switch up and down a few times, but the light would not go on. *I wonder if the power is out*, David thought, but when he saw the digital readout from his clock radio, he quickly put that idea to rest. Perhaps it was best to get his parents.

David walked out of his room, stepping cautiously into the hallway. His door closed hard behind him, the noise reverberating like a gun shot in the stillness of the house. He turned around and saw that the door was no longer there and that he was no longer in his house. He stood and stared down a long hallway. The walls were pale beige and streaked with dirt. The overhead fluorescent lights flickered and alternately changed the hallway from a low gloom to near total darkness. An antiseptic smell filled the air, with an undercurrent of a cloying odor that seemed both ripe and moist. On each wall were several doors, all of which were closed.

David scratched his head. *Had he been here before*? The hallway looked familiar, but ever since his rapid fire series of Transient Ischemic Attacks the prior year, his memories were often random bits and pieces that he had to try to weave together.

David tentatively began walking down the hallway. He tried the first door on his right and found it to be unlocked. Inside the room he saw a bed, a dresser, and a small old- fashioned television perched on top of the dresser. Someone appeared to be asleep on the bed, nestled under the covers. He walked over cautiously, not wanting to wake whoever was lying there. Reaching out a tentative hand, he firmly grasped the rough grey blanket and pulled it back to reveal an elderly woman lying prone on her back. Her face was an ashen grey and the skin was drawn tight around the skull. Her snow-white hair was sparse and fell limply over her forehead. The woman's eyes were open and glazed over, the pupils all clouded. Her mouth was agape, revealing dark gums pulled back over yellowed teeth. It took a moment for David to realize that he knew her. It had been nearly forty years since he had last seen her, but the realization came as sudden as if being doused by cold water.

"Grandma?" he said weakly. He had last seen his grandmother in the hospice two weeks before she died. His parents felt that during her last days, she was too weak for visitors and that David was too young to see his beloved grandmother waste away to nothing. The funeral had a private viewing for close family only but, again, David's parents felt that he was too young to see his grandmother in a coffin and preferred to have him stay home with a sitter. Seeing her like this right now was too much for David to bear.

David was about to turn away when his grandmother slowly sat up in the bed. She turned towards him, her lifeless eyes following his movement. She raised her withered arm and beckoned to him. "Come here, David," she said, her voice low and guttural, "let me have a look at you. It's been so long."

David froze. He stared at his dead grandmother and weighed

his options. *Did she mean to hurt him? Could he run?* David's adult reasoning was intact in his ten year old form and allowed him to decide to stay and hear what exactly she wanted from him. He moved a bit closer but managed to stay slightly out of reach, just in case.

David's grandmother grinned, but there was none of her former warmth or compassion in it. Seeing his grandmother like this, hovering on the brink of death, made David want to turn and flee right then and there. As she smiled, the skin on her face split at the edges of her mouth and tore through half her cheek. She licked her lips with a black and swollen tongue. "David," she said, her voice rough and grating, "you grew up to be such a fine young man. It's a pity I never lived to see it."

"Grandma, why are you here?" David asked. "Why am I here?"

Grandmother smiled again, her eyes seeming to shine in the dull light. She leaned forward and placed an old locket in his hand. David looked at it and sensed that he'd seen the piece before. He closed his hand over it and felt it tingle in his palm. "I came to warn you, David. A storm is coming and the decisions you make will determine whether your family lives or dies."

David froze. "What do you mean, grandma? How does this affect my family?"

Grandmother wheezed and forced herself to speak. When she did, it was as if her vocal cords were drawn over broken glass. "An old friend will come to see you very soon. What he has to say will make you question his very sanity, yet you must listen. More importantly, you must do as he says or everyone will die, including your wife and kids."

"Who will come, grandma?" David asked. "What do they want? More to the point, how will my choices affect the lives of my wife and kids?"

Before David's grandmother could reply, a man burst into the room. He was dressed all in black, with pale, alabaster skin and long, jet black hair slicked back and flowing down to his shoulders. His eyes were bright gold and seemed to be glowing. He held a spear in his hand and in a single, fluid motion plunged it deep into the old woman's left eye. She screamed and then lay still.

The man turned to David and snarled, showing his contempt. For a brief second, his face flickered out of focus and was replaced by that of a bird. *An eagle or perhaps a falcon*, David thought. The man smiled, showing perfectly white and very sharp teeth. He gestured to David's grandmother on the bed. "Consider this a warning, David," the man in black said. "When your old friend shows up, you will politely listen and then send him on his way. If you do not do exactly as I say, I will personally visit your family and rip out the still beating hearts from their chests."

David woke up screaming. His heart was racing and his shirt stuck to his chest from the heavy perspiration.

His wife sat up in bed and looked over at her husband. His eyes were wide and she was fearful that he might have had another TIA. "Are you all right, honey?" she asked, terrified what damage another such event might do to his brain. The doctors had warned them that another stroke would cause irreparable damage to his brain and permanently impair his faculties and motor skills.

David looked at his wife and held her tightly. He thought back to his dream and knew what he had to do. "I'm okay, honey, but I have to tell you something. I think I'm going to have to leave soon. If I don't, you and the kids will be in great danger."

"It was just a dream, David."

David held out his trembling hand. In it was his grandmother's locket. "My grandmother just gave this to me. If it wasn't real, or didn't happen, then how in God's name do I have her locket here with me now? She was buried with it, for God's sake."

David's wife looked at him, her expression a mix of fear and curiosity. "Are you sure you didn't have this before you went to bed? You know your memory has been spotty since the accident."

David stood up and paced the length of their bedroom. He stood at the window and looked out over their yard. He had worked hard to provide a good life for his family. He wouldn't allow anything to take that away. He turned and hugged his wife. "I'm sure, honey. Whatever is going on, it's real, and I'm somehow involved. An old friend is coming, and then I'll need to leave for a while."

"How long will you be gone?"

David hugged his wife even tighter. "I honestly don't know. I don't even know if I will be coming back." His wife held on to him and refused to let go. He felt her tremble. He wished he had the words to comfort or reassure her, but they wouldn't come.

She let him go and looked at the man she had been with since high school. He was older and greyer, but she still saw the same shy high school kid who captured her heart. "You'll be back, David. Do what you have to do, and then come home to us."

CHAPTER 9

Lasalle, Quebec. Yesterday.

Kevin awoke to find his brother sitting at the foot of his bed. This normally would not have been such an odd occurrence, but his brother Brian had been dead for years of an accidental overdose of prescription medicines and painkillers. Kevin, of course, remembered that little incident very vividly because he had been the one who found his brother dead and cold to the touch, looking like he was fast asleep in the overstuffed living room chair. Instead of the grownup Brian whose life had taken far too many wrong turns, the happy child version of him sat there. Ten year old Brian, with his whole life ahead of him, sat there smiling like he didn't have a care in the world, blissfully unaware of the horrible, mangling accident that would ruin his right arm a few months later, the first of many tragedies to befall him.

Kevin looked over at Leanne who slept peacefully beside him. She was a very sound sleeper and not even an earthquake could wake her, if Lasalle ever had them. His daughters would be asleep as well, although the older one occasionally slipped out at night to see her boyfriend. He rubbed his eyes and looked back to the foot of the bed. Brian still sat there, his smile twisted into the kind of malicious grin that could only come with youth.

"Hey, Kevin," dead Brian said cheerfully.

Kevin rubbed his eyes again, hoping that when he stopped, his brother would no longer be there. Work was tough enough, and he sometimes felt like he was at the end of his tether, yet he was always pretty grounded. He was, if anything, a very practical man. And practical men certainly did not believe in ghosts, nor did they see their dead brothers sitting on their beds trying to engage in conversation.

Kevin looked up at the foot of his bed and Brian still sat there. "Who are you?" he asked. "You're not Brian. I was there when he was buried."

Brian's ghost just smiled. He stood up and Kevin watched as he started growing older. His arm bent and withered, showing all the same signs his arm had shown months and years after his accident. He reached manhood and gained some weight. His face lost some of its healthy glow, only to be replaced by a greyish pallor. His hair turned brittle and started falling out. His skin greyed even further and was soon blended with a mottled purplish black. The skin pulled back around the mouth, exposing his teeth in a semblance of a grin. His eyes pulled back into their sockets, exposing gaping black holes. A maggot crawled from one eye socket to the other.

"Is this better, Kevin?" Brian said with rasp, his once youthful voice now raw and hollow. "Do I look the part of a ghost? Want me to float around the room and moan like something out of a cheap horror movie?" Brian then laughed and resumed his ten year old form.

"Damn it, Brian," Kevin cursed. "What are you doing here? I have enough shit in my life without my dead brother starting to haunt me."

Brian threw his head back and laughed. "You're so close-minded, Kevin." He reached out and grabbed his brother by the wrist and pulled him closer until they stood face to face. "I was brought back, Kevin, because you are going to be needed soon. Something big is brewing, something in which you will need to play a part."

Kevin tried to pull back from his brother who held him firmly in a vise-like grip. He smelled like earth and decay. *I must be dreaming*, he thought. *Yet can you smell things clearly in dreams?* "What part am I to play, Brian?"

"I don't know, Kevin," Brian sighed. His voice was a low and haunting whisper which chilled Kevin to the core. "All I know is that it was important enough to bring me back."

"Why was I chosen?" Kevin asked. "What makes me special?"

"I don't know. All I know is that I was brought back because something big is coming. You will soon get a visit from an old friend and will need to go on a long journey with him. What he's going to tell you will sound like complete crap, but it's real. Trust him and do the right thing. The lives of your wife and daughters and everyone in the world that you hold dear are at stake."

"What the Hell is going on, Brian?"

Brian stood on his toes and spun around in a mock-pirouette. He laughed and then sat back on the bed. "Don't know. I just know that you have no choice in the matter."

"Okay," Kevin said, "If I do go with him, will things be okay?"

Brian let go of his brother's wrist. He looked cold and very lonely. He seemed very tentative for a moment and refused to meet Kevin's eyes. "I won't be back, big brother. Just be ready. Your friend will be here shortly. Here, take this as a keepsake." Brian tossed a small coin to Kevin. Kevin caught it and saw that it was his brother's lucky silver dollar. *The one he had been buried with.*

"Damn it, Brian," Kevin hissed, "if I do everything that is asked of me, will things be okay?"

Brian started to fade. He looked away, his features downcast. "Remember, Kevin, trust your instincts and beware those who side with the Falcon. They only want death."

Brian did a slow fade and soon was ethereal. Kevin watched his brother fade into nothingness, the air seeming to implode before him. He looked over at his wife who still slept soundly beside him. He suspected that whatever was coming was big and, that if he went, he'd never see his family again. He looked down at the coin in his hand. Seeing it brought back so many memories that he had fought for years to keep buried. He put the coin down gently, almost reverently, on his night table.

"Fuck this," Kevin said softly. "I can always whoever's coming to see me and not go. If the shit is going to hit the fan, my family will need me here." He smiled, feeling somewhat relieved. It seemed to be the most logical decision to make. It certainly made more sense than running off on some wild goose chase prophesized by the ghost of his long dead brother. Better yet, he wouldn't even answer his door until this all blew over. Family came first, no matter what.

CHAPTER 10

Outside the House. Yesterday.

The clouds grew dark and swelled in the sky. The winds grew stronger and the trees around the House shook and bent in the storm. Fat drops of rain fell, slowly at first then building to a torrential downpour. Thunder boomed as nature unleashed all of her unbridled fury.

The grounds around the House were still. No one lived near the House and the only way one could get there was by design. You were either meant for the House, and then you would find it easily, or else you would never see it. The House had been around for ages, in one form or another, but there wasn't a soul alive who could recollect anything about it even being there. In many ways, the House wasn't there at all. It appeared but, while it shared the same physical space, it occupied many places in many times. It was also said that if you actually could see the House, then you had other things to worry about.

The ground itself was devoid of most life as well. While there were abundant trees and greenery, no animals, birds or even insects could ever be found on the grounds. The area was instinctively avoided. Nothing had ever lived there and likely never would.

So it was even stranger that on this stormy afternoon the air shimmered and split and two forms fell out of the rift in the air and landed hard on the lawn outside the House.

The first shape stood erect, perhaps six feet tall and three feet wide. It was mostly shapeless, with rudimentary stumps for its head, arms and legs. It was covered in a coarse glistening, reddish- brown fur. It had no facial features, but in the center of its chest was a gaping hole of darkness. A low, undulating moan came from its opening.

The second shape then stood. It was slightly smaller than the first with coarse shiny black fur covering its body. Like the first, it was mostly shapeless, with stumps for the head, arms and legs. It also had a gaping hole in its chest and it, too, started a low, mournful wail.

The two shapes stood to their full height and turned towards the House. They were needed as they had been for millennia. The larger one paused and tilted what passed for its head back, as if it were gauging the air around it. Something big was coming, and they sensed they would be playing a role in what was to come next.

The first shape rippled and oscillated, and then shook itself violently before flinging itself forward. It landed with its head on the ground and this split into two rudimentary stumps for legs. It pulled itself to a standing position with its former feet merging together to form a new head. The second shape followed suit. They moved as if they were boneless sacks of meat, but with a fluidity and grace that belied their appearances.

As the two things worked their way across the lawn, they left a trail of scorched and smoking grass in their wake. The devourers closed in on the House, ready to once more claim some souls.

From a window on the second floor, two brothers witnessed their appearance from the nether realm that had spawned them and felt fear.

From deeper in the house, Anubis felt a chill and knew that, once again Ammit had made it to his domain. He knew the devourer was held only tenuously in control and would soon need to be there to bear witness to the Ascension. Part of the ceremony included transference of their fealty. For now, they were here for their main purpose, the harvesting of souls.

Elsewhere, other eyes were watching, as well. They felt revulsion at the appearance of the Devourer. The creatures were unnatural and wildly unpredictable if not tethered, but they did serve their purpose. He realized how having the Devourer's allegiance would be a very nice thing to have indeed. All that was needed was to set the plan in motion and thwart Anubis. Soon, he thought gleefully, soon it will all fall into place.

CHAPTER 11

Shoreline, Washington. One week ago.

Megan had spent the better part of the day working on trying to get free. She knew that the bolt which held her chains secured to the floor was loose. Her wrists were worn raw and red from the repetitive hours she spent pulling against the chains. Even though the pain to her cut and swollen wrists was excruciating, each little bit of give which loosened the bolts made her spirits rise and she felt some dim hope that she might somehow get out of her current mess alive.

Perry had been down each night to brutally ravage her. Each night held a new degradation which made her die a little more inside. She was at her wit's end. She couldn't take any more of his cold, reptilian touch. The sight of his ugly, misshapen face and rank breath filled her with such a feeling of hate that she knew if she ever got the chance she would kill him. Just the thought of watching the life wink out of his beady little pig eyes helped her cope and keep her sanity from slipping. First chance, she thought, her dry cracked lips forming into a small tight smile.

A few hours later, Megan heard the unmistakable rattle of the locks to the cellar door being disengaged. She stopped her efforts to loosen the chains, having nearly gotten the bolts out of the floor. *One more day*, she thought. *One more day and I'll be free*. She looked at her wrists. Even in the gloom of the cellar, she could see that they were scraped and torn, with bloody strips of skin hanging in loose fringes.

Perry came down the stairs, his footsteps heavy on the wood.

He approached her and without a word took off his shirt and then pushed his pants down around his ankles. He leaned in to her, the whiskey evident on her breath. He was clearly aroused and started sloppily kissing her neck and cheek. His hand awkwardly groped its way over her body and she involuntarily recoiled in disgust.

Perry pulled back, his face distorted in an ugly grimace. "What's the matter, you worthless fat bitch. Am I not good enough for you?"

Megan bit her lower lip. She knew she should keep quiet and agree with him. She had been on the receiving end of Perry's explosive temper for the last week, and had the cuts, bruises and swollen eyes to prove it. She only needed one more day and she'd be free of her chains and could escape this house of horrors. All she had to do was smile and regress back into her safe place and wait until it was over. "I'm sorry, Perry," she said in a low voice, avoiding eye contact.

Perry sat there quietly, as if sizing her up. His mouth twisted into a snarl and he hauled back and punched her in the head as hard as he could. "Liar," he screamed, and spent the next ten minutes alternating between punches and kicks while Megan curled up in a ball and took the abuse.

Perry stood up, pulling his pants up as he did, and spit onto Megan's trembling form. He stormed up the stairs and left her crying softly in the darkness.

Megan was awakened by the sounds of the locks being disengaged at the top of the stairs. The light came on and she had to shield her eyes for a moment. Perry came down the stairs with something thrown over his shoulder. The shape cried out in terror and Megan's heart caught in her chest as she realized that he had a little girl with him. He put the girl down in a darkened corner of the room and tied her up to one of the cages. The girl let out a low sob, followed by a plea to let her go.

Oh my God, Megan thought as she heard the girl's terrified voice, *is that Jenny?*

Perry walked over to Megan and stood over her, his face breaking into a lopsided grin. "Seeing as how you don't find me attractive, Megan, I thought I'd bring along some incentive to ensure your compliance."

"What do you mean?" Megan asked as a cold knot to her gut hinted as to where this was heading.

Perry started slowly unbuttoning his orange and blue dress shirt with the Ralph Lauren label. Megan thought briefly how there was no chance that Lauren really made such an ugly shirt and that it had to be nothing more than a cheap knock off. "I figure," Perry continued slowly, savoring the look of fear and hatred on Megan's face, "If you are so disgusted by my touch, then I'll simply have to satisfy my needs in someone else." He waved his long arm to the whimpering shape on the floor.

Megan snapped. "Spit it out you sick fucking freak. What do you want from me?"

Perry dropped his shirt on the ground. "I decided to make this a family affair. For each time you don't accept my advances with eagerness, I'll take out my lust on your sister. The only difference is where I'd be soft and gentle with you, I'll be brutal and violent with your sister. And you will be there, helpless to watch as I not only take her innocence, but inflict such pain on her that she will be begging me to kill her." Perry's eyes were glazed over and he had a look of complete and utter triumph on his face.

Tears welled up in Megan's eyes. "Please. Don't do this to her. She's only seven years old. I'll do whatever you like."

"I'm sure you will, Megan. But a threat is ineffective if you don't believe in the sincerity of my words."

The weight of his words hit Megan harder than any of the punches he had inflicted on her. "I believe you, Perry. Please. I believe you. Just leave her alone." Megan wept, terrified that she was so helpless to protect her sweet little sister.

Perry turned to her, his features contorted by rage. "Maybe after this, you will not only learn who is in charge, but to show the proper respect that I'm due." He stripped down and crawled over to the girl's whimpering form.

Megan let out a banshee like shriek and started pulling at the chains which bound her. She screamed and thrashed with an animal ferocity. Her screams and yells masked the screams made by her sister as Perry began violating her.

Within minutes, and fueled by her rage, Megan succeeded in pulling the chains free from the bolts in the cellar floor. She no longer had any feeling in her hands but didn't care. Perry was so engrossed in what he was doing to Jenny that he didn't see her break free of her shackles. With a growl, she leapt forward and landed on his back. Megan wrapped the chains around his neck and pulled with all her might, pulling him free of her sister.

Perry thrashed about violently, his long arms desperately trying to pull the chains free from around his neck. When that proved to be futile, he tried clawing at her face. Megan pulled even tighter and took Perry's struggles as all the motivation she needed. She thought of the week of pain and humiliation this animal inflicted upon her and made her tighten her grip. Then she thought of what he did to her sister and knew that no matter what, no matter how much therapy she went through, she would never be the same again. She was blind with rage and she pulled even harder on the chains. She pulled and pulled until she couldn't feel her arms anymore and even then refused to let go.

"Megan?"

Megan looked up to see her sister staring at her. She looked down and was shocked to see the deep grooves in Perry's neck. In her unbridled fury, she had nearly ripped his head free from his body. She moved a shaking hand to his neck looking for a pulse and found none.

Jenny ran over to Megan and gave her a huge hug. Megan was briefly conscious of her nakedness and the mess of purple bruises and welts all over her body. Then she saw the marks on her sister, and the look of such helplessness that she let go of the rage and hugged her sister fiercely, cradling her head as they both cried together. Maybe with time they would be okay. At least they had each other and Megan swore that she would be there for Jenny as long as she lived. They would heal together, one day at a time.

CHAPTER 12

Windham, New Hampshire. Present day.

Greg stood and paced around his living room, the frustration clearly etched across his features. He had been on the phone with his brother since early in the morning, going back and forth as to what they should do. After close to two hours of throwing out ideas and arguing as to next steps, they were no closer to figuring out where there kids were. Both men were exhausted and feeling crushed by their helplessness. The police had no leads and things seemed stuck in a holding pattern.

Paul wanted a plan of action. Greg certainly did as well, but was at a loss on how to proceed. He needed to find a way to the House. His initial thinking was that the house was in Maine. He knew that their parents were killed in a hit and run accident in northern Maine and he had started dreaming of the House shortly after. He had run searches online but never found a house that even remotely resembled the sprawling mansion where he believed his parents now were and where he suspected his daughter was taken. And more to the point…why Maine? A house like the one from his dreams would be conspicuous anywhere. Greg felt pretty sure that the House was secluded, well hidden and not something that lent itself to curiosity seekers. But there was something more that made Greg think the House wasn't somewhere one could just drive to. Some intangible that made his hunch have more bearing, as if rooted in fact. It felt like an afterimage in his brain, lingering from his dreams, yet just out of reach.

"So what do we do, Greg?" Paul asked for what seemed like the twentieth time since his brother had called him.

"I don't know, Paul." Greg scratched his head. "We're missing something. There has to be some clue that will lead us to their whereabouts."

Paul sighed. His eyes were red-rimmed from lack of sleep. "I don't know. I remember the dreams with crystal clarity. The pale dream man clearly wants us there. He all but sent us an engraved invitation. Don't you think he'd tell us where there is?"

"I would think he already has. Think back. Was there anything even remotely cryptic in the last few dreams?"

Paul scratched his head and sat down on his couch with a sigh. "No. Nothing is coming to mind. Are you sure that nothing that was said in the dream struck you as odd either?"

Greg looked at the receiver, almost as if it held an answer. "No. I honestly think I'd remember."

The two brothers sat in silence, lost in their thoughts.

"God damn it," Paul cursed. "What are we missing here? First, we have the dream man as the bastard who stole our kids. Second, for years on a nightly basis we've had dreams in this creepy house. Third, the dreams seem to always focus on death. I don't know. To me, the dream guy is the key. Maybe we need to focus our energy on him?"

Greg jumped to his feet. "That's it," he yelled into the receiver, "I know what we missed. And I know how to find our kids. It's a long-shot, but everything else has fallen into place."

"Don't keep me in suspense, Greg."

Greg grabbed his coat from the closet. "I'm on my way to Toronto, Paul. I'll call you on the way to the airport and explain everything."

Greg hung up and explained his theory to his wife who looked at him in disbelief. The police had called earlier with nothing new to report so she was willing to try anything.

"I'm coming with you."

"No. I need you here. In case I'm wrong, or in case the police do uncover something, we need someone to be here."

"Damn it, Greg. She's my daughter too."

Greg hugged his wife tightly. "I know, honey. Please trust me. While I do need you here, something tells me that I need to follow my instincts on this."

Grace wiped a tear from her cheek. "Fine, do what you need to do. Just bring her back, Greg."

Greg called his brother from his car. "The dream man did give us directions. In my dream, that creepy pale guy said to me that the key of years past was needed to enter but the mighty Oak would get us there. He gave us what we need to be able to find him."

"I'm not following. How does that gibberish tell us anything?"

"I didn't get it at first either. But as you were talking, it all seemed to click into place. The key is not an object, Paul, it's a person. Do you remember my friend David Burke?"

"Of course," Paul replied, "You've known him all your life."

"Correct. Now do you remember what his nickname was?"

"No. Should I?"

Greg sighed. "Okay, back when we were kids, this guy Joel we knew who had some speech impediment or something always called him Bookie. It was his way of saying Burkie. Well, somehow we all thought it was funny and Joel's "Bookie" ended up as Key, and it stuck as a nickname."

"So? How is David supposed to help us?"

"Think. The key from years past, Paul, is what he told me. David is the Key, man. He's the key to the past."

"Now I get it. So you think that David, your old friend from long ago is also the key of years past? You know, while it's plausible, I hope we aren't reaching conclusions based on our need for answers." Paul said grimly.

As he drove, Greg thought of his brother. The image of him in the house with his kids was still fresh in Greg's mind and he had to suppress a chill. When he last saw his brother in his dream, he had glanced out the window to see these two horrific things moving towards the house. Whatever the Hell they were, they certainly scared him. Greg did not want to freak Paul out. If he knew about those creatures, he might back out. "Paul, think back to the dreams. Did you notice a common thread?"

"The dream man," Paul said, and instantly thought of the image of his kids in the man's arms.

"What else?" Greg asked.

Paul thought for a moment and absentmindedly scratched his head. "I don't know. There was the specter of death everywhere."

"Exactly," Greg said. "Now what you don't know is David Burke suffered a kind of rapid fire TIA a month ago while driving."

"What's that?"

Greg continued. "He had series of Transient Ischemic Attacks. This in itself is an issue because it's a series of mini strokes. TIA's can leave cerebral scarring and trigger other, more powerful attacks in the future. What makes David's TIAs even worse was it was a rapid fire version, where he had multiple mini strokes going off in his head at once. It was like a cascade effect, where the first one triggered the next and so on. The intensity caused David to black out and lose control of his car on the highway. Thankfully, his wife was there and managed to get the car safely to the side of the road and then drive David to the hospital. The doctor said he was lucky to be alive and that one or two more attacks would have done him in. Heck, had he been alone in the car, he probably would have died. So, Burke cheated death. See the pattern now?"

Paul sat down on his couch and stared at the receiver. David was only a year and a half older than him. The thought of him almost dying was a little too real.

"Don't you get it?" Greg cried out. "It all fits. David is the key. And he almost died. So we have the death thing. I swear, Paul, this isn't me reaching for any causal link. It feels right. Hey, I'm at the airport. I'll call you when I land."

Greg pulled into the parking lot at the airport and rushed over to departures. He soon had his ticket to Toronto and boarded shortly after.

He cleared customs without incident and headed to the parking lot at Pearson's International Airport where Paul met him.

Paul was pretty quiet on the drive back, seemingly lost in thought.

"Penny for your thoughts, brother" Greg asked.

Paul looked up at his older brother and Greg noticed how tired he looked. "Greg," Paul began, pausing between his words, "all this centers around death. I can't but help feel that the further we follow this path, the more likely we cross the point of no return. What I'm trying to say is it feels like we're on a one way trip and once we start, we're never going to see home again."

"I intend to get my daughter and head home to New Hampshire. I'm not letting a few messed up dreams dictate my life for me. I know there's a chance this ends badly, but I'm not turning back."

Paul held up his hands in a defensive posture. "Relax, Greg. I'm in this until we find the kids. I just have a feeling that things are going to get bad real soon."

Greg looked out the window and noticed the sprawling Toronto skyline. He eventually turned back to his brother. "I feel it too. But our kids' lives are at stake. What choice do we have?"

"I know. Let's hope that your hunch on Burke is a good one."

"I think it is. Nice ride, by the way." Greg remarked.

"Thanks. I wanted a Porsche, but the wife put her foot down and that was that. So I got the Beemer as a consolation."

They pulled up at David's house twenty minutes later. David had a large, sprawling home set in a nice northern suburb just outside of Toronto proper. They drove up the long circular drive and came to a large gate made out of wrought iron spikes framed by stone pillars on each side of the driveway. A video camera was affixed to the top of the fence. Greg leaned out the window and pushed the security button on the gate. The camera at the top of the pillar turned with a whirring sound and clicked to a stop while focusing on Greg.

"Who is it," the voice came from the intercom on the pillar. The voice sounded thin and strained.

Greg tried to be upbeat as he replied, "David, it's me, Greg."

There was a moment's pause. "Greg? Greg who?"

"Greg Burgess. We grew up together in Laval. Don't you remember?"

The gate clicked and swung open. "Come on in," David said, his voice shaky. "Follow the drive and park in the front."

Paul drove up the long circular drive and came to a stop in front of the steps leading to David's front door. The door swung open and David came out. He looked different than Greg remembered, having gotten thinner and greyer in the four years since he last saw him. But it wasn't the fact that David had clearly aged from his accident. What was more striking was the glowing black aura that surrounded him.

CHAPTER 13

In the House. Present day.

Perry sat up. *Had he dozed off?* He looked around at his surroundings. He was sitting in Miss Jameson's English class in Lowell High. *I haven't seen Miss Jameson in years.* Perry wondered where that errant thought came from. He had lived every one of his sixteen years in Lowell, Massachusetts. Not only had he never lived anywhere else, it was rare that he even stepped foot out of the city, even to venture to surrounding towns. He heard someone clear their throat so he looked up. Miss Jameson stood by his desk, the anger clearly etched in her features.

"Perry, were you asleep?" Miss Jameson asked, causing the class to erupt into peals of laughter.

Perry felt his face get red. He shook his head. Why did he feel that he did not belong there? He looked up at his teacher and smiled sheepishly. "Sorry, Miss Jameson, I guess I was lost in my thoughts."

Miss Jameson looked at Perry and sighed. She was frustrated with him as usual. She suspected that he was bright but he simply did not apply himself. She knew that Perry was picked on by his classmates and wished she could change that, but she also knew that kids could be cruel and always picked out the weakest ones in the pack. If she intervened too much, they would only find him after school. She made sure she kept an eye out for the kids who were bullied and although there were rumors amongst the other teachers about the cuts and bruises Perry always seemed to have on his face, no one had ever actually witnessed him being picked on. "Perry, I asked you if you were prepared to discuss your book report with the class."

Perry looked nervously around the class. He noted the blank, bovine stares of his classmates. For a brief moment he almost felt pity for the other kids, but he knew better. He had no friends in this class or even at school, and certainly not this group who teased him mercilessly. Perry frowned when he considered this. He didn't know why he put people off so much. He supposed that he felt better amongst his books and movies. At least they didn't judge him or laugh at him. It wasn't his fault he was born homely, yet his classmates reminded him of this on a daily basis. He saw the way the girls looked at him like he was beneath notice and how the boys saw him as a constant target. Perry was simply someone to be picked on and bullied at every occasion. "I didn't have time to do it, Miss Jameson."

Miss Jameson looked at Perry. "It was due today, Perry. Unless you have a very good reason, you're going to have to stay after school today until it's completed."

The class once again burst into laughter as Perry shrank into his seat. When Miss Jameson turned to the blackboard, Mitch Arnison threw a quarter at Perry, striking him in the side of the head.

"Who threw that?" he screamed, his eyes filling with tears. He stood up, hands clenched into fists, knocking his desk over as he did.

Miss Jameson whirled around. "Perry," she screamed, "Report to Principle Koppen's office right now. I won't have any more of your disruptions in my class."

"But…."Perry stammered, "I didn't do anything."

"Enough, Perry, just go."

Perry walked out of class, the laughter of his classmates echoing behind him. He felt the hot tears streaming down his cheeks as he headed to the principal's office, thoughts of revenge racing through his brain.

Perry spent the rest of the afternoon in detention. The principal had called his parents and they gave permission to keep him after school. They would have come down to speak to the principal directly, but both worked and couldn't take the time off. As he sat there, Perry's dark thoughts turned to revenge. Mitch was the ringleader. As the most popular kid in school, everyone followed his lead. If Mitch declared Perry an outcast, then that's what he would be. If Mitch stated that only a loser would be caught dead with Perry, the kids would avoid him like the plague. Well, after three years of being

Mitch's personal punching bag, Perry decided enough was enough.

Perry walked home in a sullen silence. His mind was full of thoughts of revenge as he walked the quiet, tree lined streets. He came to a small park and decided to cut through, figuring it would save him a few minutes on his walk home. He was so lost in thought that he didn't hear the boys running behind him until they were nearly upon him. He turned to see Mitch Arnison and his buddies Jimmy Holiday and Pete Breault.

"How are ya doin', stick?" Jimmy asked with a sly grin. Perry knew Jimmy Holiday well. Jimmy was a short, ferocious little monster who fought like a wild Tasmanian devil. He had a chip on his shoulder and would fight with anyone just for looking at him the wrong way. Jimmy stood perhaps five foot six, with a thin and wiry frame. He had a small head, with short cropped black hair, a small, pig-like snout of a nose and tiny, beady eyes that always seemed devoid of any intellect. When he grinned, his smile showed the missing two front teeth he wore as a badge of pride for beating up an entire gang of Hispanics from the next town over.

Perry started backing up slowly. It was bad enough that Mitch was there, but all three of the boys meant one thing. It meant that Perry was due for a beating. "Jimmy," Perry said with a forced smile. "I haven't seen you in a while. How are things?"

Pete snorted. "Hey there, Perry, ain't you glad to see me too?"

Perry turned to face Pete. Unlike the other boys, Pete Breault was well over six feet and topped the scales at over three hundred pounds. So far he had been held back three times, so he was three years older than the other kids, and of legal age. This made him very popular with the other kids as he could buy them alcohol. Pete was not fast, but was built like a linesman and was strong. He looked at Perry and frowned, his large, fleshy lips contorted into a look of pure hate.

"Sure, Pete," Perry replied, "You know I'm always glad to see you too."

Mitch walked forward and pushed Perry hard in his chest. Perry let out a small cry of pain and fell hard on his butt. The boys laughed and slowly moved forward. Perry tried to scuttle backward but was blocked by Pete.

"Where are ya going, Perry?" Pete said in a sing-song kind of way. "You'll miss the party."

Perry was terrified. He'd been picked on and bullied for years. But never like this. These guys wanted to hurt him, and there was no one about who could possibly save him. He felt his bladder loosen and looked down in shame when he realized that he wet himself.

Mitch was the first to notice the spreading wet stain on the crotch of Perry's khakis. "Look guys," Mitch said through peals of laughter, "Perry pissed himself." The other boys burst out laughing. Perry jumped to his feet and began running at fast as he could towards the outside of the park. He reasoned that if he could at least get back to the street, he may still avoid the beating as Mitch and his friends wouldn't risk harming him up in the middle of a busy street.

Mitch and Jimmy tore after Perry, with Pete struggling to keep up. Perry was fast, but Mitch was a jock and easily caught up. He tackled Perry to the ground and slammed his head down hard. Perry tasted grass and earth and spit it out quickly before Mitch got any ideas.

"Thought you'd run, you piece of crap?" Mitch said, clearly out of breath.

"What did I do?" Perry pleaded. "Come on, Mitch. We've known each other for years. You don't have to do this."

Mitch's upper lip curled in disgust and he drove his fist down hard into Perry's face. "You have no idea, do you? You little freak."

"What did I do?" Perry asked again?

Mitch got off Perry and pulled him to his feet. "We know you've been sitting outside Anne Quinn's bedroom window almost every night. She saw you, you twisted piece of shit. Bad enough you've been watching her get undressed, but taking pictures of it too?" Mitch took another swing at Perry and knocked him down again.

"Okay," Perry admitted, the tears starting to fall, "I did sit outside her bedroom window. So what? What's it to you?"

"She's my cousin," Mitch yelled. "But I'm not going to soil myself beating you. My boys will, though." Mitch signaled to Jimmy and Perry who came over and proceeded to methodically beat Perry until he curled up in a ball and lay there sobbing. Mitch walked over to where he lay and kicked him as hard as he could in the ribs. He paused, gritted his teeth and did it again. "If you ever go near my cousin again, you freak, I'll kill you. You got that?"

Perry nodded weakly, and covered his face as he lay there sobbing.

Mitch and his friends left, laughing as they walked. Perry stayed where he was, making no attempt to move. It hurt when he breathed and he couldn't feel the left side of his face. He thought that he may have lost a tooth or two. Even worse, what was he going to tell his parents when he got home? If they called the police, as he suspected they would, Mitch would surely drop the news that Perry was peeping in on Anne Quinn. He knew how things would go. People already didn't like him. If they thought of him as some kind of a pervert, then Mitch and his friends would be looked at as heroes. Even worse, the beatings would surely continue. Everyone would think that he was peeping on their sisters, cousins, girlfriends, you name it. Life would get even worse than it already was.

Perry forced himself to his feet and limped his way home. More than once, he had to stop and spit up some blood. His ribs really felt tender and hurt with each breath. It took longer than he would have liked, but he finally made it to his house and saw that the place was dark and that the driveway was empty. That meant his parents weren't back from work. Since his brother moved out a year earlier, it meant he had the house to himself.

Perry walked in and locked the door. He made a beeline for the bathroom and relieved his aching bladder. He was not surprised to see that his urine was bloody. Perry was taken aback by the strange visage staring back at him from the mirror. His right eye was swollen shut and a hideous shade of black and purple. He was missing two of his bottom front teeth. He had cuts, bruises and lacerations all over his body. When he touched his fingers to his left cheek, he found that his face was numb and that he couldn't feel the fingers on his cheek.

Perry went to his room and put a Bon Jovi record on his turntable and sat down at his desk and began to write.

Paula Christopher can home to a darkened house. *That's odd*, she thought, *why is the house so dark*? "Perry," she called out. "Are you home honey?" Paula walked through the foyer to the kitchen. She flipped on the light and saw that there weren't any dishes in the sink. She walked out of the kitchen and up the eight steps to the second floor of their split level bungalow. "Perry, are you home dear?"

Paula got to the top of the stairs and saw down the hallway that there was a light under Perry's door. She walked to the door and knocked. "Perry?" When she got no response, she opened the door and froze when she saw her son, looking bruised and bloody, swinging from the ceiling fan, with his belt around his neck.

CHAPTER 14

Toronto, Ontario. Present day.

"So, let me get this straight," David Burke said as he took a long sip of coffee from the steaming mug he held in his hands, "you're saying your children were abducted by a mysterious pale man from your dreams and that, in order to find him and your kids, I need to be involved because somehow I play an instrumental part in this?"

Greg nodded. "Yeah, that's about right."

David frowned, looked at Greg then Paul. Both were sitting there, their mouths tightly closed, waiting for David's response. No matter what was true, David realized, was that they believed it. "Why pick me, Greg?" David continued. "You know what happened to me a few months back, right? I suffered a series of strokes. My brain basically short-circuited while I was driving. The doctors said I'm lucky to still be alive. If my wife hadn't been there, I probably would have crashed the car. They said what happened to me is fatal in over ninety-five percent of occurrences. I'm still recovering, though. My memory is full of holes and my strength is nowhere near where it was before everything shorted out."

Greg looked at his oldest friend. It was true that David looked frail and a shell of the man he used to be. He knew they had to convince David to come with them. Both Greg and Paul saw the black glow which emanated from David's frail form. If anything, perhaps his near death experience meant he was more sensitive to other planes of existence and maybe that was what was needed to get close to the pale man. Greg suspected that David's brush with death changed him more than he realized and that was the reason they were there in the first place.

"David," Paul began. "Do you remember when we were kids? You were unable to skate. We all played hockey but you always bailed out because you didn't want to embarrass yourself in front of the other kids. I remember that day at my house when you asked my brother to give you skating lessons. He took you out every afternoon for a month after school and on weekends. He never told a soul he was doing it. And guess what? You became a good skater. It was your perseverance but, also, it was my brother. He was there for you, then and many other times during our youth and adolescence. He was there when you needed him. That's what being a friend was about. Look at him, David. More than anything, he needs a friend right now. Both of us really need your help."

David stood up and paced around his spacious den. He'd known Greg since they were kids. For years, they had been inseparable. Life took them to different places but, in the end, he knew Greg and trusted him. David had always been a good judge of character and, if anything, Greg had integrity and did not strike him as someone to go off on a wild goose chase. He wouldn't have flown all the way to Toronto and made the drive to his house if he didn't believe it was necessary. And if he believed it, it was probably true. "Okay, Greg. I'm in."

"Excellent. I know it sounds far-fetched but…"

David held up his hand. "There's something I have to tell you both. Last night my dead grandmother came to me in my dreams. She told me that you'd be coming and would ask me to join you on a journey. She was very clear that if I didn't go, everyone I knew would die. Showing up after not being in contact for a few years convinced me that my dream was more like an omen. So, when do we start?"

"Now," Greg replied. "Pack some things because we're going to Montreal next. From there, I'm not sure. We've been guided on our route so far. I suspect things will continue making sense once we complete the next phase of our journey."

David nodded. "I just need to call my wife and inform her of what we're doing."

Greg grinned. "So you're going to call your wife and tell her that one of your oldest friends, whom you haven't seen in years, needs you to go with him to find a pale man who abducts children by coming into their homes through their dreams. Don't forget to add that there is a very good chance that this little excursion might be dangerous."

David smiled. "Actually, yes, that was what I was going to do. We have a very good marriage. She trusts me to make the right decisions, no matter how far-fetched they appear to be. After she flips out and I can talk her down, I don't anticipate this will be any different. After two decades together, she's learned that my judgment is usually sound."

A half hour later, David, Paul and Greg were driving down the 401 for the next leg of their journey. Paul had thrown in an old Scorpions CD and, if they weren't on a mission to find their abducted kids, it almost would have felt like a road trip with a few friends out to have a good time.

The drive to Montreal was pretty uneventful. Conversation was light, more about sports and films than about what they were doing. Paul kept a steady stream of CDs going so that they always had something on, which helped fill the lulls in the conversation. David saw that Greg kept glancing his way. "Something you want to ask me?" Dave remarked.

"Nah. I was just hoping that we made the right choice bringing you along. I'm worried that this could get really ugly and that perhaps you didn't need to be dragged into all this."

"Two things I was wondering," David stated. "First, why were you given a clue to find your kids? Surely this has to be a trap? Second, why are we going to Montreal?"

Greg laughed. "I honestly don't know why we're being led to him, but clearly it's important enough that my kid and Paul's were used as bait. So, either he really needs us and can't get us there himself or he needs to get rid of us and can't do the deed. As for Montreal, I didn't want to spoil the surprise, but we're picking up Kevin Oakster."

"You're kidding, right?" Paul asked. "The guy's an idiot."

"No, I'm not. The message the pale man gave me said to seek out David and Kevin. If you remember, the second part of the pale guy's clue was that the mighty oak would get us there. That part was easy. Kevin's nickname was oak as long as I've known him. In fact, we often called him the Mighty Oak."

Paul ran his hand through his hair and let out a long sigh. "I know I haven't seen him since high school, but the Kevin I remember is not the guy I would expect to bring along on something as serious as this."

Greg smiled. "You already said that. Kevin is what he is. He's like an overgrown teenager, but he's been in a stable marriage for over two decades and has managed to raise two kids. After the turmoil he's gone through in his life, it's amazing he's ended up as well adjusted as he has. He also has seen death close up, with both parents and a brother dying all within a few years of each other. He even found his brother dead in a chair in his apartment after an overdose of medication. And, like David, he's a critical link to us finding our kids."

Paul nodded and opted to look out the car window in silence. He muttered some crack about a *very* overgrown teenager and chuckled quietly to himself.

They arrived in Ville Lasalle and found their way down the grid of streets to Bannantine where Kevin lived with his family. Greg remembered the set-up that Kevin had. He and his family lived in the upper duplex owned by his wife's father and, although they were never charged rent, Kevin paid in many other ways. His mother-in-law constantly meddled in their affairs and his father-in-law frequently entered their home unannounced. Yet, somehow, he managed to rise above it and raise his family. Quite the change from the socially awkward teenager who Greg remembered always being on the outside looking in.

They parked the car and walked up to Kevin's door. Greg rang the bell and waited.

"Is he home?" David asked. "If he's not, we can manage this on our own."

"I don't know. Let me ring again." Greg was about to ring the doorbell again when the door swung open. Kevin Oakster stood there, arms akimbo, in the doorway.

"For Pete's sake, Greg, what the Hell are you doing here?" Kevin came up and gave Greg a big hug. Kevin hadn't changed since high school. He stood about five foot nine with a very stocky build. His hair was cut short, almost a military buzz cut, but it was clear it held very little grey. He was wearing the full military garb of his unit, the Black Watch, including kilt and even spats over his shoes. What was more noticeable was the fact that, like David, Kevin also had a black glow emanating from his person.

Paul noticed the black glow around Kevin and looked over at his brother who had a huge grin. It was clear they saw it, but it was just as obvious that David did not. Greg was thrilled that they had made the right choice in coming to see Kevin.

"Kevin," Greg said, "we have a problem and it seems you are part of the solution. Can we come in?"

Kevin paused for a moment. "Sure, guys. Come on in."

Greg, Paul and David followed Kevin inside and up the stairs to his house. They walked into the living room and sat down. Greg proceeded to tell Kevin why they were there and how he fit into the whole story.

Kevin raised his eyebrows, clearly not buying into the story. "So, let me get this straight. A guy came through your dreams and stole your children by disappearing back into the dream. And he left a clue indicating that you seek David and myself out to help find them and help get your kids back."

"Pretty much," Paul added. "Yeah, I know it seems far-fetched. But we were having the same dreams for over a decade until the day that this shadowy guy stepped out of the dream, and changed our lives forever."

Kevin stood up and held the door open, indicating that Greg, Paul and David should leave. "Guys, it was good seeing you all again. But this is simply too much to swallow. I remember the pranks you guys played on me in high school this sounds like the same shit. I'm not in high school anymore and don't have to take this crap."

"Damn it, Kevin," Greg said angrily, "do you think we'd fly into Toronto, then drive all the way to Montreal just for a fucking laugh? Cut me some slack. Our kids are missing and we really need your help."

"Then call the police," Kevin said coldly.

Paul looked at Kevin, muttered something under his breath, and left the apartment.

David stood, and walked over to Kevin. "Listen, Kevin. I believe Greg and I trust him. I don't know how I am supposed to help, but I trust my instinct. I left my family back in Toronto to do so and help Paul and Greg save his kids. We've been friends far too long to not be there when the others need a helping hand."

Kevin turned his head, not wanting to meet David's gaze. David put his hand on Kevin's shoulder and the room seemed to explode with a black, pulsating light.

Paul ran back into the apartment. "You're not going to believe this." He stopped short when he saw Kevin's apartment glowing from the black light which emanated from David and Kevin.

"What's going on?" Greg asked.

"Just come with me." Paul headed back outside and was quickly followed by Greg.

Greg stared across the street in shock. The two duplexes seemed to have moved so that there was now a road, enshrouded in mist, between them. It was hard to tell where it went because the road vanished into the swirling fog.

"Paul, what happened here?"

"I don't know. One minute I was heading to our car; the next, the houses across the street started sliding apart and then this road appeared, all covered in a thick mist."

Greg thought for a moment. "You know, when David touched Kevin, there was a huge flash of black light. I bet their touching, or connecting, was what brought the road. It looks like the words the pale man said in my dream are what we need to get us to the end.

The two brothers heard a scraping sound and turned to see Kevin and David standing there, hand in hand. Both of the two men's eyes had rolled back in their heads, so that their eyes appeared to be solid balls of white. The black glow pulsated wildly from both of them.

They turned as one and pointed in unison to the road across the street. "This is the highway of Lost Souls. It's where we need to go if you ever want to see your kids again."

CHAPTER 15

Egypt. 2,566 BC, 4th Dynasty.

Khufu managed to see a bit through the tiny slits formed by the stitching over his eyes and saw with horror the thing that was coming through the fabric in space. The long arm came through first, followed by another. Each arm was long and sinewy, covered in a glossy black fur and ended at nasty looking claws. The fingers on each claw were long and gnarled and ended in sharp talons. Khufu had no doubt that those talons could shred a man in mere minutes. He wasn't afraid of anything in life, but this was something he never would have encountered while he still lived. It was amazing that it took his death for him to learn the meaning of the word fear.

The two claws grasped the edge of the rip in space and began pulling it wider apart. It then forced its head through the tear and Khufu felt his bladder loosen. It was as if the universe were giving birth to a demon. He had never feared another mortal soul and yet the monstrosity that was clawing its way into the room chilled his blood. He supposed that had his heart still beat within his chest, the sight of the creature would have been enough to still it forever.

Ammit put its large head through; an extended stump covered a large void where the mouth should be. Tufts of oily black fur covered its head and cascaded down over its body. The body was wide and shook and undulated as it tore its way through the rift. It made a low keening noise which seemed to echo off the walls of the Great Hall.

Anubis was chanting, his head back and his arms in the air, evoking Ammit to breach the dimensions and claim his soul. Golden lights danced over the God and seemed to feed off his energy.

Khufu realized that if he was going to act, it had to be now. He charged forward and ran for the scale. He grabbed the Canopic jar and threw it as hard as he could at Anubis. It hit him square in the chest and fell to the stone floor, shattering into countless tiny shards. Anubis' concentration broken, he stopped chanting.

The rift in the air began slowly closing and Ammit roared in fury as it fought to pull apart the very air to let it enter the Hall of Anubis. It slammed its stump into the stone floor to get some purchase and began pulling itself forward. Inch by inch, Ammit fought its way deeper into the Great Hall, seemingly oblivious to the forces which were pulling him back to his own nether realm.

Khufu grabbed the scale and threw it forcefully to the ground, causing it to break into several pieces. He snatched his heart and shoved it back into his chest. The heart started beating once again and began reattaching itself to his circulatory system as tiny threads wound their way inside him, connecting atria and ventricles to arteries and veins. Fascia spread out from the chest cavity and began surrounding the heart. Blood started flowing back through the heart and once again through Khufu's body. The bones then knit together, followed by the sheeting of muscles and finally skin.

Anubis roared in fury. "How dare you, you petty little mortal! Your heart and soul were no longer yours. They belong to me. You lost your claim on them the moment you died. Do you honestly think you can defy the will of Anubis?" His eyes blazed with a golden fury.

Khufu grabbed the central rod of the scale and jammed it into Anubis' chest. It pierced him just above the heart and went clean through. Anubis looked down at the metal rod which jutted out his back and growled. He grabbed Khufu by the neck and threw him across the hall. Khufu hit the wall with a shuddering crack. He tried to rise but found that he could not move.

Anubis walked over to the fallen Pharaoh and picked him up by the hair. "You have caused trouble today, Khufu. Surely you didn't think that a mere mortal could best a God. This is a level of presumption I have not seen before. Still, it matters not. You humans have an allotted time and then your souls belong to us."

Anubis forced Khufu down to the floor on his knees. With one hand, he pulled the rod from his chest and looked at it sadly. Holding Khufu by the hair with his left hand, he plunged the rod down through

Khufu's neck all the way through his body, pinning him to the floor.

"You wished for more time, Khufu?" Anubis growled. "Then you shall have it. For the next several hundred generations, your bloodline will never see the afterlife. Upon their deaths, they will be brought to the Great Hall for judgment. But, instead of judgment, their souls will be forfeit. Ammit will then come through and rend their soul asunder. You, on the other hand, my dear Pharaoh, will remain here in the Hall, knowing that whenever one of your bloodline comes before me that there won't be anything for them but the complete and utter annihilation of their soul. You will be able to watch but, with your broken body pinned to the floor like some pitiful insect, you will be helpless to do nothing but observe. Then, after the hundreds of generations have passed, at the time of the Ascension, I will free you from your prison so that your soul can finally be claimed by Ammit. I know you can no longer move or speak, Khufu. And that is how you shall remain for what seems like an eternity. You are lucky I feel merciful today. You will now have many lifetimes to imagine what I could have done instead."

Anubis saw the single tear fall from the sewn lid of Khufu's eye and laughed. Khufu wasn't the first to try and escape, but he was the first to have dared strike him. And while Anubis did consider himself a fair and impartial God, sometimes one needed to set an example.

CHAPTER 16

In the House. Present day.

The Other felt the stirrings in his muscles like short, painful electric bursts of energy. It had been so long since he had moved that the thought of ever moving again had long since dissipated from his thoughts.

Most men would have been driven mad by his predicament but, over the many millennia, the Other had managed to not only maintain his sanity, but he felt he had learned much being in the presence of the God.

A cool breeze blew through the Great Hall and the Other felt his hairs stiffen as the damp and chilly air caressed his skin.

The time of Ascension is coming, a voice boomed in his head. The Other has heard countless voices over the long millennia, but this one, more powerful and assertive than the others, was almost real and not a part of an overactive imagination. *You will have one chance for this*, the voice continued. *If you fail, you will finally be allowed to die, but if you succeed...ahhhhhh...the wonders that will be afforded to you.*

The Other forced his features into a weak smile. He was still so very frail that even moving his facial muscles was a huge strain. He wondered what it would be like to move again, to walk, to run, to swim, and to fuck. Living in his mind for as long as he could remember allowed him to create a universe around him where others could congregate. He built cities and lived countless lives all within the confines of his mind. He married and watched his wives and children grow and age before his very eyes, ending up as dust.

The Other opened his eyes a tiny crack and the brilliant light was far too much for him. He tried to howl in pain, but not a sound came forth from vocal cords not used in several millennia. He was aware that this was the most he had moved in many, many years. He didn't know why he hadn't aged a day since the time he had found himself in this cursed situation but, if the tides were changing, then he needed to take advantage. A chance at freedom when he had nothing left to lose. It almost seemed too easy. The Ascension was coming and if he could free himself from his exile before then, he'd exact his vengeance for the millennia of misery he has endured. *Quiet*, the voice cautioned the Other. *He comes.*

The man appeared at the entrance to the Great Hall. He seemed to glide out of the shadows. He was tall and thin with pale, slightly grey skin and long, flowing white hair. His features were very gaunt and he seemed to be preoccupied. He barely even glanced in the direction of the Other. In all reality, he hadn't even given more than a passing thought towards the Other in centuries and had far too much to consider doing so now. The Ascension was coming and the One hadn't been identified yet. Even with the added incentive of bait, he mused. He turned and watched the three children following him slowly, their movements stiff and awkward, their eyes glazed over and unseeing. He hoped the parents were on the way. There were too many factors at play and everything needed to be resolved. The Ascension was coming and there needed to be proper succession, and that could only happen if it was done willingly. Otherwise, the results would be beyond disastrous.

The man walked to a great chair and sat down. He needed to think of a contingency plan if the One did not reveal him or herself. He motioned for the children to sit at his feet and, with a wave of his hand, he sent them to sleep. Time was running short and he needed to think.

CHAPTER 17

Lasalle, Quebec. Present day.

The grey storm clouds cast a darkening pall over the city. The once blue sky had changed to a steel grey and the clouds took on a darker, more ominous appearance. A sharp wind whipped leaves and small bits of detritus around the streets.

David and Kevin stood there at the doorway to Kevin's house, still as statues, their eyes rolled back in their heads, pointing to the road that had materialized across the street between two houses. A thick, white mist hung heavily over the road. "The Highway of Lost Souls," they said in unison, in a low and moaning tone. "That is where we must go."

Paul turned to Greg. "Holy, shit. I didn't really know what to believe with the whole dream imagery stuff, and only went along because I was grasping at straws. I mean, let's face it…our kids vanished without a trace or a single clue as to their whereabouts. I wanted to believe the whole premise that a man came through our dreams and took our kids, but that seemed to be far-fetched at best. I'm sure that you had your doubts as well, Greg. I mean, how could you not? But this," he said while pointing to the ghostly road between the two duplexes, "this is really messed up. A road opens up between houses and we're just supposed to follow along?"

"I know," Greg replied, "every fiber of my being is telling me that this is a very bad idea. Here's what we know. We're now being guided to follow a road which, for all intents and purposes, doesn't exist. So, let's assume we follow along, and then something happens to either David or Kevin. Will we even be able to get back home? And, even forgetting that little bit of paranoia, how do we know where the road will even take us. Perhaps the pale man is not leading us towards the kids, but making sure we are far enough away from them."

"What do you want to do, Greg?" Paul asked, clearly tired of the entire exchange. "Personally, I want to go home, crawl in my bed and stay there, but I won't. My kids are with that man and I'll take this road straight to Hell if I think that it will get them home safely. So, I think we need to keep moving on. I don't see any other options presenting themselves. Do you?"

"No. We're clearly being maneuvered forward in this. We were guided to David and Kevin and then this road appears out of nowhere. It seems we really don't have any choice in this. Paul, let's get the zombie twins into the car and get going."

Greg guided Kevin and David towards Paul's BMW 328 xi and put them in the back. They got in the car easily and without any effort. The black glow around them started pulsing with a brighter intensity. Paul decided that he would drive and Greg would keep an eye on the two guys in the back, plus watch out for any new threats. Greg suspected that his neurotic brother did not trust him with his pricey new ride and he simply felt that if he were driving there would be less chance of an accident.

Paul checked for traffic but found the road strangely empty. Greg had visited Kevin here many times over the years and had never seen this street without any traffic. It was as if the appearance of the Highway of Lost Souls somehow didn't just come to Paul and Greg's plane of reality, but rather created a split where this world was somehow just outside of their own. Paul drove directly across the street, went over the sidewalk and lawn until his front tires were on the lip of the shadowy, mist-enshrouded highway. The mist was thick and roiling and hid whatever lay beyond. "Point of no return, Greg," he said with some hesitation, "We can still turn back".

"If we do, we've lost the only lead we have in finding our kids," Greg said and pointed towards the road. "Let's just get this over with." He hoped that they were making the right choice instead of heading down into an unknown which could kill them all.

Paul nodded and put the car in drive. He drove slowly forward, and eased the car onto the Highway of Lost Souls. The front of the car entered the mist and the front windshield started to frost over. He drove straight ahead, making sure that they kept to the road. He felt the back tires leave the lawn and cross over onto the paved surface of the road. As he did, Greg turned around and saw that Kevin's house was gone and that the only thing that was now visible was the thick, swirling fog.

Greg put his hand on his brother's shoulder. "Paul, I think we can only go forward at this point. I can't see Kevin's house anymore. Screw that. I can't even see Lasalle or anything else, either." He stared out the frost-covered windows, noting that the car was surrounded on all sides by the thick, unnatural fog and the only option was to keep moving forward down the dark road.

Paul put on his headlights and their light pierced through the thick fog, sending shapes scurrying off into the mist.

They drove in silence for a while, not really feeling as if they were actually moving. The quiet thrum of the engine and the soft hiss of tires on pavement seemed to be the only sounds they heard. Due to the thickness of the fog around them, they had no perception at all of motion. Time seemed to blur and when Greg checked his phone to get the time, he saw that the screen was flickering and that none of the functions worked anymore. After what felt like an eternity driving through the fog, they spotted a figure up ahead walking in the middle of the road. Paul turned the car to drive around the man. The brothers stared at him as they passed. His skin was pale and slightly grey, and his eyes were glazed over with a thick, cloudy film, making them look dull and opaque. He walked stiffly and slowly, his motions jerky and forced. As the car passed him, he seemed to come awake and reached out slowly as if to grab them. Almost in unison, Kevin and David turned to the blind man and hissed.

"Do not stop for the Lost," Kevin and David screamed as one. "They are those who have passed on but have lost their souls. They cannot be judged so they are doomed to wander the Highway of Lost Souls for all eternity. They constantly search for souls to claim as their own because the living energy given off by a live soul draws them like a beacon of light. They will devour a soul and it will take away their chill, but only for a short time. Before long, the energy that was stolen from the living will fade and they will once again feel the cold emptiness of their existence. An eternity spent searching for new souls is all they will ever be. Theirs is a fate far worse than any Hell."

Greg suppressed a shiver. "What will happen if we stop for them?" Greg asked.

"They will tear you apart and devour your heart. Once they eat your soul, you will then be as lost as they are, always searching… always needing more to fill the void lost by your own soul."

Paul turned and looked at the two men. "Why would they do that?

Kevin and Paul continued as if in stereo, "The Egyptians believed that your soul was contained within your heart and that if someone devoured it, they would take possession of your soul, but only momentarily. They would then feel emptier than before. The devourer consumed the damaged souls so only the purest of souls would move on. The Lost are like that. They have no souls and are drawn to the heat that emanates from the heart. If they can eat a heart, they will be filled with enough life energy to regain a semblance of life for the briefest time. If they eat enough souls, it's believed that they will be able to find their way to the House for proper judgment instead of wandering the highway for eternity."

"Has that ever happened?" Paul asked.

"No," Kevin and David replied. "They devour a soul and the life force soon fades. The House is too far for those without souls to reach. More likely, they would find themselves a way back to the natural world."

Gary slammed his hand down on the dashboard. "So now you're telling me that we are driving through a stretch of road filled with walking dead who want to eat our hearts?"

"Yes," Kevin and David replied. "The only other way to get to the House is to die and arrive there for judgment. Just keep driving and steer clear of the Lost."

"How did they happen to lose their souls?"

"There are many ways to lose one's soul. Suicides are the most common of the Lost."

Paul turned the lights down to low. The high beams were reflecting off the fog causing visibility to worsen. He kept the car at twenty miles per hour, at least according to the odometer. Of course, he suspected in this odd place which housed the highway that technology might not be functioning correctly. Almost as if on cue, Greg cursed.

"What is it?" Paul asked.

"Something is going on with my watch. It's going backwards. First my phone started acting all screwy, and now the watch. Paul, don't you get it? Our phones, watches and other items we carry keep us tethered to the world we know. It's as if the further we go down this road, the more detached we get."

"Greg, it's likely just a strong magnetic field we're driving through. That would cause the watch acting oddly and the lack of cell reception. Trust me. It's nothing more than that."

Greg smiled weakly. "That's what I initially thought. Then I realized something. The longer we are away, the less I remember about my life. Quick, Paul, tell me the names of your wife and kids."

"Easy. My wife's name is…Uh, I…I…wait. My wife is Nicole and my kids are Mikey and Beth. Jesus, for a moment, I couldn't remember their names."

"I know. I'm having difficulty holding on to things that are part of my life, as well. What really scares me is will we remember that we have a life outside of this place? Will we even know we have a home to go back to?"

Paul reached into his pocket and took out his cell phone. He turned it on and noticed that the time showed 00:00 and the date as 99/99/9999. "It looks like my cell is out as well."

"Let's hope we don't run out of gas, Paul." Greg said grimly, "I have serious doubts we're going to see a service station anywhere along this cursed road."

Two of the Lost suddenly peeled themselves from the thick fog and slammed themselves against the windows of the BMW. They started smashing their fists against the side window, desperate to get to the souls inside.

Paul put his foot down hard on the accelerator. The vehicle shot forward, leaving the Lost behind, sliding back into the fog. Paul waited a minute or so before slowing down. He turned to his brother and smiled weakly. "I think we lost them."

"Paul," Greg screamed, "Look out!"

Paul turned back to the road and slammed down hard on the brakes. Walking along the highway in front of their vehicle were dozens of the Lost. They turned as one, as if the living inside cast a bright beacon which called to them, and then as one they advanced.

CHAPTER 18

In the House. Present day.

Perry woke up. He was momentarily disoriented and not sure where he was. He remembered trying to kill himself and then everything got hazy. *No, that's not right*, he thought, *there was a girl. No, there was a girl and her sister. They were his trophies. And then....*Perry shook his head. Where had that thought come from? The image of the girl and his sister had left him aroused. Embarrassed, he pulled the blankets up to his neck in case his mother came in. Bad enough he had an erection. Last thing he wanted to do was explain that to his prude of a mother.

Perry put his hand to his neck. It felt sore and it hurt to swallow. He got out of bed and walked over to the mirror that hung on his bedroom wall. Perry hated that mirror. It was a daily testament to his ugliness and the misery that life afforded to him. He looked closely and saw that his neck was raw and swollen with what looked like a rich purple band on his neck where the rope had been.

Perry sat back down on his bed and looked around his tiny room. There were books piled high on his dresser, both fiction and non-fiction, many of them found on weekends at local flea markets. Comic books were stacked neatly on the table next to his bed. Prominent on top was the latest issue of Superman. Perry was a huge comic book fan, another thing he kept secret from the kids at school. Bad enough he took regular beatings for being so ugly, but he also got laughed at for the way he dressed and his love of Dungeons and Dragons. Adding comic books to the list would be like pouring gasoline on an already raging fire.

He couldn't miss another day. He had far too many absences already and he was at risk for being held back, something he knew he could never handle.

Perry picked up a pair of khakis from the floor and a pink and white striped shirt. To that he added a red tie with yellow rose blooms adorned on it. He knew he was fashionable and, besides, he just did not feel comfortable in jeans and concert tee-shirts like the other kids did. He knew he was tall and had virtually no ass, so jeans made him look even more awkward than he already was.

With the tie done up, he could barely see the purplish black swelling on his neck, which was good. One less thing to explain in case anyone asked. He quietly made his way down the hallway from his bedroom. He heard his mother on the phone in the kitchen, so he was able to slip out the front door without any effort. Once out, he ran as fast as he could in case his mother happened to look out the window.

Perry was lost in his thoughts and did not hear the car pull up next to him. It was a Mustang convertible from the mid-seventies, and painted a glossy black. Perry looked up to see Mitch behind the wheel and Pete Breault sitting next to him. He tensed, ready to run if he had to.

"Hiya, Perry," Mitch said all smiles, "want a ride?"

Perry knew that Mitch would never give him a ride. He was being set up for something. "No, Mitch," Perry said while still walking, "I don't need a ride."

Pete stood up in the passenger side and glared at Perry. He then hurled an apple at him, striking Perry hard in the cheek. Pete and Mitch burst out laughing. "We weren't going to give you one anyways, Perry," Pete added. He picked up another apple and then threw that one at Perry. This one was a bit off in its aim and struck Perry in the top half of his forehead.

Perry turned and ran. He made a hard left and cut through the yard of the house across the street. Mitch and Pete could not catch him by car. If he was smart, and Perry prided himself at being damn clever, he should be able to make it to school without Mitch catching him.

Perry ran through a few more backyards and paused in the back of one to catch his breath. He bent forward and spit out some phlegm.

His heart was hammering in his chest. It suddenly came to him what he had to do. It was so simple.

Perry waited until it got dark and slipped out his bedroom window. His mother thought he was asleep in his room, and would be the perfect alibi. He got his bike and made his way to Mitch's street. The roads were all dark and silent, as if everyone had decided to call it an early night. The streetlamps offered some welcome spheres of light to the darkness. Every shadow seemed to pose a threat and Perry felt very alone and vulnerable as he rode towards Mitch's house.

When he got to a few houses down from where Mitch lived with his father and step-mother, he stopped and hid his bike in a neighbor's bushes and then kept to the shadows as he made his way over. He looked around the neighborhood. The streets were dark and not a soul was out. Perry could see the glow of televisions from living rooms up and down the street.

Perry looked for Mitch's car. He hoped it wasn't in the garage. Luck was with him. He spotted Mitch's mustang a bit further up the road, parked in front of the next door neighbor's house. He crouched down and ran over to the car. Perry got on his back and eased himself under the front of the vehicle. Pulling his penknife from his pocket, he went to work cutting the brake cables. When they were nearly cut through, he pocketed the knife and eased himself out from under the car. Grinning maliciously, he ran to his bike and pedaled to the Texaco at the edge of town. He parked his bike next to the phone booth and then called Mitch.

The phone rang six times and Perry was about to hang up when a tired voice answered. "Hello," Mitch said, his words slurred. It was clear he was half asleep.

"Mitch," Perry said, using his best impression of Pete that he could muster. "What's happening? I didn't wake you, did I?"

"Nah, don't worry about it. I was just chilling on the couch. You okay, man?" Mitch asked. "You sound kind of funny."

Perry smiled. Thankfully, Mitch was not known for his intelligence. Still, the fact that he bought Perry's impression of Pete meant he was probably half in the bag too. This would be easier than he thought it would be. "Yeah, I'm good. Hey, what's going on? I'm at this kick ass party at the quarry just outside of town. There are tons of college girls here, too. Dude, it's getting pretty wild. Some of the girls here have started stripping down to their panties. I figured that you'd want to be here."

"Are you serious?" Mitch asked. He looked at his clock radio by his bed. It wasn't that late. He could sneak out for a few hours, especially if hot girls were involved. "Okay, I'm in. I'll be there in a few minutes."

Mitch got dressed, worked some hair gel in to his scalp to give him that just woke up look and finally checked himself in the large mirror above his desk. Yeah, he looked hot.

Mitch left his house careful not to wake his parents. He always parked a ways up the street so he could sneak out at nights. The Mustang's big engine would have woken his parents had it been parked in their driveway. He started the car and took off at a clip for the quarry. *How the Hell did Breault manage to get invited to a party without him?* Mitch wondered. Still, if there were college girls, he stood a far better chance than Pete to get lucky.

Mitch looked at his Casio digital watch and checked the time. He was making great time. It had only been five minutes since Pete had called and he was already almost there. He turned into the quarry and raced down the road. *Odd*, he thought, *there seems to be no one here. Where are the lights and cars?*

As Mitch raced down the road, he saw someone ahead pointing to his left. He turned to follow where the person was pointing and continued. As he got closer, he saw that the person who was giving him directions was Perry Christopher. *What was he doing here?* He turned to look back at Perry and saw that Perry had stopped waving and instead was giving him the finger. *Son of a bitch is dead*, Mitch thought as he turned back to face the wheel. He realized he was going way too fast and was heading for the quarry. He slammed his brakes as hard as he could. It wasn't enough as the car had too much forward momentum and slowly slid over the edge of the quarry to the murky depths below. As he plummeted downwards, his last thoughts were of how he had been played for a fool and hoped that Perry would rot in Hell.

CHAPTER 19

Fall River, Massachusetts. Last week.

He liked to hear them beg.

Brett had followed his usual routine. He left his home in Portsmouth, New Hampshire, telling his girlfriend that he was going fishing with some buddies. As always, she believed him. And why wouldn't she? He was a big teddy bear of a guy, a near clone of the actor Kevin James. People automatically warmed up to him due to his infectious grin and bubbly and effervescent personality. Of course, Brett had no intentions of going fishing. He would, on the way back, stop at a fish market to buy his weekend catch to ensure that his girlfriend never questioned what he really did on his weekend trips. No, he had much darker purpose in mind. He was going hunting.

Brett had driven down to his usual hunting grounds in Fall River, Massachusetts where he would cruise the strip in his beat up black Ford F-150 looking for some local talent. He liked the Ford as it offered enough anonymity from the local yokels who drove them in droves.

Driving up and down the strip for the last half hour, Brett hadn't seen anything he liked. He wanted a certain type of girl and any old streetwalker simply would not do. He liked them petite and blonde, a trait they all shared with his mother, although Brett quickly erased that image from his mind.

He was about to call it a night when he saw her. She stood on the side of the road, hip jutting out seductively. She was about five foot two with long, straight blonde hair which fell lazily about her shoulders. Thigh high black leather boots, a black mini skirt and a leopard print sleeveless blouse completed her outfit. She was perfect. He turned around slowly. He didn't want to appear too eager. He wanted them at ease around him. It made what happened later that much more fun.

Brett pulled up next to the girl. Up close, she looked barely eighteen. He smiled. He did like them young.

"Hi, there," Brett said, giving the girl his biggest smile, the one that always charmed people.

"Hi, yourself," the girl said smiling.

Brett looked the girl over. She had a nice, clean white smile. Her light brown eyes sparkled with obvious intelligence. "You want a date?" he asked in his most charming voice.

"Are you a cop?" the girl asked. "You have to tell me if you are."

Brett managed to look shocked. "No, of course I'm not a cop. So, are you available?"

The girl climbed into Brett's truck and extended her hand. Her fingers were long and delicate with the nails perfectly manicured. "I'm Kirsten."

Brett smiled. He was sure Kirsten was not her real name. They never gave their names, but that didn't stop Brett from finding out. "How much do you charge?"

He's done this before, the girl thought, *straight to business.* "It's fifty for a hummer, one hundred for the works. I don't do kinky or anal and will tell you if I find anything objectionable. One other thing, I insist that you wear protection. Do we have a deal?"

Brett felt the rage build up in him and he quickly suppressed it. Who was she to tell him what he could and could not do? She'd find out in due time the error of her ways. "You bet."

"You got a room?" Kirsten asked.

"I've got one better," Brett replied. "I'm down for the weekend doing some fishing. I've got a campsite with a nice tent that is very comfortable. Does that work for you, Kirsten?"

He seemed like decent enough, affable, and certainly non-threatening, so she agreed. Brett drove them to the campsite and made small talk along the way, talking about everything from the Red Sox to the president. He kept conversation light and made sure to avoid any potential topics which could trigger an argument. Even though Kristin was a working girl, and likely to pretend to agree with whatever Brett said, he made sure that he came across as a nice, genial college guy which helped keep his girls at ease.

Brett pulled off the main road and onto a small dirt road. He followed the road for a while until he came to a small campsite. He parked the truck and they both got out.

Brett looked at Kirsten, pointed to the campsite and said "Say, who's that over there?"

Kirsten followed where Brett was pointing. "I don't see…" she began when she felt something hard strike her on the side of her head. *Did he just hit me,* she thought as everything went black.

When Kirsten came to, she found that she was gagged and bound to a tree. It was still dark out, so she estimated that she hadn't been unconscious for too long. She knew that if she didn't get home by eight AM, her roommate would know something had happened and call the cops. She doubted the local police would not likely be too concerned for another missing streetwalker.

"Glad to see that you're awake…Jill," Brett said. He sat in a beach chair in his shorts and nothing else. He was sharpening a twelve inch hunting knife slowly over a smooth stone. "I hope you don't mind my looking through your purse. I do like to know who I'm dealing with."

"What do you want from me?" Jill asked, trying to sound brave, her voice cracking ever so slightly."

Brett smiled at her and Jill felt a cold shiver run up her spine. On the surface, he looked like an overgrown frat boy. She now realized that he was something else. The look she saw in his eyes indicated that she would never leave these woods alive. She thought of her little two year old son who was living with her mother until she could find some means to care for him and realized she'd never hear him laugh again. She felt the tears start to fall.

"Please, Brett," she said slowly, trying to keep herself together, "I have a son. Please let me go. I won't tell anyone about this. I promise. "

Brett walked up to Jill and put a finger on her lips and gently shushed her. "It's okay," he said, gently stroking her hair while she sobbed.

Jill looked up at Brett, a glimmer of hope forming. "Will you let me go?"

Brett took his thumb and wiped the tears from her eyes. He

smiled again and said softly "No. I plan to cut you into pieces. Then I'll eat your organs, starting with your heart."

Jill started thrashing about and screaming for help. She screamed and yelled until she was hoarse and then just fell back against the tree, sobbing silently. Brett liked to give them a degree of hope and then take it away from them. Their suffering only added to the thrill he felt.

Brett took his shorts off and stood before Jill completely naked. He passed his large hunting blade from hand to hand, doing a small dance and making a grand show of being menacing. He felt like Michael Madsen in Reservoir Dogs.

Brett took the knife and easily cut through her blouse. He eased it over her shoulders and watched it fall to the ground. He then slid the blade under the straps of her bra and sliced through them one after the other. He took a step back to admire her.

Brett advanced on Jill and gently stroked the blade over her taut belly. She tensed, waiting for the cut which didn't happen. Pulling back, he then lightly scraped the tip of the knife to her breasts and circled them, causing slight scratches, but nothing more. He started humming and then, with a quick slashing motion, cut a shallow furrow in her left arm. He repeated the motion on her right arm.

Jill screamed. She tensed, waiting for the next cut and saw in horror what came out of the woods and stood menacingly behind Brett. Behind him, casting a long shadow was a tall, nearly naked man with a perfectly chiseled bronze body and the head of a falcon. The man's shadow fell over Brett and he turned to see the tall man raise his arm, a large silver sickle-shaped sword in each hand.

"You are needed," the tall man said in Coptic Egyptian. Brett didn't understand the falcon-headed man's words, let alone have time to scream as the two *khopesh* were brought down and neatly severed his head from his shoulders. The spray of blood from her dead tormentor rained down on Jill before he collapsed to the ground.

Jill stared in horror at the tall man as he approached. She waited for the man to raise his sickle-shaped knives and take her life as he did with Brett. He tilted his falcon's head to the side and seemed to study her with cold, liquid black eyes. Then he said something that sounded to Jill like gibberish before he turned and walked away, leaving her bound to the tree.

Sobbing, Jill worked her bonds. With time they came loose enough for her to free herself. She stared at the decapitated corpse by her feet, noticing the head which had rolled under some bushes a few yards away. She found Brett's shorts on the ground where he had dropped them. It took all her effort to reach into his pockets and take his car keys and wallet. All she wanted to do was get as far away as possible. Using the shorts as a makeshift towel, she wiped the man's blood from her face and body. She then put her ruined shirt back on and drove away in Brett's truck. She knew one thing, though. She'd never walk the streets again.

CHAPTER 20

The Highway of Lost Souls. Past, present and future.

The cold, grey mist swirled around the vehicle and seemed to caress it. Frost patterns spread out across the metallic surface and stretched to the edge of the glass. The heat inside the BMW kept the ice at bay and allowed enough visibility through the windows. Greg put his hand to the glass and shuddered at how cold the surface was. They had the heat going inside but, even with the heat at full blast, they couldn't shake the nether chill that seeped into the vehicle from outside.

The Lost circled the BMW and pounded against the windows with their fists, desperate to get their hands on the four travelers to feast on their souls and on the momentary heat that the living offered.

"Drive, Paul," Greg said. "If we stay here, those things will get in, this whole trip will have been for nothing and we'll have failed our kids."

A middle-aged man scraped his hands against the glass on the driver side door. He begged to be let in. His eyes were clouded over and his skin was greyish in hue, and flecked with crystals of frost. Aside from that, he looked like any normal business man. How could he simply drive over these people?

"God damn it, Paul" Greg hissed through gritted teeth. "These people are dead. They are dead and soulless. Whatever it was that made them people has left the building. You need to drive and drive hard, because I'm not losing my kids only to be stopped here in the middle of purgatory."

The middle-aged man slammed his fist against the window and the car shook. They clearly felt no pain, Paul reasoned. He eased his foot down on the accelerator and pushed the BMW forward. The multitude of bodies of men, women and children pushed forward and seemed for a moment to block the car from moving ahead.

"Damn it," Paul cried, "There's too many of them."

"Hit the gas and don't take your foot off the pedal for anything," Greg yelled.

Paul pushed his foot all the way down on the pedal. The front tires spun uselessly for a moment then seemed to gather traction on the road's surface. The car punched forward and pushed through the crowd of the Lost who stood in front of the vehicle. Paul and Greg felt the bodies being crushed under the wheels. With his brother's urging, Paul kept the accelerator pushed all the way down and kept going. What he found most disconcerting was that, though they were crushing the Lost who had fallen beneath the vehicle, none of them uttered a sound. He made the mistake of looking back and saw that several of the Lost who had been crushed beneath the wheels managed to get back up and, though broken in several places, continue on after the car.

After what seemed like hours, driving through the endless mass of the Lost, they made it through the crowd and came to a relatively clear patch of road. Paul kept his foot down on the accelerator and managed to put some distance between their car and the growing masses of the dead who now followed them. Eventually, he slowed down and faced his brother.

"What do we do now? Do we keep driving?" Paul asked.

"I honestly don't know," Greg answered. He turned in his seat and looked to the back. David and Kevin were sitting there silently. "Have you guys got anything to add?"

Both Kevin and David stared ahead, as if in a trance. Neither of the men moved. The only evidence that Greg had that his friends were even alive was their slow and rhythmic breathing. For a moment he worried that his friends were becoming like the Lost, that maybe crossing over to the Highway of Lost Souls had robbed them of their own souls. Greg reached back and put his hand to Kevin's forehead. It was cool to the touch, but he definitely felt alive. He hoped that this state of catatonia that his friends were in was only temporary.

"I guess we drive," Greg said to his brother. The all-encompassing silence was starting to get to him. Greg was a guy who was used to noise all around him. A steady stream of outside noise allowed him to think. This kind of total silence only served to make him more uncomfortable. He looked over at his brother who was looking ahead, his attention focused on the road.

"I'm a bit surprised, Paul," Greg stated. "You're the one with the temper. I know you're impatient and easily angered. How are you so calm through all of this?"

Paul thought for a second, running his hand through his thinning hair. "I suppose it's because I still feel detached, somehow, from everything. This doesn't feel real. It feels like at any moment I'll wake up in my bed and that my kids will be home with me. I suppose that if I really start thinking about things, I might have to face the fact that our kids might already be dead."

Greg was about to answer when he noticed what looked like a road branching off from the main road. "Paul, look over to the right."

Paul turned and saw the road. It was a narrow path that seemed to spread out into the twilight gloom. "Should we?"

David and Kevin turned in unison. They pointed to the road and said, "The way to the House is there. Follow and all will be made clear."

Paul turned off the side road and drove into the darkness. The swirling mist seemed thinner here, but that didn't help any. The darkness was absolute and even with the BMW's high beams on, which seemed to get swallowed up into the liquid black of the night, they couldn't see more than a foot or so beyond the vehicle. Paul slowed down accordingly. If they went off the road here, he suspected that the journey would end for them and that they'd join the Lost in their endless wandering down the Highway of Lost Souls for all eternity.

The darkness suddenly fell away and they found themselves on a quiet, tree lined boulevard. The road was well paved and even. The sun was high and bright in the sky overhead, which had become a rich blue filled with soft, cumulous clouds drifting lazily in the breeze. Paul rolled down his window and felt the fresh air around him. After being trapped in the BMW with the windows closed, he enjoyed the feel of the sun on his skin and the sweet smell of fresh country air. "Where the Hell are we?"

Greg smiled. He was only guessing, but it *felt* like they were home in New England. "I don't honestly know. If I had to guess, I'd say we're close to our destination."

They drove down the quiet road for a few miles and came to a long driveway that led off the road. At the driveway's edge was a big wrought iron double gate. A tall, ten foot high brick wall went from the gate and extended as far as the eye could see on both sides, giving the property plenty of privacy.

Paul drove up to the gate and Greg got out of the vehicle to check. It was unlocked, so he pulled it open wide enough for Paul to drive through. He was about to get back into the vehicle when Paul called out, "You probably should close the gate behind me. I suspect it was left open because we're expected."

"Why do you think that?"

"Not sure," Paul added. "It's just a feeling I have. Think about it, what is the reason to even have a gate? It usually means that it is to keep people out."

"It also might be to keep people in, Paul. Until we know what the Hell is going on, I suggest we err on the side of caution."

Greg closed the gate and climbed back in to the car. They eased down the driveway and soon the House came into view. It was a large, gothic style mansion, made from grey stone and built back into what seemed like a natural rock face, giving the home the impression of being a natural, organic part of the land. The front of the House boasted a wide staircase that led up to a covered porch framed by grey marble Doric columns. It stood two stories high with many windows. Although none of the windows boasted blinds or any other kind of window treatment, the glass caused enough natural reflection that it was impossible to see the interior. The House seemed to stretch on for as far as the eye could see in either direction, but both brothers assumed it was an illusion created by the way the home was built into the rock.

They got out and were followed by David and Kevin. At some point between arriving at the gate and pulling up to the House, David and Kevin pulled apart. They both seemed dazed and had no recollection of anything that had happened since being at Kevin's place. The four men walked up the massive staircase to the front door in silence, lost in their thoughts. The double door was a rich dark oak with a large wrought iron handle and knocker.

"So," Paul asked his brother, "Do you think we should knock?"

Greg smiled. "I think we're expected. Let's go in and take our chances." He turned to his two friends. "You ready for this, guys?" They both nodded. It was time to enter the House.

CHAPTER 21

Burlington, Vermont. 1985.

Nicky Jepson cranked the radio up to high, and peeled out of the convenience store parking lot. He had the radio tuned to CHOM FM out of Montreal and the host, Claude Rajotte had just announced that they we're going to play Twisted Sister's big hit 'We're Not Gonna Take it'. Nicky was a huge rock fan and that song happened to be one of his absolute favorites. He reached into the bag on the seat beside him and grabbed a Twix bar. He ripped off the wrapper with his teeth and swallowed the cookie, caramel and chocolate in two bites.

He felt good to be alive. He had over a thousand dollars in the bag, plus snacks. The robbery of that gas station's convenience store had been a piece of cake. Only one cashier and customer were there when he had stormed in and demanded all the money. The sawed off shotgun in his hands ensured that they would listen and cough over the cash, no questions asked.

Of course, the kid behind the counter had to be a hero and pull out a gun. So Nicky had shot him. He giggled when he thought of how the kid had flown back into the display case of yodels with his chest blown wide open. That was when the middle-aged guy took off. So Nicky shot him in the back and literally blew him out of his penny loafers. He then bagged up the cash, easy as can be, took a bunch of snacks and beer, and hit the road. Heck, he'd be in Canada before the cops even got wind that anything was wrong.

Nicky gunned up Shelburne and roared onto route 189. The song he was listening to ended and the opening riffs from Iron Maiden's Two Minutes to Midnight kicked in. He cracked open a cold beer and took a long swig. He pushed the pedal down and felt his Mustang 5.0 shoot forward. He edged the odometer to 90 mph and marveled at how smoothly his car hugged the road.

Just before he reached the on ramp for I-89, he saw a cop hidden off to the side. *Shit*, he cursed. Nicky realized that he only had two options. Option one would be to play it cool and hope the cop didn't search his car. If they did, they'd find the sawed off shotgun, the bag of cash and the empty beer bottle in the back seat. Or, his other option would be to make a run for it. That wouldn't work as the Vermont State Troopers were a serious bunch of pricks and would surely manage to get a roadblock in place if he ran.

Nicky slammed his hand on the steering wheel. Fuck it, he yelled, punching the dashboard until he saw his knuckles were bleeding. He pulled over to the shoulder. The Trooper pulled up behind him and angled the nose of his cruiser out towards the road. He seemed to take forever, leaving Nicky to sweat it out. Finally, the driver's door opened and the Trooper stepped out. Nicky watched the man in his rearview mirror and wanted to laugh. The guy was a freaking caricature. He had on mirrored sunglasses and wore riding pants, flared out at the thighs. On his head was the typical Vermont State Trooper hat, the green, borderline cowboy looking hat with the badge plastered dead center on the front. He even wore the polished black rider boots that went up to his knees. He lowered the window and waited for the Trooper to arrive.

The Trooper came up to the window and bent over to get a good look at Nicky and inside the car. "Good afternoon, sir," he said slowly, "would you mind turning off the radio please."

Nicky hated to shut the radio off. A classic from the Scorpions was playing, but he decided better to be safe than sorry. "Sure thing, officer," he said while flashing his most charming grin. "Is there a problem?"

The Trooper gave Nicky a scowl that Nicky assumed he likely spent hours in front of the mirror practicing. "You were speeding, sir. I have you clocked at going ninety-five miles per hour. The posted speed limit is fifty-five."

Nicky feigned surprise. "I'm sorry, officer. I just had dropped my cigarette and must have inadvertently picked up more speed. Can you give me a break today? It's been a real tough day." Nicky gave the

Trooper his most sincere smile and waited for the Trooper's reaction.

"I see," the Trooper eventually replied. "Normally, I would, but driving that high over the speed limit necessitates you coming back to the station with me. Please step out of the car, sir."

"Sure," Nicky replied. He pulled out the sawed off shotgun he had kept between his leg and the door and aimed it at the Trooper who saw the gun and was frantically trying to pull his service revolver from its holster. "Bang, you're dead," Nicky roared with laughter as he shot the Trooper twice in the chest.

He started the car and turned the radio back on as he peeled out on 89 north. He was forty minutes from the border. If he gunned it, he might make it before they found the dead Statie. He revved the engine and the car raced along the highway, steadily gathering speed. He had the car at one hundred and was pushing it even faster. Traffic was sparse and what cars he did see appeared to be standing still as he roared by them. He soon passed a sign that said he was only six miles from the Canadian border. He looked at his watch and saw that he had gotten this far in less than twenty minutes. It looked like he would make it in plenty of time. Once in Canada, he knew of an old girlfriend who could put him up for a while and help him get off the grid.

Nicky reached down to grab another beer and chocolate bar. When he looked up, he saw a deer trotting across the highway, directly in front of him.

"What the....," was all Nicky managed to say as the car, doing over one hundred miles per hour, plowed into the deer. The impact crushed the front of the Mustang and flipped the deer over the hood, landing hard on the windshield. The glass from the windshield shattered and rained in on Nicky. He took his hands from the wheel and tried to shield his eyes, causing the wheel to jerk to the left. The mustang turned too sharply and flipped over, rolling down I-89, eventually coming to a stop in the middle of the blacktop. Nicky was bleeding from dozens of cuts from the shattered windshield. His arm was broken and, when he looked down, he saw that the steering column had impaled his chest.

Nicky looked out at the clear blue sky. *Seems like as good a day as any to die*, he thought. His vision was getting dimmer when he saw the air in front of his car shimmer and then split. A tall man with the head of a bird stepped through the rip in the sky. He walked over to the car and ripped the door off its hinges. The man with the bird's head then reached in and pulled Nicky free from the car, sliding him easily off the steering column. For some reason, he didn't feel any pain. He looked at the bird-headed man with reverence.

"Are you God?" Nicky asked.

The bird-headed man threw his head back and laughed. "You should be thankful I got to you before God. No, I am not him nor am I here to offer judgment on your soul. Instead, I'm offering you the gift of eternal life. All I require is your allegiance and that you perform a simple task for me. I must have your answer, Nicholas Jepson. What will it be? Will you come with me and live forever or die alone on this lonely road?"

Nicky smiled. Eternity with the bird man sure beat going to Hell. "You got it, friend." He looked down at his ruined chest and broken body. "What about the damage?"

The bird-headed man waved his hand over Nicky's chest and the gaping wound sealed up. Nicky's arm straightened and, with a brief snap, was back in one piece. "Come with me, Nicky. We have much to do."

The two then walked through the rip in the air, which sealed up the moment they were through. Later, when people came upon the wrecked Mustang, they would see the blood all over the seats and steering column, the crushed front end and glass and twisted shards of metal all over the road and wonder how anyone could have survived a crash like that and walk away.

CHAPTER 22

In the House. Present day.

It is time.

The Other heard the voice echo around his brain. It was the same voice which had kept him company and whispered in his ear for the many millennia he had been trapped in the Hall. The voice had kept him sane and filled with a purpose. He welcomed it as one would welcome a lover. The stranger's voice was both warm and caring. The Other knew that he would do anything for the voice.

Khufu, the voice said a bit more urgently. *I need you to awaken. The time we have waited for so long is finally upon us. The Ascension will happen within the next twenty four hours. We must be there as our part in this drama has yet to play out. I have assembled all the players we shall need to stop this travesty from happening. It's time.*

The Other, Khufu, forced his eyes open. His vision slowly came back into focus. He saw the powerful figure standing before him. When he looked up, he saw that the figure had a perfect, bronzed and well-oiled body and the head of a falcon. Khufu would kneel before the God, but he was still held prone by the metal rod which pierced his body from his shoulder through his groin and held him pinned to the floor like an insect on a specimen table.

"Mighty Horus, my life is yours to command. I live to serve you and only you," Khufu said so softly, so reverently, he hoped the God would approve. Of course, his lips were sewn shut and his throat was parched, after not having spoken in more than a millennia. Still, he hoped that he pleased the God that loomed over him.

Horus threw his avian head back and roared with laughter. "Dear

Khufu, favored, son, I already know that. But tell me, Khufu, how can you serve me pinned to the ground as if you were next to nothing?"

"Please, mighty Horus," Khufu begged, "Free me and I am yours for eternity."

Horus leaned over Khufu and with a long, taloned nail, sliced through the bindings which held his lips sewn together. He then went about removing the bindings from his eyes. "There," Horus' voice boomed, "now you look more presentable. Of course, I do need you to be mobile. Horus crouched down and looked Khufu straight in the eye. Khufu wanted to turn away. He knew he should never look upon a God directly, but Horus' liquid black eyes were so hypnotic he could not look away even if he tried. "I see that I can trust you, Khufu," Horus said as he grasped the metal pole protruding from Khufu's shoulder. He gave a small tug and pulled it free of the ground and Khufu's body.

Khufu looked at the hole in his shoulder and was amazed by the lack of blood. He bowed his head and swore fealty to his God. "Thank you, oh mighty Horus. I am your eternal servant. If it is not too bold, why do I not bleed? Am I dead?"

"It is this place," Horus said. "It is a place after life but before death. It is Anubis' realm. But it won't be for much longer. The Ascension is due. It is time for a changing of the guard and you, my dear Khufu, will be helping me make this happen."

Khufu forced himself to stand. He was a fairly tall man, or had been in life, but he was dwarfed by the imposing stature of Horus. That Horus' own brother Anubis, had imprisoned Khufu so many years back, yet Horus was so willing to free him, meant that there was no love lost between the siblings. Khufu smiled. He'd store that knowledge away for later. Perhaps there would come a point where he could use that to his advantage.

Khufu took in his surroundings. The Great Hall looked as it had when he had stood there many millennia before with his Canopic jar in his hands waiting for judgment. The throne was on the far end of the room as before. A similar scale to the one which Anubis used to measure souls was off to the side of the throne. It contained a new steel pole much like the one Anubis had used to imprison him for all these many years. To the other side of the throne was where Ammit, the Devourer of Souls, had breached this world. He shuddered, thinking of what that creature would have done to him. He would not go anywhere near that thing if he could avoid it.

"I'm ready, mighty Horus. Tell me what I need to do."

Horus tossed him a small cloth and rope. "Use these to cover your nakedness, Khufu. We have a lot to do." He waited while Khufu put on the loincloth and properly covered himself. "Come, Khufu. We are going to leave this Hall. We must hurry, though. Anubis is far too occupied with the coming Ascension and he has failed to notice that we are in his realm. We must go to the House where his souls are judged. It is there that we will change history."

Horus walked to the edge of the Great Hall, waved his hand and a door appeared in the stone wall. Horus grasped the handle and ushered Khufu through. Khufu passed through from the great Hall to a narrow hallway with a pale cream carpet and walls painted a soft white, with dozens of doors running the length of the two walls. He turned and saw Horus standing on the other side of the doorway.

"Aren't you coming?" Khufu asked.

Horus let out a long and low sigh. "I cannot. It is not my realm. I can at best manage brief periods in the Great Hall, as can our father Osiris. But that is the extent of it. Do not worry, Khufu. What comes next requires very little of you, but will set in motion a chain of events that history will never forget."

Khufu felt nervous. The place he was in was certainly strange. What was this odd fabric on the ground? And the walls were clearly not stone or even wood. Even stranger were the doors. There were more than he could count, all identical and they extended down a passageway as far as he could see.

"What should I do, oh mighty Horus?"

Horus beckoned Khufu to come forward. Khufu walked to the door and Horus passed him a scimitar through the threshold. "Take this weapon, Khufu. I need you to follow this passageway, counting the doors on your right side. When you get to the twenty- fourth door, you are to open it. Inside, you will find a man who will help us. He is the first of two men you will recruit. Be careful with these men, Khufu. They are jackals and will turn on you at their first opportunity."

"Then why should we use them? Surely we two are enough to disrupt the Ascension and change things to your needs?"

Horus tilted his head affectionately. "That is very brave of you,

Khufu. But my accursed brother is no fool and has already set in motion plans to bring to the House those he will engage as allies. So, we have no choice in the matter. As untrustworthy as the men are, we need them, Khufu. But you are in charge. Remember that when the men try to take control. Now go quickly. Time is drawing short and there is still much to do."

Khufu started down the hallway and paused. Once he found the first man, how would he know where to find the second? He turned back to ask Horus, but found that the portal to the Great Hall was gone and there was another hallway with countless doors stretching out before him.

Khufu turned and began walking down the hallway, counting doors as he went. When he got to the twenty-fourth one, he stopped. He put his ear to the door and listened. When he didn't hear anything, he decided to open the door and see who might be inside. He pulled the door open and was shocked to see that it did not contain a room as expected. He stood in disbelief as he watched the scene that was unfolding before his eyes. He wanted to turn and run, but had made a promise and would not betray Horus. Khufu gritted his teeth and crossed the portal into a nightmare.

CHAPTER 23

In the House. Present day.

Greg opened the massive front door and stepped into the house, followed by his brother Paul and then David and Kevin. Once through the doorway, it swung shut behind them. Kevin ran over and tried the handle only to find it locked.

"Guys," Kevin said, his voice trembling, "I think we're locked in."

Greg went over and tried the handle, but it wouldn't turn. They were trapped in the house. He kicked the door and saw that it didn't even move. "Kevin's right, guys. We're locked in and the door is pretty solid. I don't see us getting out this way, so it means we have to explore the House and try and find another way out. Right now, we need to stick to the plan and find our kids. Let's hope we can find the kids and a way out without running into the guy from our dreams. I'd rather avoid any encounters which could in any way hurt the children," Greg added.

They stood in an elaborate vestibule with a thick Persian rug on the floor. Beyond the rug, the floor was a grey marble reminiscent of the classic Roman style. Mahogany wing chairs with plush red seats lined the walls. An elaborate chandelier hung overhead, with dozens of candles casting their flickering fingers of light in dancing patterns over the walls. The walls themselves contained crown molding and were painted a rich cream color. A cherry wood buffet table stood against the far wall beneath a large mirror with an ornate gold frame. On the buffet were two pewter candelabra, and each one held lit black candles. Greg noticed that they must have been recently lit, since there was virtually no wax drippings visible down the candle's stem. Clearly, they were expected. The marble floor extended down a long hallway, with several branches going off in either direction from the main hallway.

"This place is huge," David remarked. "Anyone have any idea as to where we should go?"

"I'm kind of thinking we head home," Kevin remarked. "This place is seriously creepy. On the surface, nothing seems out of place. It's just that there's a kind of vibe that makes me feel as if we shouldn't be here."

"I feel it too," Paul remarked. "It's like people don't come here. There is no reason for a living person to ever set foot through those doors. This whole house looks like it was made to be an illusion of life. The only ones who come are the dead and that's to complete their final journey. If I had to guess, they don't walk through these front doors."

"So what are you saying then, Paul?" Kevin asked, clearly visibly agitated.

Paul paused. He wanted to be sure he expressed himself in the clearest, most coherent manner. "I think our walking through the front doors was symbolic. Same as the whole journey down the Highway of Lost Souls. I think we passed from the realm of the living, when we left Kevin's house in Lasalle, to a midway point or way station en route to the afterlife."

"Why would there even need to be a mid-point?" David asked.

Greg rubbed his chin, something he frequently did when engrossed in thought. "I think I agree with my brother. Look at us. We're not dead. I, for one, feel very much alive. But you can feel that this place is completely devoid of life. Look at the candles. They burn yet no wax drips. There is no smell to this place. It's as if it were a sterile prop to make us feel at ease. Life does not belong here and yet here we are. But it all makes sense if you think about it. The dreams Paul and I had were all about death. We dreamt these same dreams for a decade. Was it coincidence or was someone trying to get a message to us? If that was the case, why did we have to go through the whole song and dance needed to get here?"

"I get it," David added, "we had to come here the long way because we're not dead and only the dead can be brought here. That means that this whole thing is an illusion. I have to admit, it's a very realistic one." David walked over to the candelabra and put his hand over the flame. "There's no heat. So, it makes sense that if everything here is nothing more than an illusion for our benefit, we can safely assume that the door wasn't there either even though we all swear we saw it open. Our trip down the Highway of Lost Souls took us here to this place. Our minds processed it in such a way that we can accept it."

"Then how are we all seeing the same thing if it's an illusion?" Kevin asked.

David shrugged. "I don't know. I'm as much in the dark as the rest of you. It helps to try and understand as much of our situation as possible."

"Then how did our kids get brought here?" Paul asked, "Because we know they are not dead. And I'm pretty damn sure they didn't come here via the same route that we did."

"Maybe," David said, expanding on his theory, "the rules differ for children? Perhaps their souls are not fully defined or are purer and, because of that, they can enter this place freely."

"Sounds like you guys are reaching," Kevin added. "Can we just get on with this?"

Greg walked over to Kevin and gently pulled him aside. "What's going on?"

Kevin sighed. "Greg, I know how these things play out. In books and movies, it's always the bit players who are expendable. I wasn't keen on this trip and, somehow, by touching David's hand I became an unwilling participant. Now it looks like we're in some way-station between life and death or even Earth and Hell, and there is no way back. I don't want to be the fucking Star Trek character in the red shirt. I have a family and I'd like to see them again."

"I don't know what to say here, Kevin. I honestly don't. Right now, though, we're all in this together. None of us wants to die. We all want to return home to our families. I've known you since we were kids. I've seen you laughed at, rejected, go through adversity and hardship and then come out stronger on the other side. Compared to all the crap from the past, this should be easy. Besides, I need you, we all do. There's a reason we are all here together. Let's keep moving forward and find the kids and get the Hell out of here."

Kevin refused to look at Greg. "Whatever."

The two men walked over to where Paul and David were standing.

"Is everything okay?" David asked.

Kevin nodded. "Like sunshine in July."

"All right guys," Greg said. "Find something you can use as a weapon. We're heading out."

Paul grabbed one of the two candelabra from the mantle. He found it to be surprisingly heavy and he reasoned that whoever he hit with it would be sorry. Besides, he liked the light the candelabra gave off. In a huge gothic mansion like this, light was always a good thing. The rest of the guys smashed one of the Queen Anne chairs and made makeshift clubs out of the legs.

Once armed, they walked down the long hallways. They passed several passageways which branched off the main one. Each branch extended as far as the eye could see, with doorway after doorway. On many occasions, they could swear they heard screams of terror and cries of pain coming from the depths of the shadows which made up the dark recesses of the many branches off the main hallway. It didn't take long for the men to be completely overwhelmed by the enormity of the place. When they looked back, they could no longer see the foyer which they had entered. They hoped that it was merely due to the foyer being absorbed by the shadows. It was far better than the alternative.

The four men eventually came to the end of the main hallway which ended at a long spiral staircase that rose up into the shadows.

Greg slowly climbed the stairs, quickly followed by his brother. When David started up, Kevin grabbed his arm and asked whether it was such a good thing to be going upstairs. David shrugged and kept up the pace set by the two brothers. Kevin sighed and followed David up.

The staircase was much worse than the ground floor as the darkness seemed to envelop them by the time they were midway up. Only the light of the candelabra allowed them to see where they were going.

Eventually they came to the top of the staircase which opened into a huge landing. The landing extended to both the right and left which gave the option of exploring the top level of the house in two halves, both of which were substantially larger than anyone had imagined.

"Anyone want to select a direction?" Paul asked.

"Let's go right. Typically, when faced with this type of choice, people usually choose to go left. For what it's worth, I'd like to have the element of surprise here, if possible," Greg added.

David looked at his friend. "Only surprise is if we make it through this in one piece. All signs point to the fact that we're expected."

"I know," Greg sighed. "It was really just me trying to convince myself that what we're doing is the right thing."

Kevin laughed. "Well, if you really want to have us do the right thing, we should find a television, order a pizza and watch the game."

Greg just shook his head and started down the hallway to his right. It was dimly lit with hidden recessed lights. The dim lights cast menacing shadows over the cream-colored walls. On each side of the hallway were many identical doors. Greg tried the first door and found it to be unlocked. He started to open it when he heard a blood-curdling scream from further down the hall. He took off running to investigate, followed by Paul, David and Kevin.

After a while, they came to a hallway which branched off the main hall and continued on straight ahead. They paused, listening for more screams, but none were forthcoming. Moans, shrieks and other sounds were heard coming from behind the multitude of doors.

"So what do we do now?" Paul asked his brother. He found the cacophony of screams behind the many doors unsettling but refused to give in to his terror.

"Keep going straight." Greg walked on, keeping to the main hallway. After a bit, he stopped. "These doors are bugging me. It was behind a door like this where I dreamt of my parents as rotting corpses." He then grabbed a handle and pulled the door open. Inside was a small boy huddled in the corner, staring off into space. He was watching something play out on an invisible screen in front of him. Greg stepped into the room and saw the walls melt around him. He found he was in a small cornfield with the boy who was being chased by a large man wearing nothing but overalls. The man was huge, at least six foot two and weighing at least two hundred and fifty pounds. His long hair was matted with filth and there were several days' worth of stubble on his cheeks. His eyes blazed with fury as he chased the small boy. In his right hand, he held a pitchfork.

The boy was screaming and crying out for help, and kept turning to see if the man was gaining on him. When he saw Greg, he stopped and stared. The man chasing him did the same.

"Who are you?" the man growled in a low, gravelly voice. "You don't belong here."

"Leave the boy alone, mister," Greg said, hoping he sounded braver than he felt. He turned to the boy. "Are you all right, sonny?"

The boy seemed confused. "I don't remember you. But that's odd because why should I?" He looked back to the man in the overalls. "I remember him. Me and my buddy found him sleeping in the shed in the back of my dad's farm. He scared us, so we took off. My buddy and I split up and he ran after me. And then..." the boy paused and wiped tears from his eyes. "Then he...." The boy burst into tears. He ran to Greg who comforted him.

The man's features darkened with rage. "He and his little friend threw rocks at me. They called me a worthless bum. They said they was gonna get the cops. There is no way I'm going back to jail for vagrancy. So I decided to put a little fear into them. Teach them some respect for their elders. So I chased him and," he paused, "I seem to remember him falling and hitting his head on a rock in the field." The man looked at Greg. "How can I remember him falling and splitting his skull open? That hasn't happened, yet if I think about it, I can see it clear as day."

Greg looked around. There was nothing but cornfield around him. *Where was the door that let him into the room? How would he get back to the House?* "I shouldn't be here," he said, backing away from the boy in the direction he had come. "This is wrong. I shouldn't be here."

Greg felt hands around his collar and turned in time to see his being hauled out of the cornfield through a golden slash in the air, back into the hallway. The door slammed shut behind him. He turned and saw that it was his brother who had pulled him out of the room.

"Are you okay, Greg?" Paul asked. You stepped in to the room and I saw you fade away, the deeper you went in. I followed you and felt myself being pulled from the room itself into a whole other universe or something. Frankly, it was a miracle that I was able to grab you at all."

Greg sighed. "I think I was in a snapshot of someone's life. The two people there seemed as surprised to see me as I was them. They both seemed to sense that I didn't belong there, even though they, in fact, did. It was pretty intense. A boy was being chased by a homeless guy. Both seemed to remember that the kid trips, hits his head and dies, even though it had yet to happen. Notice the whole death thing again? I feel that we're close, but that elusive piece is still missing."

The group kept walking down the main hallway, ignoring the moans and cries coming from behind the other doors. At one point, Kevin made a beeline towards a certain door and was about to open it when Greg interfered.

"Don't open any of the doors!" Greg yelled and grabbed Kevin's arm and pulled him back forcibly.

Kevin's eyes were red and wet with tears. "I heard my mother, Greg. She died when I was little. She was calling to me, asking me to come and be with her."

"This house messes with your mind, Kevin," Greg said grimly. "I dreamt of this place every night for several years. It feeds on your emotions and somehow pits them against you. Keep the doors closed. In my dreams I saw my dead parents and they wanted me to stay with them too. Of course, they wanted me to stay forever."

"So why did you just open a door, Greg?"

"As I said, Kevin, it called to me. You see, the little boy I saw in the room was one of my best friends as a kid. He and his family moved away to a farm when we were eight. We kept in contact by writing letters and by phone calls when our parents allowed. Well, the summer I was ten, I was invited by his family to spend a few weeks there. I was thrilled. We had the best summer. We went swimming, bike riding, built a tree house. You name it. One day, we were messing around in the cornfields and came across an old shed. Inside, a filthy bum was curled up on the floor sleeping. Well, Jimmy picked up a small rock and threw it at the bum. It hit him in the forehead and he woke up right away. Well, he grabbed a pitchfork and swore he was going to kill us. Jimmy started taunting him, calling him names and said his dad would get the police. The bum was screaming in rage by this point. I grabbed Jimmy and we took off.

"Well, we split up and the bum followed Jimmy. I made it back to the barn but Jimmy didn't. We found Jimmy dead in the cornfield, his head smashed on a rock. The bum was caught outside of town within twelve hours and was jailed. Of course, small town justice prevailed and the men in the town, all wearing masks, broke into the local jail, dragged out the bum and delivered their own brand of justice.

"I hadn't thought of that day in years. I had nightmares about Jimmy, wondering if he would have still been alive if I never had visited. To this day, I still blame myself for his death. What's worse, when I walked past the door, I heard Jimmy in my head calling to me, pleading and scared, asking for me to help him. I couldn't stop myself. I had to go in."

"It was the same for me," Kevin added. "My mother's death hit me hard. I wasn't around when she died and always felt guilty about that. Hearing her calling to me, it was like I couldn't stop myself from going in to see her."

"Then we all need to watch each other's backs," David said. "This House, like everything else on this odyssey, is a lot more than it seems. We need to stay together, watch out for each other and be smart. We have only one job that we need to focus on. Get the kids and get out."

They started down the hallway, keeping to the main hall and ignoring the many branches that led off into the darkness. No one said anything. They were all lost in their thoughts. The recessed lights gave them enough illumination to see a good distance ahead and behind them, so they felt secure enough that they wouldn't be surprised.

Soon enough, they came to the end of the main hallway which ended at a large double door. Paul tried the handle and found it unlocked. The door swung inward and led to a huge stone hall. The walls were adorned with lit braziers that cast warming shadows across the room. The floor was a gleaming black polished marble which reflected the light from the braziers. Across the large hall was a huge throne set atop a dais and was partially hidden by the shadows of the room. Lying across the throne with a spear through his chest was a man.

The men cautiously approached the throne, watchful that whoever had done this to the figure on the throne wasn't still around. As they got closer, the figure stirred and slowly moved to a sitting position. He sat up and gritted his teeth together as he pulled the spear from his chest and casually tossed it aside. The figure stood on shaky legs and slowly walked over to the group. He kept his head down and, when he got within a few feet of the men, he straightened up to his full height and lifted his head to stare at them with a regal gaze. Greg and Paul froze as they recognized the gaunt features of the man who haunted their dreams. The same man who had abducted their children.

"I welcome you to my home, Greg and Paul. You may call me Anthony for the time being." Anthony turned to face David and Kevin and smiled. "I applaud your resourcefulness in managing to find your way here. You four are the first living beings to ever enter the Great Hall. I sincerely apologize for the clandestine means in which you were lured here, but it is a matter of great importance and we simply don't have much time."

"Where's my daughter, you son of a bitch," Greg yelled as he lunged at the pale man.

The man easily dodged Greg and turned back to the others. "Hear me out. Then, and only then we shall discuss the children." He glared at Greg who grudgingly walked back next to his brother. Paul saw that Greg was trying to hold it together.

"Why were you lying there with a spear sticking out of your chest? Why aren't you dead?" Kevin asked, trying to change the topic.

The man hissed. "My cursed brother did this. He caught me unawares. It won't happen again." His features hardened and the four men saw the flicker of a face behind his visage.

"He's not human, Kevin," Greg stated. "But he obviously has his weaknesses or he wouldn't be so desperate to get my brother and me here."

Anthony smiled. "Greg is correct, Kevin, on all counts. I am not human. And, yes, there is a reason I brought you here. You are needed to prevent what could be a catastrophe unlike the world has ever seen."

Paul looked around, then glared at Anthony with his coldest stare and grabbed him by his collar. "Let me ask again what my brother already asked you, Anthony. Where are our kids?"

Anthony sighed and removed Paul's hands from his person. "I took your kids to get you here. It was the only way. We both know that if I asked you for your help, your answer would certainly have been no. It seems that there is now a new a wrinkle to things. You see, when I was attacked, your kids were taken from me by my brother and he will use their lives as leverage to ensure that the reason I brought you here never happens."

Paul approached Anthony. "We don't care why we were brought here. It doesn't involve us and we want no part of it. We want our kids and we want to go home."

A look of despair crossed Anthony's delicate and pale features. "I don't think you understand me, Paul. The people who have your kids will kill them one way or the other. All they care about is stopping what has been set in motion since the dawn of time."

"And what if they do?" growled Greg.

"It will be the end of your world and everything you hold dear."

CHAPTER 24

In the House. Present day.

Ari awoke and saw that he was in a dimly lit tunnel. The walls were slightly damp and had a faint odor of mildew. Green fluorescent lichen lined the base of the walls, creating enough light by which to see.

Ahead of him, down the tunnel, Ari saw what looked to be a body. He approached carefully, making sure that his shoes did not make a scraping noise which could alert anyone to his presence. He finally came to the body and saw that it was that of a young man. *His name is Eric*, Ari thought. *No*, he thought, *my name isn't Ari here. I'm known to these people as Jason.*

Ari shook his head, clearly confused. How did he know that young man? Even worse was the fact that the young man was torn to shreds and yet he didn't feel even remotely bothered by it. He saw that the poor young man's ribcage had been split open and that his internal organs had been laid out before the body like some warped pagan offering.

He stood up, his decision clear. He couldn't stay here. Whoever or whatever had killed the young man might be back. Either way, he did not wish to come across it. Ari knew that his focus should be on survival. He had survived the suicide bomber at that café in Israel. *The one that killed my beautiful wife*, he thought bitterly. He had survived his stint in the Mossad, and still had the scars from the various bullets he had taken and the year of torture he had endured in a Syrian terrorist camp. He would survive this. His first order of business was to establish where he was and then find a way out. Based on the dampness in the air and the faint earthy smell, Ari surmised that he was in a tunnel below ground. Getting out shouldn't be that difficult, then.

Ari followed the tunnel, making sure he kept to the shadows. On more than one occasion, he came to an intersection and had to debate whether to stay the course or take one of the turns. A bit further on, he came to another body. It belonged to a short, stocky woman who, like the young man he had seen earlier, was torn to shreds with her internal organs placed almost reverently in front of her corpse. *Her name was Suze*, Ari thought. *How do I know this?* Ari felt his chest tighten. It hit him that he was reliving a portion of his life, and that what he was reliving was clearly of some importance.

He paused to reflect. *If I'm reliving my life*, Ari thought, *does that mean I'm dead?* He held out his hands and looked at the backs and the palms. The hands were smooth, the same hands he looked at every day of his life. He balled his right hand into a fist and punched the wall. A searing pain shot up his arm.

I can't be dead, he reasoned. *After all, the dead don't feel pain.* He kept walking down the tunnel, using the fluorescent lichen as his only source of light. The air itself was cool and damp and left a moist, earthy taste in his mouth.

After walking for a good ten to fifteen minutes, Ari was sure he was going in circles. There were too many twists and turns and the tunnels seemed to go on forever. He was beginning to feel frustrated. He was a man of action. Inactivity or simply wasting time bothered him. He needed to feel like whatever he was doing served some meaningful end.

Ari walked down a long corridor and was about to turn the corner when his instincts kicked in and made him stop. He advanced carefully and peered around the corner. He saw a man-shaped figure bent over someone else. There were glowing characters on the thing's body which Ari recognized as Hebrew letters. He couldn't believe his eyes. It was a golem. No, scratch that. This was The Golem. Ari froze as the memories came flooding back to him. *This just happened*, he thought. I helped unleash this monster on the world. *So how is it here?*

He took a step back, moving behind the safety of the wall so he was no longer visible. His heart felt heavy. How had he allowed himself to be filled with so much hatred that he could be part of such a horrific plan? Rachel had been his life and, when she had been cruelly taken from him, he had spiraled deeper and deeper into despair. He supposed that by the time he was captured by Al-Qaida, and held and tortured in Syria, he was already so emotionally empty that nothing would be able to touch him.

Perhaps he could at least right this wrong. After all, he had been instrumental in carrying it out. He knew that his name was not written on the parchment that was placed in the Golem's mouth, so he could get close. As long as he didn't make any overt, threatening moves towards the creature, he'd be safe.

Ari moved slowly around the corner, staying close to the walls, hoping to stay hidden in the shadows. He would wait for the right time and then strike. The Golem was still busy with something in front of him. It made wet, tearing sounds. Its crude hands were drenched in blood, which looked almost black in the near darkness. A thick white mist swirled about the creature. It seemed to emanate from the Golem.

Suddenly, the creature stiffened and stood erect, its arms hanging loosely by its side. The Golem seemed to glare directly at him. Ari saw a word etched into the creature's forehead. Like all the letters carved all over its' body, they glowed brightly. The word was in Hebrew, and meant truth.

Ari saw the ruined figure of a man on the ground behind the creature. The Golem took a tentative step towards Ari, then another. *It senses my presence but can't see me*, Ari thought, *as long as I stay completely still.*

Ari shivered as a cold mist seemed to swirl and emanate outward from the creature. He heard a voice at the back of his head, grating and tearing into his brain. The creature seemed to be whispering something to him, telling him of his sins and promising absolution. Ari wanted to run. Every fiber of his being screamed for him to turn and flee, yet his body was frozen in place. A single tear rolled down his cheek as the Golem pulled his sins from his memories and passed its judgment. Ari screamed and the Golem turned in his direction.

The Golem moved closer and grabbed Ari and hurled him against the wall. He hit the wall hard and slumped down on the floor. Everything hurt, but at least the spell was broken. He tried to stand

and found that he couldn't. *So this is how it ends*, he thought. He supposed he deserved it, but found he still wanted to live.

Behind him, a bright doorway opened. He turned to see a tall, gaunt man framed by a halo of light. Behind him, stood four other men, all of whom looked like they would rather be anywhere else.

"Ari Friedman," the man said, his rough, papery voice echoing in the stillness of the tunnel. "Would you like a chance to earn redemption? Would you like to be reunited with Rachel once more?"

Ari nodded, his eyes welling with tears. He knew he'd give anything to have her back. "Yes," he whispered. "I would."

The pale man smiled. He reached out and grabbed Ari by the collar and pulled him into the light. The Golem stayed in the shadows and howled with fury at being denied its prey.

"Thank you," Ari said.

"Don't thank me just yet," the man said. His features flickered and Ari was sure he saw something else beneath the skin. It looked like a dog, or something else, something older. "You have a difficult task ahead of you and, if you fail, you'll end up with a fate far worse than what you just left behind."

Ari gritted his teeth. "Bring it, then," he growled. If it meant getting to see his wife again, he would go to Hell and back. He didn't know how close to the truth that very sentiment was.

CHAPTER 25

Windham, NH. Present day.

Grace sat up in bed. She looked over at the clock radio on the nightstand next to her bed and sighed. It was only two- thirty in the morning. She was exhausted but knew she wouldn't fall back asleep. Since her daughter had been taken in the middle of the night and Greg and his brother had taken off on what she suspected was a useless trip in search of their kids and the monster who abducted them, she hadn't managed to have a good night's sleep. She knew the lack of sleep was killing her. Just that morning, she had drifted off behind the wheel on her way to work and almost went off the road.

Grace was by nature not someone who sat still, and the lack of anything new by the police was killing her. Even her husband seemed to have vanished off the face of the earth. He wasn't answering his cell and her calls and texts went unanswered. She had called his brother's wife and she was in the same boat. She decided that tomorrow she'd go to the police and push the issue. Her daughter was gone, and maybe now her husband. The time to passively sit back and wait was over.

Grace lay back down and tried to fall asleep. She wouldn't admit it to anyone, but being alone in the big house made her feel alone vulnerable, feelings she had repressed since her childhood where she had lain still in her darkened room under the safety of her covers while her parents screamed and yelled at each other.

A sound from downstairs caused Grace to sit up, her heart hammering in her chest. It wasn't the house settling, she thought. It was far too loud. She was pretty sure she had set the alarm before she had gone to sleep, so anyone forcing their way in would have set it off.

She quietly got out of bed and wrapped her terrycloth robe about her. Grace slipped on her slippers and walked out of the bedroom and out to the hallway. She looked at the alarm box and saw that the alarm was still on and active. Feeling foolish, she was about to return to bed when she heard a loud noise from downstairs.

Grace stopped. *Where was the dog?* They had a hyperactive black lab and the slightest noise would usually set her off. She looked about the bedroom and Lucy was nowhere to be found. She was sure that the dog was with her in the bedroom. Grace always kept the bedroom door closed out of habit, so the dog shouldn't have been able to get out of the room.

Grace kept the lights off and quietly made her way down the staircase to the ground floor. She peered into the living room and saw that it was empty. She crossed over the dining room to the kitchen and breathed a sigh of relief when she saw that it was empty too. She quietly walked across the kitchen to the great room and froze when she saw that the floor lamp was on. She was certain that before she had gone to bed, she shut every light in the house. Someone had turned it on…but how? No one could have breached the perimeter without setting off the alarm. God knows she had accidentally set it off herself on more than one occasion, usually when she took Lucy out in the morning and she had been too tired to remember to key in the code. She softly crept into the great room and peered into the shadows, making sure that no one was there. Darkness spilled from the corners and seemed to taunt her to come closer into their murky depths. The guinea pig ran around his cage and seemed to stop when he saw Grace.

In the corner of the room, Grace saw Lucy lying on her bed. Did she come downstairs and then curl up on her bed to sleep, Grace wondered? She walked over to the dog and scratched her on the back of her head. Lucy didn't stir and Grace felt something sharp sticking out of the back of the dog's head. She felt something cold and sticky all over the dog's fur. When she pulled her hand back, she saw that it was covered in blood.

"Lucy?"

Grace felt her world start to slip away from her. The house was empty and yet someone had viciously killed the dog. She wished Greg were home. She always prided herself on her strength, but she certainly felt safer when her husband was there in the house with her. She was about call the police when she noticed a movement behind her. She turned around to see a figure seated in the black leather chair in the corner. It was a man of just under seven feet tall. He sat there casually with his legs crossed, as if he were at a social function instead of sitting uninvited in someone's den. He wore a black suit, with a black shirt and tie. Even his shoes were a polished black. His skin was a rich olive color and his black hair was glossy and swept back. Most distinctive were his dark, liquid black eyes with flecks of gold.

"Hello, Grace," the stranger said in a rich and mellifluous voice. "Have a seat." He gestured to the couch which was directly across from where he sat.

"Who are you?" Grace asked hoarsely, desperately trying to figure a way to escape.

The stranger smiled. His teeth were very white and stood as a stark contrast to the gloomy darkness of the room. "Please, sit. I mean you no harm."

"How the Hell did you get in?" Grace asked, hoping to keep the tremor out of her voice. "The house is alarmed, and why did you kill my dog?"

The stranger let out a low chuckle that was devoid of any sense of mirth. "Your house might have an alarm as means of security, but I came by…less conventional means."

Grace backed up slowly, carefully scanning the room for anything she could use as a weapon. All she saw were her daughter's toys and her husband's books. "What do you want?"

The stranger stood and smiled. "Not one for small talk, eh Grace? I like that. You want to get straight to the point. Here's the deal. Your husband has gotten himself involved in matters that do not concern him. I want you to persuade him that it is in all of your best interests if he returns home."

"Why should I? Our daughter was taken and my husband went to get her back."

The stranger's eyes darkened and Grace saw his features shimmer and shift. His skin appeared to be momentarily translucent and Grace saw the face hidden underneath. In that split second, Grace saw the stranger's true appearance. *He has the head of a bird*, Grace thought. *What the fuck is going on?*

"I never said you had a choice in the matter," the stranger hissed. "Now, are you going to come on your own volition, or do I need to be…a bit more persuasive?"

The stranger advanced on Grace and she blindly reached out to grab the lamp on the coffee table beside her. She swung it with all her might and connected solidly with the stranger's head. The lamp shattered, spraying the room with tiny shards of ceramic. The stranger recoiled and fell backwards, landing awkwardly on the hardwood floor. His face was a mess of cracks and in a few areas the pieces had actually fallen off, leaving the true face of the man available for scrutiny.

"Who are you?" Grace screamed. "What are you?

The stranger roared in anger. "You dare lay hands on my person?" He grabbed her by the throat and lifted her off the ground. Grace felt herself choking beneath the stranger's vice-like grip. She saw his eyes blaze with fury and then, as quickly as his rage was unleashed, it subsided. He put her down slowly and let her go.

Grace slumped back into a chair, rubbing her throat.

The stranger said in a low voice, "It's time Grace. We're going to your husband and you will get him to come home."

"And if I don't?" Grace asked. She hoped there was some trace of defiance still in her voice.

The stranger smiled. "Then I will show you an eternity of pain and I promise you, you will never see your husband and daughter again. Do I make myself clear?"

"Crystal," Grace said through gritted teeth. Her hands were tied for the moment, but she was resourceful and she would find a way to make things right.

The stranger waved his arm and a crack appeared in the air. The crack widened into a rift and Grace saw a large, cavernous room beyond. He pushed her forward and everything went dark.

CHAPTER 26

Lasalle, Quebec. Yesterday.

The man stepped through the rift and turned and watched it close behind him. He stood and stared blankly at the odd buildings. He was so cold even though it was a beautiful summer day. The sun was high in the sky and the lawns a bright emerald green. The man felt chilled to the bone.

He came to the realization that he did not know his name. He felt lost and alone amidst the alien surroundings. Why had he come here? He had seen the light through the rift and watched from the shadows in fascination as the strange carriage had come through with four shining beacons of light and heat contained within. Two of those points of heat were rimmed with black and looked to be cooling. But one of them was as bright as anything he had ever seen. It drew him forward, but others of the Lost beat him to it and surrounded the carriage, their need for the heat palpable in the cold mist of the road. He did not know why, but instead of following the four heat sources, he instead sought out where they had come from. His dim intellect was no longer capable of reason. Instead, he was drawn to the source, his primal sense of need forcing his steps. He turned and walked through the rift into another realm.

He stood on the street and marveled at the serenity of the place, yet he felt directionless. He did not know what to do or where to go. Without any other option, he just stood there. After some time, the man sensed a presence other than his own. He turned and saw, off in the distance, a heat signature. The man felt a need stirring within himself. He did not understand what it meant, but something about the heat signature made every nerve aware and set forth a primal response that he had to follow.

Mary Georgakis walked down Bannantyne lost in her thoughts. School had not gone well today. Not well at all. Jimmy Kokkelis had tripped her on the playground and caused her to fall into a puddle, soaking her new dress in the brackish water. All the kids laughed and when she went to tell her teacher, Miss Ledoux, not one of the kids would back up her story. Jimmy was, after all, the most popular boy in class and all the other boys followed him without question. Even the girls seemed enthralled by his presence. Ten years old and he owned the schoolyard. Mary, on the other hand, was short, heavyset, and socially awkward. Her parents had divorced years earlier, and she lived with a mother who was not only physically absent most of the time due to her holding down two jobs, but was also emotionally absent as well. She had no time for her daughter. It seemed to Mary that her mother was more interested in the steady stream of men who came to take her on dates, than on her own daughter who needed her.

Mary had started her period the previous month and, while for most girls this was a special time of bonding with their mothers, Mary had no one to share this with and learned about the whole process from the internet. She did have one friend at school, Lucie Ferrier, another social outcast like herself, but she did not know how to broach the more intimate areas of her life with the other girl.

Mary was so lost in her thoughts of today's humiliation that she almost bumped into the man who slowly approached her on the sidewalk. She afforded only a passing glance in the man's direction and, although the age-old warning of *don't talk to strangers* echoed in her ears from the few times her mother actually bothered to be a parent, the man seemed more lost and helpless than anything else.

Mary stopped. Something about the man seemed off. His face was a pale white with a slight bluish tinge. His hair was short and brown, with traces of grey running through it, and cut in what looked like a very hip style, especially for someone of his age, who Mary guessed to be in his mid-forties. What really struck her as odd were his clothes. He was dressed in some kind of a tunic and actually wore sandals on his feet with straps running up his calf. He looked like an extra in that movie Gladiator, which she had watched one night while her mother was out late on one of her many dates.

"Hello?" Mary asked the man in a cautious voice. "Are you okay?"

The man stared at the girl in front of him. He saw her only in outline, her features vague and indistinct. What he did see was the heat source emanating from her. It warmed him and made his need grow and become more palpable. It screamed as it rose in intensity, blocking out anything else from his mind.

Mary felt the warning bells start to chime in her mind. The man stared at her hungrily like she was a piece of meat. Mary knew that while she might be unpopular, that didn't matter to men who preyed on children. She took a step backwards and said to the man in what she hoped was her bravest voice, "You better not try anything. I live right here and know all the neighbors. One scream and they will be out here in a flash."

The man took no notice and, instead, smiled broadly, showing yellowed teeth. For the first time, Mary noticed that his eyes were vacant and clouded over. Mary felt her bladder loosen, the urine running down her leg. She knew without a doubt that this man was not a pedophile. Instead, he was clearly something much, much worse. She turned to run but the man hissed and grabbed her by the shoulder. His grip was like steel and his hands were so cold that she felt her shoulder burn beneath her sweater.

The man spun her around and threw her to the ground and straddled her in one fluid movement. Mary barely had time to react and sobbed uncontrollably. Tears streamed down her cheeks and she pleaded with the man not to hurt her.

The man heard her cries but did not care. Her heat source pulsed and burned brighter than ever. He balled his hand into a fist and punched through the girl's ribcage and wrapped his hand around the heat source and felt it pulse and throb in his hand. The heat flowed from his hand and up his arm until he actually had sensation in his fingers. He tightened his grip and wrenched the heat source from the girl's chest cavity. She shrieked in agony but he was oblivious.

The man quickly pulled off his tunic and stood there naked in the street, his skin a pale bluish white. His chest had a gaping hole where his heart should be and he quickly shoved the girl's still beating heart deep within the cavity. He threw his head back and screamed in ecstasy as the ribs grew back over the hole, followed by the muscle slowly roping its way across the newly grown ribs. Adipose tissue and skin followed and soon the man's chest was whole, as if the gaping cavity had never existed.

His skin grew warmer and soon it took on its natural tone, a light olive with a mild pinkish hue. His eyes were no longer a liquid black but instead were a deep ice blue. He felt the neurons in his brain reconnecting and vestiges of memory started coming back to him. His name was Gaius Claudius and he was a member of the Senate in Rome. The memories began flooding back. It was late and he had been walking back to his villa when three low born men had approached him. There was something about how they had fanned out when he approached. He should have been more wary when one of the three asked for directions. It was late and his mind was on seeing his wife and, as he had let his guard down, one of the other men had circled behind him and stabbed him in the back, puncturing a lung. The other two men rushed him, stabbing him repeatedly before robbing him of the denarii he carried. As Gaius Claudius lay there bleeding out on the cold marble surface of the city road, he wondered whether his wife and daughter would be taken care of in his absence. He had cried then, his life blood slowly pooling beneath him for his lost opportunities and he bemoaned times lost where he could have spent more time with his family instead of constantly feeding the political machine until his world was enveloped in darkness.

Gaius Claudius took stock in the strange surroundings. These were buildings unlike any he had ever seen. Most were built with a rectangular reddish stone. They all were virtually identical and, while very narrow, seemed to extend up quite high. Even more curious were the metal chariots which lined the road outside the structure. He saw the four wheels were thick and black, and very unlike the wooden spoke wheels on the chariots that he knew. He peered through the window and saw the seats and wondered how such a conveyance propelled itself forward. Where did they attach the horses? Even more confusing was how could a team of horses actually pull such a vehicle? It looked far too heavy to be practical.

It was then that Claudius realized that he was standing naked in the street. He bent down to pull up his tunic and saw the body of the girl at his feet. Why hadn't he noticed her earlier, he wondered? While his mind seemed to be coming out of a great fog, his thoughts and memories were patchy at best.

The girl lay there on the ground, the pool of blood beneath her already starting to dry to a burnt copper under the hot sun. Her chest was a ruined mess, with a fist- sized hole where her heart had been. He saw the ragged ends of the aortic arch and the various arterial and venous systems which had once connected to the missing heart and had once provided the vital life- giving blood to the rest of her body. Worst of all was the look of agony etched on her young features. She had died in a lot of pain. That much was clear. *Had he done this*, he wondered. He tried to sift through his memories but could not remember.

Gaius Claudius looked around. The road was deserted. Not a soul was in sight. If he left now, perhaps no one would connect him to the killing. He didn't know what the authorities were like here, but there was always punishment for the taking of a life. Claudius hated leaving. It felt cowardly and, in his entire life, he had never...He paused. He had never what? What had he been thinking? He looked down and saw the corpse of the girl and wondered what had happened, yet at the same time grew more detached. He felt something like claws rake across his brain and a searing pain followed. He felt his skin tighten and looked down and was horrified to see the natural olive hue turn to a bluish white on his fingertips and spread down his hand and up his arm.

A violent tearing sensation followed on his chest and Claudius dropped his tunic to see. He was horrified to see the skin flay back in strips, exposing the raw muscle beneath. Then the muscle shriveled and began pulling back, exposing the ribs beneath which were already pulling back themselves. He saw the...the...he could not remember what it was shrivel and blacken in his chest. His features tightened as ice blue veins knitted their way across his face and body and bleached his skin of all color, leaving only a pale white with bluish tint. The fact that he was naked did not bother him. Nothing did anymore. He stood there, driven by an insatiable hunger that could never be assuaged. He looked around but there was nothing in any direction. The girl had been a source of heat, he dimly remembered, but that was gone. He looked down and saw her rise, her skin the same whitish blue as his. She was oblivious to the gaping hole in her chest, as he was to his own. Her liquid black eyes mirrored his. She no longer burned bright, that light was gone forever. She now was like him and felt a need within her that formed a kind of kinship with the man. All he felt was hunger, as he somehow knew she did as well. So they began to walk. They would need to find more sustenance. All he could remember was that the heat from the living brought an end to the hunger and pain, and he was so very hungry.

CHAPTER 27

In the House. Present day.

Amy was scared. It wasn't like showing up at school and having to talk in front of the class. Oh, no. This was much worse. Ever since the grey man with the dog's head had grabbed her from her bed, things had gotten strange. First, the dog-head man had taken her and her cousins to a big room and told them they were to remain there for a while. Then, a bird- headed man had taken them somewhere else, somewhere scary. She was in a very weird house surrounded by very bad men. She wanted to go home so badly. Every time she thought of her mom and dad, she felt the tears starting to well up in her eyes.

Amy looked over at her cousins. Mike was sitting on the floor, mumbling something to himself. Every so often, he would softly chuckle, almost as if he were enjoying a private joke. Beth, on the other hand, was having nothing to do with her captivity. She was throwing a fit and screeching at the top of her lungs.

The bad men stood off to the side, huddled together. One of them, a tall, ugly man with greasy black hair, kept staring at her. Amy didn't like the way he looked at her. He looked like he wanted to hurt her...badly. He scared her. Even though he wore a shirt that looked like a candy cane, he was anything but friendly. She made a point to not turn her back on him. Another of the men reminded her of one of the actors in a movie her dad liked. She seemed to remember it was called Grown Ups. The man looked just like the funny fat guy from the movie. She would have thought he was nice, except she saw him get angry with the candy cane man, and his anger really scared her. He looked like he was going to hurt the candy cane man, and that might have been okay.

The third guy was the one who terrified her the most. He wore a skirt of some kind and sandals. He had almost brown skin and a funny beard that was tied with a gold string and looked like a thick black rope coming out of his chin. Around his eyes and mouth were multiple holes that Amy couldn't take her eyes off. What was the worst, though, were his eyes. They were black and dead and when Amy looked at him, she got the sense that whoever used to live there was long, long gone.

The fourth guy didn't seem so bad. He reminded her of the pictures of her daddy and his brother when they were younger. He almost seemed silly. But she knew better. If he was with these other men, then he was a bad guy too.

The tall man with the face that was sometimes a bird and sometimes a man looked over at Beth. His eyes blazed with fury. "I want her quiet. Now!" he roared.

Amy saw the tall, ugly man walk over to Beth. He smiled a lopsided smile and bent down so his face was nose to nose with the girl's. "Little girl," he hissed, "you will stop screaming right now or I'll rip your head off your shoulders and eat it."

Beth's eyes went wide and her lower lip started to tremble. Amy could tell she was trying not to cry, but it wasn't successful and, within a few minutes, she was crying uncontrollably. Tears streamed down her cheeks and mucus bubbled from her nose.

Amy ran over to the tall man and kicked him hard in both shins. He dropped to the ground, clutching his legs. The bird-man and the man with the dead eyes said nothing, but the angry fat man burst out laughing at Perry's misfortune.

Perry stood, gritted his teeth against the pain and then swung a haymaker at Amy's head. With a scream, she fell soundlessly to the ground, a thin trickle of blood dripping from the corner of her mouth. She lay there unmoving. Mike and Beth saw this and both started screaming in terror.

"What did you do?" the bird man roared. He swiftly crossed the room and checked Amy. He turned to Perry who stood there grinning, clearly enjoying the pain he had inflicted on the girl. "She lives. No thanks to you. We need her alive until after the Ascension. You are not to touch her again, you understand?"

"Why?"

Perry started to argue and the bird-man grabbed him by the throat. "So help me, if anything happens to her, I will make sure that Ammit gets to devour your soul." Perry lowered his eyes so they wouldn't look the bird-man in the face and nodded meekly. "If she is the One and is killed, the Ascension will move to one of the other siblings. If all the kids are killed, I have no way of predicting who would then be chosen. This is why they all must be kept alive until after the Ascension so that the ritual cannot be done and it ends once and for all with his bloodline."

The bird-man looked over to Khufu, Nicky and Brett. "See to the other kids. Quiet them, but they are to remain unharmed…for now." He added in Coptic for Khufu, "And please keep an eye on these fools. You are the only one I trust".

Khufu bowed reverently and said in Coptic. "Your wish is my command, my Lord." He walked over to Mike and Beth, followed closely by Brett and Nicky and set about trying to quiet the screaming children. Perry went off to a corner of the room, clearly enraged by being reprimanded in front of the others.

Horus paced the room. The Ascension was in a few hours. He had the children so all was going according to plan. Thing was, he didn't trust his brother. Anubis was always a crafty being. He must not underestimate Anubis. That kind of thinking would lead to failure.

Horus looked at the men at the other side of the room. To think he was putting his trust in this collection of degenerates. What happens here during the Ascension will set the tone for the next millennia. Khufu had his uses and might be of some value after the Ascension, but the other three…well perhaps Ammit should just dispose of the waste. He smiled again. Yes, perhaps that would be best, after all. They could join his worthless brother in oblivion.

CHAPTER 28

In the House. Present day.

Anubis paced his throne room, the look of consternation clearly etched into his grim visage. He still wore his mortal guise, as it seemed the most comforting to the humans who currently occupied the throne room with him. He looked over at Greg, who was watching him intently. Greg leaned over and whispered something to his brother, Paul, who then looked up at Anubis and scowled. Kevin was actually seated on Anubis' throne, clearly enjoying himself, while David stood silently by Greg and Paul's side.

Anubis' attention was diverted by Ari who paced the room, momentarily stopping to look at something in the distance with a greater degree of attention. Ari was very sharp, and Anubis was concerned that adding him was a mistake. He had learned to trust his instincts and, while Ari was destined to be devoured by Ammit with the remnants of his soul being returned to the primal forge with other souls of failed beings, he sensed there was something more in the troubled man, some need for redemption that he could make use of. Nevertheless, he would have to be watched very carefully. He had some ability in scrying, as time was an open book, yet Ari's role was still clouded over and undefined. He supposed it would all be revealed soon enough.

Greg walked over to where Anubis stood, his brows furrowed and a frown creasing his features.

"Anthony," Greg said, "we need to get everyone up to speed. For example, why were we brought here and, if what will be the ramifications be if we decide not to help you?"

Anubis sighed. He walked to his throne and motioned for Kevin to step down. Kevin looked over at Anubis with disgust and grudgingly walked over to stand with Paul and David. Anubis climbed the stairs and sat down on the throne with a barely audible sigh. Everyone looked up at him expectantly.

"Everyone", Anubis said, his voice booming, "Come close. We have much to discuss."

The men all moved closer and sat on the floor before the large throne. They looked up expectantly and waited for Anubis to continue.

Anubis sat there silently watching the men as they waited. After a few minutes of silence, Anubis waved his hand across his face. His features changed to reveal the head of a jackal. The men all were stunned and began to back away from the throne.

Anubis stood and slowly walked down the steps. He approached the men. "Stop, I mean you no ill. It is time we discuss why you have been brought here and the roles we all must play. All of you know me as Anthony. Greg and Paul have been dreaming of me and this House for over ten years. I was the one who manipulated their dreams. It was necessary as I needed to find my way to their homes to get the children and bring them back here."

Paul jumped to his feet and had to be held back by his brother. "Tell us why you had to take our kids. I'm fed up with all the bullshit. I want answers or I'm done with this. Then you can do whatever you need from us by yourself."

"My name is Anubis. I am the Lord of the Dead. Where we're all sitting is the Great Hall where I judge the souls of the dead."

Kevin spoke up. "We're not dead, right? So how can we be here?" The other men nodded and made mumbling noises indicating they were wondering the same thing

"You're the first living souls to ever step foot in my realm", Anubis admitted and cast a glance at Ari, "Well, most of you, anyways. Normally, the dead come into my Great Hall, carrying their hearts, which contain their souls, in a portable container. The Egyptians used to carry theirs in Canopic Jars. They then stand before me while I weigh their soul against that of a feather. If their soul is heavier, Ammit, the devourer, will come and devour them and tear their souls apart. The soul-shards will be collected one day be recombined to create new souls. All trace of the former individual is gone forever. But, if their soul is lighter than the feather, they are judged worthy and move on to a higher plane of existence."

"Spare me the mythology lesson, Anubis," Paul interjected. "Why did you take our kids? What do they have to do with your judging the dead?"

Anubis stood up and paced back and forth in front of his throne. His eyes blazed with a golden fire. "This is a complex situation and I'll try to manage an explanation that you will understand. You see, the existence of Anubis, like all Gods, is finite. We have a starting point as well as an ending point. Before I made the ascension to Godhood, I was as mortal as all of you. And then the role of Anubis was presented to me and I needed to make a decision. I chose to become Anubis, the God of the dead and with it, forfeit my humanity. Now my tenure as the God of the Dead is coming to its end and I need to ensure that a proper member of my bloodline undergoes the ritual and takes my place. That's where your family comes in. It is critical that the ritual gets done during the Ascension. If it doesn't, everything you know and love will be lost."

"How is that?" Paul added. Greg waved him off. "Surely you're not implying what I think you are."

"I am," Anubis replied. "Your family is directly descended from mine. You are my bloodline and, therefore, it is to your family that the mantle of Lord of the Dead must pass. No one else will suffice. The mantle of Anubis must pass to one of my blood, or it is lost to us. I know another has been coveting this for millennia."

Greg looked confused. "First off, why should we believe anything you say? You took our children and are now telling us you want our help? Even if you are telling us the truth, why do you suddenly need to transfer over your divine responsibilities? Most importantly, what happens if we refuse? Frankly I just want to get the kids and go home."

Anubis slammed his fist on the arm of his chair. "You dare ask questions? Time grows short and if we do not get your children back, the human race is doomed."

"No." Greg stood up, his hands balled into fists by his side. "We've been patient, but we've gotten nothing but the runaround from you. You haunt our dreams and then you steal our kids and you have the fucking gall to ask for help?"

"You dare?" Anubis roared. He grew in size and his voice echoed and reverberated off the walls. Red fire blazed from his eyes.

"Yeah, I dare," Greg answered. "Far as I can tell, you need us. If you were so powerful, you'd have resolved this by yourself. Instead, you steal our kids and threaten us. I want the truth or you get nothing from any of us."

Anubis sighed. He seemed to deflate. "All right, here's what's going on. My brother Horus, who is the God of War, has wanted to control the dead for many, many years now. He knows that while he is very powerful, he could not hope to steal another God's powers. But he is a crafty one and is aware that during the Ascension, at the point of transference, the hold on the mantle of power is at its most tenuous. If he were to block the transference by cutting out the bloodline, the power would have nowhere to go and he'd be free to absorb it into himself."

"Why does he want it?" David asked.

Anubis chuckled. "Why does anyone want power? Just because one is a God doesn't mean one is above petty jealousies. Horus is the God of War and Vengeance. Imagine how powerful he'd be if he had control over life and death as well.

"Horus would no longer judge men's souls after they died. Instead, he would release the soulless dead back unto the Earth."

"I don't understand," Kevin asked. "What would that serve?"

Anubis smiled, "As I said, Horus is a crafty one. He's a violent, volatile being, which comes as no surprise since he is the God of War. My power is enticing for him, but it is not his endgame. Instead, he seeks power over life and death to go to war with the one whose power he has sought all along."

Ari stood and glared at the jackal-headed God. "You pulled me from my own judgment to take part in this? I've stayed quiet because I've been trying to understand why you would need someone with my particular talents. I think I finally understand. Horus' end game is to dispatch your father Osiris and usurp his power, is it not?"

Anubis threw his head back and roared with laughter. "Very astute, mortal, and you are correct. Horus, the God of War desires what our father, Osiris, has. He wishes to be the Lord of the Underworld. With my ability over life and death, if he were to also rule the Underworld, he will be the most powerful God that ever existed. Life as you know it would cease to exist."

"How would he do that?" Greg asked.

"He would begin by absorbing the powers of the God of the dead," Anubis said as he stood and moved to stand amongst the five men. "With my powers, he would release the soulless dead onto the Earth. The dead crave the essence found in the souls of the living. They would attack and destroy everyone they came into contact with, creating an army of the dead for Horus to command. With billions of dead at his disposal, he would attack Osiris and take control of the Underworld and, in the process, steal Osiris' energy, thus becoming near invincible."

"So let me get this straight," Kevin said, his voice trembling with rage. "If we don't help you, your brother will rob you of your essence when your powers are being taken away from you. Then he will unleash an army of the dead on Earth, killing everyone. All so he can control Hell?"

"Close enough," Anubis said. "Except it isn't Hell as you know it. The Underworld is where all who die and who do not move on to a higher plane end up. Ammit devours the soul and the body moves on to the Underworld. You saw a glimpse of the outskirts of the Underworld on the route you took to get here. Once the soul is gone, the dead are nothing but shells of their former selves. So, yes, bad people do end up there, but good people do, as well, who may have made questionable choices in their lives.'

"How much time do we have?" Paul asked.

"Not long," Anubis answered. "We only have a matter of hours. If the time of Ascension comes and the Bloodline is not available to receive the power of Anubis, then the energy will disperse and be free for Horus to steal."

Greg stood up and walked over to Anubis. He looked into the God's liquid golden eyes and fought to maintain his courage. "You left out one detail, Anubis. Why did you kidnap our children? I don't buy that it was merely to get us here."

"No, it wasn't to get you here," Anubis growled. "One of your kids is the proper member of my Bloodline and will be the next Anubis. I took them all because it has not been revealed to me which one will ascend in my place. They were taken to ensure their safety from Horus and make sure that they are available for the Ascension."

"Looks like you underestimated your brother, Anubis," Greg screamed. "I've had enough of the cryptic bullshit. I want the truth."

"Because," Anubis hissed, "you were led here to ensure that the Ascension takes place. You are here to get your children back from Horus and make sure that, when the time comes, they are there to receive my divine essence. Your roles in this have been written long before you were even born. I care not if you live or die. You are all inconsequential. A bigger game is being played and you all have a part to play in it."

Paul put his hand on his brother's shoulder. He felt how tightly knotted the muscles were. He supposed his own stress levels were as bad. "Greg," he said softly, "we don't have a choice. If we do nothing, Horus will kill the children, and everyone we hold dear will die back home."

"Assuming this piece of crap isn't lying to us."

"Why hasn't Horus killed the children?" Paul asked Anubis.

Anubis shook his head. "He needs to ensure that the children are alive at the time of the Ascension. Otherwise, the power that makes me the God of the Dead will be diverted to someone else in the bloodline, just someone whose lineage is not as direct. If the Ascension comes and the children are still alive and the One is not there to receive it, Horus can claim it. I am tired of this existence and ready to move on. Horus is too impatient to wait. Now is his chance. All he needs to do is keep the children alive until the Ascension passes. Of course, he is working with some seriously evil people who will likely kill the children once the hour of the Ascension has passed and he has claimed my powers and no longer needs them."

"It seems like we've been left with no other options," David said. "Let's go and find the children. Where would they be?"

Anubis smiled. "At least we have that as an advantage. All of the henchmen that Horus has employed were men whose lives have ended. They could not exist anywhere but here in my realm until they go through judgment. In fact, one of the men was currently undergoing his own judgment but somehow Horus managed to get him out. No matter how he got the men, there are rules that must be followed. That gives us an advantage. It means that they have the children within the House."

"That's good, right?" Greg asked.

"To a degree," Anubis said. "The House contains thousands of mortals being judged at any one time. If they are hiding within another's judgment, it might be difficult to find. Even more challenging is that there is the risk they jump from one judgment to another. Then, even if we find them, they won't give the children up without a fight or, if pushed, may even kill them."

"I still don't understand how this Ascension plays into all of this," Greg asked.

"It's like this," Anubis said softly, "When a soul is judged, he or she is either deemed worthy, and ascends to a higher plane of existence or is deemed unworthy and has his soul torn apart by Ammit the devourer and is deposited as energy in a soul repository. When someone is born they receive a soul created from the energy of former unworthy souls. As you can imagine, eventually this energy repository gets depleted."

"So where does new energy come from?" Paul asked.

"This is where the Ascension comes in," Anubis added. "Every time I allow a soul to move on to a higher plane, only a small piece, the main essence of the soul, moves on. The rest gets absorbed into me. This goes on for ages until the repository is down to the last bits of energy needed to make one more soul. I would then need to transfer all the energy I absorbed from souls over the last several millenia back to the repository. This is done during the Ascension. You see, when I transfer the soul energy, most of what makes me the God of the Dead gets transferred as well. What remains is the piece that will be transferred to my successor and the piece of me, the core essence which will move on to a higher plane of existence." He saw the confused expressions on the men. "It may seem somewhat abstract, but it is part of the cycle of existence."

"Okay," Paul said. "You have our attention. How do we get the kids back?"

"I have a plan," Anubis said, and proceeded to tell the men his strategy. As he listened, Greg started making plans of his own. Maybe Anubis was convinced that one of the kids was the next one to become a God but, if Greg had his way, he'd get the kids home and to hell with Anubis, Horus and everyone else in this nightmare.

PART 2

Into the Mouth of Madness

The whole world is a dream, and death is the interpreter
–*Yiddish Proverb*

To sleep: perchance to dream: ay, there's the rub:
For in that sleep of death what dreams may come,
When we have shuffled off this mortal coil,
Must give us pause: there's the respect
That makes calamity of so long life
–*William Shakespeare*

CHAPTER 29

Laval, Quebec. 38 years ago.

Greg finished his day of elementary school and went to the front door of the school to meet his neighbor Mikey so they could walk home together. Normally, all the kids from their neighborhood walked together, led by the older sister of one of the girls in the neighborhood. Today, though, the girls were both sick so it looked like it would be just him and Mikey.

Greg paced nervously on the front steps. *Where was he*? He realized that he didn't know the way home and, while he didn't want to admit it to anyone, he was pretty scared.

Greg watched the children stream out of the school, yelling and screaming, celebrating freedom for another day. After a while, he saw the grown-ups begin to leave as well. He knew some were teachers and others were from the administrative staff. Some nodded to him as they passed, others walked by as if he were invisible, being lost in their own thoughts.

After waiting for what seemed like an eternity, he realized that Mikey was not coming. He also realized, with a sickening twist of fear that he was all alone. No more students were around and even the last teacher had left long before. It was starting to get dark and he realized that he had to go home by himself and hope he found the way.

Darkness was starting to creep in. The streetlights turned on and cast a sickly yellowish pall over the encroaching gloom. Long shadows from trees and buildings seem to stretch out towards Greg, threatening to pull him into the shadows to be consumed by the darkness.

Greg shoved his hands in his pockets and started walking, casting furtive, fearful glances over his shoulder. He hoped he was going the right way but, at eight years old, his world didn't often extend that far beyond his house and family.

He reached the end of the street and had the option of turning right or continuing straight down the next block. Greg knew whichever way he went, it was a guess. He decided to turn right. He wasn't sure why, but it seemed to feel like the correct way to go.

He was lost in his thoughts and didn't even notice the car until it stopped alongside of him. The passenger window rolled down and Greg saw the outline of the driver. He didn't know why, but he got the impression it was a man, and he was smiling.

"Hey, little boy," the man said from the inside of the car. His voice was soft and silky yet carried a sense of menace beneath the words. "Are you lost?"

"No," Greg replied. "I live right here." He didn't know why he lied. It certainly wasn't something he usually did, but he was alone and scared and this stranger gave him the creeps.

The man laughed. "I saw you walking from the school, constantly looking back as if second guessing the route you're taking. I don't think you don't live anywhere near here. I also think you're lost."

Greg froze as he heard the man open the door on the driver side of the car. When the door opened, the light briefly illuminated the interior of the car. The man was huge, easily twice the size of Greg's father. He was bald and had a soft, doughy face that was pale and pockmarked. His eyes were large and watery and he had thick, fleshy lips which seemed like they were perpetually wet. And, worst of all, were the teeth. Greg stared in terror as the man smiled and walked around the car towards him. His teeth were large and so very white, almost blinding in their brightness. It made Greg think of a creature that needed big teeth to rip their victims apart.

The man put a thick, fleshy hand on Greg's shoulder. His hand felt cold and clammy and Greg recoiled in disgust. "Get in the car, kid. I'll take you home."

Greg's eyes got wide and he tried to back up. The man gripped his shoulder and Greg found he couldn't move. "Leave me alone," Greg cried out, tears welling in his eyes.

The man licked his thick lips and they gleamed with spit. "Get in the damn car, kid. You go in easy, or you go in hard. But either way, you go in."

In a blind panic, Greg kicked the man as hard as he could. His kick connected with the man's groin and he recoiled as he screamed in pain. Greg turned and ran behind the closest house and through their yard to the yard of the house behind it. He ran from one house to the next, staying in the shadows of trees, and hiding under decks or behind bushes. For a while, he heard the man crashing through the bushes a few houses back, but Greg was young and small, and easily darted between fences and stayed hidden in the shadows. Eventually, he made his way to a house with a large, spacious yard. He recognized it as a neighbor's yard and knew that he was close to home.

Greg was about to cross the street when he saw the car coming down the road. He ducked back in the shadows and crawled under the front porch. He waited with bated breath as the car slowly passed. After several minutes, Greg felt safe enough to venture out. He ran the rest of the way home, frantically ringing his doorbell when he got there. His father opened the door, a copy of Tolkien's *The Two Towers* in his hand. He grunted a brief acknowledgement to Greg and walked back into the house, plopping himself back on the couch as he continued his reading.

Greg realized that his parents hadn't even noticed that he was as late as he was. He could have been taken away by the fat man, and no one would have ever been the wiser. He slowly climbed the stairs and went to his bedroom where he curled up on his bed and cried himself to sleep.

Greg awoke in a panic. He stared around the room and felt disoriented as he tried to get his bearings. He was in the House and with his brother, his two friends and a once dead Israeli soldier. They were here to rescue his daughter, niece and nephew from a God who had gone mad and some dangerous side-kicks he had recruited.

He looked around the room and saw that everyone except for Ari was fast asleep. Ari sat off in the corner of the room, lost in his thoughts. He noticed that Greg was awake and nodded at him.

"Did you have a bad dream?" Ari asked. Greg nodded. "It's the House. We're here for judgment. Our past comes alive and we confront it and are judged on how we handle ourselves."

Greg frowned. "That might be the case for you, Ari. But that's because you're dead. I'm still alive. My soul isn't being judged."

Ari grinned. "I don't consider myself dead. I'm still around, still drawing breath. And I still feel. Sure, I'm here for judgment, but so is everyone in this place. The fact you are feeling alive has nothing to do with whether you still hold your soul. It's the nature of this place. We are here to be judged and then we move on. Whether you like it or not, the longer you stay in the House, the more of your past you will be forced to relive, as if you were among the dead waiting for judgment."

"You can wait to be judged, Ari," Greg growled, "I'm only here to find my daughter and my brother's kids and get the Hell out of here. I don't care what tale Anubis is spinning."

Ari put a reassuring hand on Greg's shoulder. "I'm here to help. I'll do whatever I can to make sure you find the kids."

Greg looked suspiciously at Ari. "What's your angle? I don't know you. Why risk your life for my family?"

Ari sighed. "I did some horrible things in my life. Several years back, my wife and unborn child were killed right before my eyes by a terrorist attack in Israel. I didn't realize it at the time, but I wanted revenge as badly as a person could. I found a man who was carrying his own demons around with him and I tricked him into taking me into his confidence. While I helped him get his revenge on those who had wronged him, I was setting up my own revenge by unleashing a horror unlike anything the world has ever seen."

"I don't understand. What horrors did you unleash?"

Ari looked perplexed. "I created hundreds of Golems which I set loose with the sole purpose of destroying every living thing with whom they came into contact. I realize now that I'm likely going to have my soul devoured by the Soul Eaters but, if I can atone even somewhat, then perhaps I can find redemption prior to judgment. If not, at least I can go to my end with my head held high."

"I didn't hear anything about Golems. Are you sure that it happened?"

"Oh, it happened all right," said a gravelly voice behind them.

Ari and Greg turned around. Anubis was standing there in his true form. He stood a few feet taller than either Greg or Ari, with a sculpted and muscular, bronzed physique. He didn't wear his human form and, instead, looked at them through the unfeeling eyes on his jackal's head.

"I don't understand," Greg said.

"It's simple," Anubis said. "Time does not exist in this house. You see, for Greg, the present for you is 2015. Ari, on the other hand, was killed in late 2016. Therefore, the apocalypse that Ari unleashed is the past to him, but hasn't happened in Greg's frame of reference."

"So, what I'm being told is that this prick will kill us all in a bit over a year."

Anubis replied, his voice grim, "I'm afraid so. Millions will die before a stalemate can be reached."

"So how can he be dead now if he isn't scheduled to die for another year? Is there anything I can do to prevent this?" Greg asked.

Anubis looked ahead stonily. "No. All you can do is bear witness to what will transpire and record it for posterity. You see, as I've explained, time does not work the same way here in the House. All of the past, present and future converge here as every time beyond the veil into the world of the living."

Anubis looked at where Paul, David and Kevin slept. "They will not all survive this, Greg. The time, place and means of their passing had been written long before they were even born."

"I can't accept that," Greg replied. If we can be here to fix things, then it means that time is not immutable and can be altered."

Anubis gave a semblance of a grin. "I am impressed. You can grasp the concept. There is one small paradox to the entire rationale of trying to correct or fix time. There are things within this House that can exist across all times. Like me. I need to exist in the past, present and future, as there is a need for someone to harvest the souls of the dead. My brother, Horus, is another, as is our father Osiris. You and all of mankind, on the other hand, have your lives tied to a small stretch of time where you interact with others and create whatever legacy you were destined to create. Once you perish, your souls are brought here to my domain where you await judgment. Of course, the more evil the soul, the longer that judgment must endure. For example, someone who was a good soul in life would have a short and simple judgment. A person who perpetrated many misdeeds in his or her life would be made to relive those misdeeds over and over again until some semblance of understanding would take place. Then that soul could be brought before me for final judgment. That is the reason why there are some dead souls who have been here for many hundreds of years. I cannot judge them until they see and, perhaps understand, upon what they are being judged."

Greg nodded. In a strange way, it made sense. Of course, in perspective to all other recent events in his life, having a jackal-headed God tell him that all time is as one hardly seemed out of the ordinary. "So, when are we going after the kids?"

"Let us wake the others," Anubis said while beckoning Ari over. "It is time."

CHAPTER 30

In the House. Present day.

The two men stood outside the door. It looked like the many thousands of other doors that they had seen in the House, yet they knew that this one was different. A small, glowing red "x" was on the door, marked by Anubis to easily allow them to find the judgment where the children were held.

Anubis had told them that while Horus could manipulate the dead, even to some degree within his domain, Anubis was all-seeing and could counter anything Horus did, except perhaps interfere; hence the need for Greg, Paul and the others.

Anubis told them that the children had been separated into two groups and were held in two separate judgments. What the men needed to do was to go into the judgment, find the children and bring them out. This was easier said than done as each of the two rooms held a very specific judgment that was unique to the individual. Aside from Horus' minions, no one else in the self-contained universe of the judgments was aware that he was in anything but the waking world. This meant there was the unknown to contend with, and that unpredictability made it very dangerous. Horus seemed to believe that hiding the children in these virtual worlds would guarantee that the Ascension passed before the children were ever found. Then, his helpers could do to the children as they pleased.

Anubis also warned them that if they were hurt in the rooms that those injuries would be real and would still exist upon leaving the room. If they were to get killed by anyone in those rooms of judgment, they would be doomed to be a part of the House for eternity, never being able to move on, as there would not be any soul to judge. Therefore, while they needed to hurry, they also needed to ensure that they were careful and aware of their actions. Also, in order to best blend in with their environment, they would only carry weapons that were easily concealed. Ari was surprised that weapons were readily available in the House, but Anubis assured him that over the millennia, everything eventually made its way inside. So, Ari chose a long serrated knife and a Desert Eagle 50 AE, a handgun with which he was intimately familiar. Ari outfitted Paul with a similar knife and a Beretta 96A1, which seemed to be a gun that Ari felt Paul could handle. They both wore jackets which could easily hide the weapons. Ari smiled, the building adrenaline made him feel alive again. They were good to go.

Ari looked over at Paul. For all his earlier bravado, he now seemed to be withdrawn and visibly nervous. Ari understood this quite well. They had no idea what they would be facing. "Are you ready?" Ari finally asked. Paul grimly nodded his assent. He took a deep breath and grasped the door handle. "Okay, Paul. Let's do this. We go in, we find the kids, and we get out. Do you have any questions?"

Ari looked at Paul who shook his head. He looked as if he were about to speak, but bit his lower lip instead. Paul opened the door and the men went in. Once they were in, the door disappeared behind them. Paul turned and saw that the door was gone, replaced by a simple wall.

"How are we supposed to get back out?" Paul asked.

Ari shrugged. "Anubis said the door would be in the same spot as where we entered it. I expect that when we're ready to leave, the door will be here."

"I hope so. I didn't plan to spend eternity inside someone else's Hell."

They stood in a fairly nondescript hallway. A pale brown carpet lined the hallway, which was painted a light cream color. Recessed lights kept the building well lit. They could see a door a bit further up, and decided to investigate.

The door was a rich mahogany with the company name, 'Alliance Consulting Group', affixed to the door on a golden plaque. The number 1021 was inscribed in the wood above the name of the company.

"So, what do we do?" whispered Paul.

"Ari was quick to answer. "I guess we go in. We have to start looking somewhere, right?"

A loud ping from around the corner signaled that an elevator had arrived at their floor. The two men paused and saw a short, stocky man in an expensive suit and running shoes come hustling over towards where they stood. His face was flushed and his thin blonde hair was plastered to his forehead with perspiration. He came to a stop outside the door next to Paul.

"Hi," the man said while smiling. He wiped his palm on the pant leg of his suit and extended his hand to Paul, then Ari. "Are you the men from the Cormorant Corporation?"

Paul put on his best smile and extended his hand and firmly grasped the stranger's extended hand. "We sure are. And you are?"

The stranger tried to regain his composure. "I'm John Potter. I'm the one who is assigned to your team. I was supposed to meet you here at 8:30. He looked at his watch and frowned. I'm sorry I'm late. My wife and daughter are both sick and I was up all night with them. I… I'm sorry," Potter, said, "my personal issues are not your problem. I really appreciate your patience. Please, come in." Potter opened the door to the office and ushered the two men inside. He led them to a spacious conference room with a large picture window overlooking New York's impressive skyline. "Please, have a seat. I'll go round up the team and we'll be in to join you in just a moment. Would you care for some water or coffee?" The two men shook their heads.

Potter walked out and Paul looked at Ari. "This is really weird. I feel like we're really in this guy's office. I wonder if this is his judgment or someone else's."

"Does it really matter? If it is his judgment," Ari remarked, "then this day is somehow very relevant for his life because his afterlife is being judged in part on what he did on this day. Remember, I myself was in just such a place and, while some elements might feel off, you don't realize that you are dead and that none of it is real."

Ari walked to the window. He put his hands on the glass and quietly swore.

"What's wrong, Ari?" Paul asked.

"Paul, get over here now!" Ari screamed.

Paul hurried over to the window and stared in utter horror at the plane that was rapidly heading towards their building. "What is it?"

"Shit," Ari cursed, "I don't believe it. We're in the fucking North Tower."

It took a moment for Ari's words to sink in. Paul looked pale. "Are you sure?"

"Very. I was in the Israeli military on this day. I spent many hours watching and re-watching the footage of the attacks."

"Oh God," Paul replied, "That means we're reliving someone's judgment on September 11, 2001. If we're in the North Tower, it means the plane will hit just below floor one hundred and then collapse about an hour and a half later."

The plane flew closer and the two men ran from the conference room and out of the Alliance Consulting Group's Office. They braced themselves against the wall for impact. The plane hit, shaking the entire building. They felt like they were in the middle of an earthquake. The walls cracked and broke and plaster fell to the ground in chunks. The drop-ceiling tiles and some of the fluorescent light tubes crashed randomly to the ground. Dust was everywhere and the remaining lights began flickering on and off. Alarms sounded everywhere throughout the building. Screams could be heard from the floors above and below them. The panic was real and very palpable.

"We need to get out of here," Potter screamed as he exited the office. He was followed by a dozen others from his office, all professionally attired and in full blown panic.

"The stairs," a pretty young Asian girl in a well-tailored navy business suit yelled. "The elevators are too risky. If the power goes out, we could be trapped. The stairs are our best bet."

"We're on the 102nd floor, Ann," a heavyset, middle-aged woman in a long skirt and dark blouse replied angrily. I can't make it down a hundred and two flights of stairs."

"We don't have a choice, Mary. You can stay here if you want, but I'm going." Ann looked around to her co-workers. "Is anyone coming?"

The staff of Alliance Consulting Group looked at each other and then followed Ann to the stairwell. Even Mary went, although it was clear that she disagreed.

Potter looked at Paul and Ari. "Are you coming? It's not safe here."

Ari looked around, surveying the damage. The kids were here somewhere. As real as this felt, it was someone's judgment and they had an exit. "We're staying. We'll wait here for help."

"Are you sure? You're better off coming with us" Potter said, his face flushed with panic. "I don't want to leave you guys here, but I have to get out. I have a family, you see." Potter then turned and followed the others down the staircase.

"We should have gone with them," Paul said angrily.

"Damn it, Paul," Ari snapped. "Have you forgotten why we are here? Also, we're on the one hundred and second floor. No one made it out from above the one hundredth floor. Not one single person. Those people are all dead. They will all die when the building collapses in an hour and a half. What that means is that we have a very limited time to find the kids or we are trapped here in this hell forever. At least you will be. My soul is already awaiting another judgment and, from what Anubis implied, it's quite significant."

"Sorry," Paul replied. "It just seems so real. I panicked."

"I get it. I'm here because I want to help. I can't change what I did, or will do, to your timeline, but I can try and atone for my sins."

Paul added. "We're both on edge. Listen, we have a very short window in which to find the kids. Smart money is that they are on this floor, or at least one very close to it. After all, this is someone's judgment. So for better or worse, where we need to be is here. Also, Anubis said he would make sure we entered the judgment close to where he sensed the kids to be."

"My money is on Potter," Ari replied. "It has to be. He was willing to leave two men to die due to his own cowardice."

"Maybe," Paul said. "But I would guess it was someone else. Remember, he thought we were someone else who clearly hadn't shown up, so on the day he died, he never met the two men he was expecting. Therefore, he couldn't be judged for leaving two men to die who were never there. There must be something else."

They looked out at the hallway before them. The air was thick with dust. The lights were flickering and, in some cases, were hanging down by their wires. The walls were cracked and broken and pieces of plaster from the walls and from the drop-ceiling littered the floor everywhere. They could smell smoke and were sure that fires were already starting in the building. "So," Ari asked, "Where should we begin?"

CHAPTER 31

Elsewhere. Present day.

Grace awoke and found that she was held securely to the cold stone wall behind her by thick metal shackles. She tried to look around and get a better idea of where she was, but she was in complete darkness and couldn't see even a foot beyond her. From the way her arms hurt and the lingering stiffness in her neck, she was convinced she had been shackled here for hours. *What was the purpose? What did that bird-headed prick have in store for her?*

She tried again to move and grew increasingly more frustrated by her lack of success. Grace was a doer. She was very detail-oriented and, while she didn't always have much patience, she was highly organized and efficient and always managed to get things done. Being held against her will, both powerless to help herself, but also powerless to help her daughter, ate at her like a cancer. She felt the rage boil up inside of her, but she fought hard to keep it suppressed.

Grace knew that she often got angry and, when she did, she let her emotions run loose. This was not the time to lose it. She knew that she had to keep a level head and, when the right opportunity presented itself, she would take it.

A low voice, almost musical, whispered in her ear yet seemed to be coming from everywhere. "Ah, I see you are awake."

"Where are you?"

Grace noticed a flickering light that danced and swayed in the inky darkness. The light appeared to be far off in the distance and then space seemed to fold in upon itself and the flickering candle light was right next to her. In the dim yellow glow, she saw the outlines of Horus' bird-head profile.

"Why am I here?" Grace screamed. If she weren't shackled to the wall, she would have thrown herself at Horus and attacked him mercilessly.

Horus walked over to Grace and leaned in close. He smelled like cloves and spices to Grace, scents that were at the same time both pleasant and noxious. His eyes were close together and were liquid black. Grace had to look away as she felt disoriented staring into his cold, dead eyes. His beak grazed against her skin and she felt an involuntary chill pass through her.

"Why am I here?" Grace asked again.

"Insurance," Horus replied. "Your child, or those of your brother's kin, can never be allowed to be the one from the Bloodline to become the next Lord of the Dead. You are here in case things start getting out of control and if the child needs further incentive."

Grace looked quizzically at Horus. "I don't understand. What does my daughter, or my brother-in-law's children, have to do with anything? Is my husband here as well?"

Horus roared in anger. "Your husband will die by my hand for the affront he has shown me. I will tear him to shreds while his child watches. He thinks he can stop what has been in motion for millennia? As for the prophecy, it is still unclear as to whether it will be your daughter, or the boy or girl from your husband's brother. For now, they are hidden from my scrying until the time of the Ascension. Once the Ascension passes, their fates are irrelevant to me."

Grace still didn't follow what Horus was saying, but decided her best course of action was to pretend that she did. "So how am I insurance?"

Horus looked at Grace. "Why, that is simple. If your husband somehow manages to get your daughter to the Ascension, then you will be responsible to stop that from happening."

"What happens if it is to be my nephew or niece?"

"Then you are to ensure that they are in no position to ascend either. Or, if that fails, then you are to get close and kill them."

Grace glared defiantly at Horus. "You want me to kill my daughter or my niece or nephew? Good luck with that."

Horus smiled at Grace, his beak twisted in what could best be called a lopsided grin. "I thought you might feel that way. So, I brought some insurance." He threw his hideous bird head back and roared with laughter. He then extended his arm so that his closed fist was directly in front of Grace. He slowly opened his fist to reveal a large, glistening black scarab beetle. It was huge, at least as big as a plum, and divided into two shiny black sections. The top part of the scarab had two multi jointed, chitinous mandibles that were connected to the head on either side. They twitched eagerly when they got close to Grace, as if her scent suddenly triggered something in their rudimentary nerve net that passed as their brain. The back half of the beetle was also a shiny black carapace, with two vestigial arms on each side of the top end of the rear segment. In the back were two large and chitinous legs which would help the beetle's motility. It smelled of rot and fecal waste and Grace recoiled at the sight of the beetle.

"What are you going to do with that thing?"

Horus' eyes twinkled with both malevolence and glee. "I'm not going to do anything. I suspect the scarab will do quite a bit, though."

Horus grabbed Grace's face with one of his powerful hands and held it still. She tried to shake him off but couldn't get free of his vice-like grip. He applied pressure, slowly forcing her jaw open.

"Please," she begged, a tear trickling down her cheek.

He pulled her mouth open and held his palm flat and waited as the beetle crawled across the hand and into her mouth. She gagged at the foul taste but couldn't do anything as the beetle worked its way to the back of her throat. She felt it starting to burrow and she screamed as a lightning bolt of agony shot through her. She felt the creature work its way up the back of her throat and then burrowed in, tunneling deeper until it started to probe at the base of her brain. It crawled in, tearing and rending the soft tissues as it went. Grace screamed and screamed until she eventually passed out.

CHAPTER 32

In the House. Present day.

Greg stood in the hallway with Kevin and David and looked at the white door with the pulsating red 'x' emblazoned upon it.

"What are the odds that this is the door?" Kevin said with a chuckle, "X marks the spot, eh."

Greg punched Kevin in the shoulder. "Damn it, Kevin. My kid's life is at stake. It's hardly the time for jokes."

Kevin snarled, "Listen, Greg. We might be walking into a trap, or even to our deaths. So if I feel like trying to lighten the mood and make things a bit less grim, I will. Now back the fuck off."

Greg balled his hands into fists and was about to reply to Kevin when David stepped between them. "Guys, I understand that things are a bit tense right now," he said in his usual good natured tone, "but take it down a notch. You're both friends and have been so for many years. There's something here in this House. It makes you feel things at a deeper level and read into everything. Don't let it get to you. We'll get the kids out, I promise."

Greg and Kevin lowered their heads and both apologized to each other.

"Good. Now let's go and get your kids home safe and sound."

Greg grasped the handle and opened the door. It swung silently inward. A wall of darkness lay before the three men.

"Now that's encouraging," David said with a hint of bitterness and then he stepped through the doorway and vanished, swallowed up by the darkness that spread before them. Greg took a deep breath, looked at Kevin and followed David into the room. Kevin stepped back and managed a quick look down the hallway. He saw how deserted and silent things were in the House. He wished he were back at home with his wife and kids. Sure, they didn't listen and often ridiculed him to his face, but they were his own and were a big part of his safe place. He muttered a short curse under his breath and followed his friends into the room.

The men found themselves in a dense jungle in the middle of the night. The air was thick with moisture and redolent with the many smells of vegetation. There was also a damp, earthy smell and they knew they had to be near a river or stream. Large insects flew thickly around them and the men found themselves swatting incessantly at the bugs to keep them out of their eyes and mouths.

The leaves and high grass was damp and smelled fresh, as if a cleansing downpour had recently happened. Underneath it all, though, was the stench of cordite and rot and decay, and even death. The men realized that the ground was soggy marshland and, as they walked, they often found themselves up to their waists in the foul, brackish water. Greg suspected that there were a lot of bodies submerged under the thick, filthy muck which lay just underneath the water, but decided to keep his thoughts to himself. Morale amongst his friends was already low. Last thing he needed was to set one of them off.

The men walked through the submerged fields for what seemed like a solid hour. Occasionally, they heard screams or gunfire off in the distance. Thankfully, none were even remotely close to their location.

"I feel like we're in a set of Full Metal Jacket," Kevin remarked.

"Why's that?"

Kevin turned to look at Greg. "Are you serious, Greg? I've been in the reserves for twenty years. I've seen every war movie ever made. I don't have to have ever been here to recognize a rice paddy field."

"Okay, Kevin. We'll take your word for it," David added, "Besides, it's not like my damaged memory has any recollections of any of this. Heck, I barely have any memories of you and Greg."

Kevin sighed. "Think about it, okay? It all makes sense. We're in a rice paddy field in the middle of the night in a wet and cloyingly sticky climate. We've heard gunshots and explosions off in the distance. If I had to guess, I'd say either Vietnam or Korea."

"Okay, guys, let's just focus on finding my kid. If we're in the middle of a war zone, we better be damn careful."

The three men waded through the rice paddy field. The water was up to their waists and had a foul smell. Mosquitos assaulted them incessantly, and they had to keep swatting at the miserable insects. Greg was sure he passed within mere feet of a water snake and almost lost it as it slithered past. Periodically, they heard more gunfire off in the distance, sometimes followed by screams of the dying.

After what seemed like ages trudging through the marshlands, the men came to dry ground. They followed a trail which led off into a dense forest. They stopped to pause at the edge of the woods, with Greg taking the lead. Kevin wiped his brow with his sleeve and grimaced with disgust as he saw the fat leech which now clung to his sleeve. He picked it off his sleeve and walked over to the woods. Just as he was about to hurl the leech, he felt his foot sink in the ground up to his knee. Kevin fell over and hit the ground face first.

"God damn it," he screamed.

David and Greg rushed over. Kevin was face down on the ground with his leg sunk into the earth. Greg helped Kevin get free and peered down into a dark tunnel opening.

"Is that what I think it is?" Greg asked.

Kevin peered down the tunnel, his embarrassment over stumbling into the tunnel forgotten. "I think it is. In the Vietnam War, the Viet Cong had entire networks of tunnels which they used for guerrilla warfare. In some cases, these warrens of tunnels were practically underground cities."

David got down on his knees and peered into the tunnel's opening. The darkness was absolute and as hard as he tried, he couldn't see anything which might indicate that any of the children were being held in the murky depths below.

"So, what do you think?"

Kevin looked at Greg. "I think we have to go down. There might be many places they could have the kids hidden down there."

"I agree," David replied. "What worries me is that we could be walking into a trap. Horus' men could be lying there in the darkness, waiting to take us out."

Greg wiped the perspiration from his brow. He knew that there was a good probability that they were walking into a trap, but what choice did they have? It was either go into the tunnel and risk getting jumped by Horus' minions or walk away from what seemed like the best place to hide the kids. As Anubis stated, the Ascension was rapidly approaching. Hiding the kids in the tunnel seemed like the obvious choice. He knew that they were working against the clock. The kids would not be out in the open, so the tunnel seemed to present the best option.

"Okay, guys," Greg said in a low and ominous tone. "We're going in."

Greg started towards the tunnel and lowered himself down. David and Kevin paused for a moment, waiting to hear if there were any signs of a struggle below.

Kevin turned to David. "I'm going next. I've been in the reserves for over twenty years. I studied this stuff. If they are hiding in any secret chambers, there's a good chance I'll find them." Kevin didn't even look back at David. He turned and climbed down into the pit. David watched as he disappeared into the darkness. He waited for a few minutes and, not hearing anything, descended into the tunnel after Kevin.

David climbed down the ladder into the darkness. He soon found himself at the bottom. He looked around and noted a faint light source off in the distance. He couldn't see Greg or Kevin, so he assumed they were up ahead. He headed off towards the light. He didn't dare call out as it would give away their presence to anyone who might be lying in wait. The tunnel was only about three feet high at the ladder's base, so David crouched down and followed a short tunnel to a well-lit room. A single bare bulb hung suspended from the ceiling by a long wire. Greg and Kevin were at a table in the center of the room poring over some documents.

Greg saw David and motioned him over.

"What's going on?" David asked.

"Well, I know where we are, Kevin replied. "We're in Vietnam during the Vietnam War. So I estimate that this is sometime in the mid nineteen sixties. This is a VC tunnel, and these plans seem to indicate an attack of US friendly locales. We were trying to see if there is anything which might indicate where the kids are being held. Unfortunately, we're no better off than we were before we found the tunnel.

"Let's keep moving then," Greg said as he stood and walked towards the tunnel opening at the back of the room. Kevin and David followed. The tunnel twisted around a few bends and then widened out in what looked like a kitchen.

Standing ahead of them, with one hand clutching a gaping wound in his stomach, the other holding a Kalashnikov AK-47, was a visibly shaken Viet Cong soldier. Greg put his arms up and Kevin and David followed suit.

"*Bạn là ai?*" the soldier cried out. "*Bạn có với những người khác?*"

"Any idea what he's saying?" Gary asked. Both Kevin and David shook their heads. He turned to the wounded soldier. "Do you speak English?"

The soldier stared at Greg with a blank expression. He held the rifle out in front of him, moving it back and forth to show the men that he had them all covered. His hands were shaking as he tried to take a defensive posture. He was clearly terrified. He took a hesitant step back and fell to the ground. Kevin rushed up and grabbed his weapon while David and Greg went to check on the soldier.

"How is he?" Kevin asked.

"Not good," David replied. "He's been shot and I can barely feel a pulse. It doesn't take a doctor to tell that he looks pretty far gone."

Greg scratched his chin. "What are the odds that this guy here is the one who is receiving his judgment?"

"Why do you ask?" David replied.

"Because if it is his judgment, what happens if he dies?"

Kevin looked horrified. "If he dies, do you think we'll cease to exist? We are, after all, in someone's own private judgment, except we are not part of it. So if our soldier friend here happens to die, and move on to face Anubis, then does this world disappear? Even worse, if the world winks out of existence, what happens to us?"

Greg snarled, "Then let's hurry up and find the kids and fast, because this guy doesn't have long to live and I don't want to be around to find out what happens to us if he dies."

They left the kitchen and followed the tunnel which branched off both to the right and left.

"Anyone have an idea which way to go?" Kevin asked.

"Well, the tunnel goes in three directions and there are three of us. I think that's the approach we should take."

"I don't like it," David complained. "We stand a better chance to survive by sticking together."

"I agree. The problem is if we pick the wrong tunnel, my kid could die."

"We have to play the odds, Greg. We can cover more ground separated, but we have no idea what's in store for us. One wounded soldier wasn't much of a threat but remember what Anubis told us. His brother Horus has recruited others to help him keep the Ascension from happening. The kids stand a better chance of being rescued if we keep to strength in numbers."

Greg sighed. "I hope you're right. Let's go, our time is running out."

The three men hurried down the middle tunnel when gunfire erupted from all around them. Greg felt a bullet graze his shoulder. "Get down!" he screamed. The men fell to the ground and tried to figure out where the gunfire was coming from. They were being shot at from at least two directions and were being slowly pinned down. If they didn't think of something quick, they would never get near the kids.

CHAPTER 33

In the House. Present day.

Ari and Paul ran back into the offices of Alliance Consulting. They decided that it made sense to begin where they had started and search these offices first to see if the kids were there. After meeting Potter and his co-workers, he felt reasonably confident that the kids were elsewhere. Still, they needed to be sure. They only had one chance to save the kids, and they wouldn't mess it up by cutting corners in their search.

They stepped inside the office and saw that it was in worse shape than the hallway. The lights were out and the ceiling had fallen onto the reception desk. They walked back to the conference room where they had been originally seated and were horrified to see that the entire picture window overlooking the city was gone. It was as if someone had roughly cut away the side of the building leaving an ugly, gaping wound that was exposed to the elements. Paul and Ari took a few tentative steps towards the edge and were able to see where the wall had been. The sky outside was thick with smoke from the fires and dust from the ruined building. Intermittently, something would go sailing past, plummeting to the ground below. In some cases, it looked to be office furniture but, in others, Paul saw that it was people from the floors above them. The floor still rumbled and lurched once or twice while they stood there.

Paul took a step back and gently took Ari's arm. "Come on, Ari. This whole place looks like it will come crashing down."

Ari looked sadly at Paul. "It will. In a little over an hour, this whole building will collapse, killing everyone still inside, crushing them under tons of debris from the building."

Paul and Ari turned and left the conference room. They explored the rest of Alliance Consulting's offices, checking anywhere that a child could have been hidden. After fifteen minutes, they were convinced that the kids were not there and decided to try another office on the floor.

The next office they found belonged to Cantor Fitzgerald. Ari tried the door and it opened easily. He walked into the offices followed by Paul. At first glance, these offices did not look in too bad shape. The lights were flickering off and on and there were some cracks in the walls but, otherwise, the space looked to be in fairly good condition. Ari was impressed with how opulent the office must have been.

"What do these guys do?" Ari asked.

"Financial services and investment banking," Paul replied without missing a beat.

Ari turned to Paul. "Seriously, how did you know that?"

"I work as a lawyer for one of the largest credit card companies in the world. We deal with companies like Cantor Fitzgerald all the time."

Ari smirked. "Never would have guessed. You don't act like any lawyer I've ever met."

Paul reddened a bit. "And how do lawyers act, anyway?"

"Relax, Paul. I was making conversation. Most of the lawyers I've had to deal with cared only about making money, and not the people they were supposed to be helping."

Paul relaxed a bit. "You sound like you're speaking from experience."

Ari felt the rage building inside himself. "I am."

"Maybe one day you'll want to talk about it?"

"I doubt it," Ari hissed and turned his back to Paul.

The two men walked around the offices and didn't find anything. They found it unsettling being in the large space with no one there. Cantor Fitzgerald was not only deserted, it actually felt empty. If it weren't for the occasional shaking of the building, they could have doubted the reality of their situation.

The rumbling began anew and the building started to shake harder. Some of the ceiling panels came crashing down. A long jagged crack appeared on the back wall, causing the window to shatter. The floor buckled and before either man could react, a whole section of the wall and floor fell away from the building. The dust and smoke filled their lungs as they ran out of Cantor Fitzgerald's offices.

"Shit. Did you see that?" Paul asked.

Ari nodded. He could not believe that they had been mere feet away from dying a horrible death by plummeting over a hundred floors down. "Let's try another office."

Paul and Ari walked down the hallway, getting frustrated by the lack of offices.

"Damn it," Paul cursed, "there must be somewhere else."

"Hey, Paul," Ari said while pointing down the hall where another door was visible, "there's another office."

They hurried over to see a door with the name Paine Webber written on it in gold letters.

"Let's try here next," Ari said. He walked in followed by Paul. Unlike the offices of Cantor Fitzgerald, the Paine Webber space was in bad shape. The lights were completely out and the air was thick with dust and smoke. Several small fires could be seen burning. The ceiling panels were mostly down and, in some cases, it looked as if the entire thing had collapsed, with exposed wires and cabling hanging down loosely. Some of the walls were cracked and others had actually collapsed.

They walked in carefully and turned down an adjoining hallway when Ari put his hand up and motioned them to stop. A woman lay on the floor in front of them. She was lying on her back with her eyes wide open and staring. Her throat was torn open, indicating that her head had nearly been severed from her body. Her hands were up in what looked like a defensive posture.

Ari looked grim. He bent down and examined the woman's corpse. He gently touched the wound in her throat and looked at the still damp blood on his fingers. He motioned for Paul to come and kneel by him. Paul complied.

"This woman was killed within the last few minutes," Ari said softly. "Her blood hasn't fully dried and coagulated yet. Someone took advantage of what is happening to mask this murder."

"So what does this mean?"

Ari sighed. He said in a low whisper, "Paul, either we've stumbled across a random murder or the people we are looking for are here. They probably came here and chose to hide out in this office when the woman accidentally ran into them, forcing them to kill her and eliminate a loose end. Her throat was cut and my guess is that whoever did it was very strong and used a very sharp blade."

"Shit. Well, what are we waiting for? Let's get the bastards and find the kids," Paul responded, his voice low and menacing.

They took a more defensive stance and slowly advanced down the hallway. At the first door, Ari paused. He motioned for Paul to stop. He put his ear to the door and, hearing nothing, slowly opened it. Inside was what had once been a plush office. A bookcase had fallen over, with numerous texts strewn over the carpeted floor. At the back of the room was a large mahogany desk with a man lying face down on it. Two leather chairs were in front of the desk, one of them lying over on its side. Papers were everywhere and a thick dust covered every surface.

Ari walked over to the man and prodded him with the nose of his gun. The man did not move so Ari grabbed him by the hair and lifted his head up. Paul let out a small gasp when he saw the man's face. The throat had been slit. Even more disturbing was that his eyes had been gouged out. Paul gently placed the man's head back down on the desk.

"Holy shit, Ari, they cut out his eyes," Paul said, his voice threatening to rise above a whisper. "Why would they do something like that? Wasn't it enough to just kill him?"

"Paul, you know that these people are not real, right? They are memories brought to life to assist in someone's judgment."

"I know. I know. It's just that it seems so real and that what they did goes way beyond the act of murder. Whoever killed this man took a certain pleasure from the act."

Ari shook his head. "Perhaps, but I suspect in this case, it's something else. It's almost as if they were desecrating the bodies to send a message. Either way, it really doesn't matter. These people have shown that they are very dangerous. We can't afford a single mistake. When we find them, we take them out with extreme prejudice."

Paul thought for a moment. "Anubis never told us what the men who took the children looked like. How will we recognize them?"

"Look for those who don't fit or don't belong in this judgment universe. We're in the World Trade Tower. This was a building of professional service companies, banks, investment firms and other professional organizations. The people working here are all professionals or admin and clerical support for those companies. Keep your eyes peeled for those who seem out of place."

They closed the office door and walked past an area with a few dozen cubicles. They found a few more bodies, all of which had been murdered; most had been grotesquely mutilated. With each body discovered, Paul felt himself growing angrier. These killers were animals who had no regard for human life. He swore he would get the kids and then he would kill the murderous bastards.

They came to another door. Ari swung it open, his gun at the ready. Inside was what had once been a conference room. It was in total disarray, with a fire burning in the far corner and papers strewn all over the floor. The entire back wall was gone, the floor ending with a drop into the New York skyline. What got their attention, though, was the man standing at the edge of the floor. He was tall and lanky with a small, doughy mid-section. His black hair was slicked back and his face held a lopsided grin. He wore a red, blue and yellow checkered shirt and tan khakis. In each arm were Paul's children, which he held upside down by the ankles, dangling them over the precipice.

"Hello, guys," he said, his voice surprisingly calm and ordinary. "I'd advise you to step back, or I drop the kids." He grinned and glanced over his shoulder. "And trust me when I say that it's a long way down."

CHAPTER 34

In the House. Present day.

Another round of shots hit the wall behind David, spraying him with slivers of dirt and stone. David moved forward to take advantage of the cover the angling of the tunnel provided.

"You okay?" Greg called out to David.

David looked a little pale and nodded.

"We need to find out where the shooters are," Kevin yelled over the din of gunfire. "If we can, we can fight our way out of here. If we don't, sooner or later one of their shots will hit home."

Kevin aimed the AK-47 in the direction of where some of the gunfire was coming from and shot back, laying down a wall of return fire. He let out a howl and kept firing.

David looked at the gun he was given and then over to Greg. "I don't know if I can kill anyone."

Greg fired three quick shots from his handgun. "Damn it, David. These people aren't real. They are the recreation of someone's memories. So put a bullet in them before they put one in you because, if you get shot, you will die. Do you understand?"

David nodded and gripped the gun tightly.

The shots seemed to be getting closer. Pieces of the tunnel wall sprayed over them as the gunfire continued.

Kevin pointed to holes in the walls just past the tunnel entrance a little further into another room. "The shooters are on the other sides of those holes. I'll draw their fire and you two make a run for the door across the room."

"We'll be sitting ducks if we open ourselves up like that."

"Do you have any other ideas, Greg? I'm the one with military training and, to be honest, the only one of us who can actually shoot a gun and hit the target. All both of you would be doing is wasting the few precious bullets we have."

Greg shook his head. He hated having Kevin risk himself for their cause and being exposed to their enemies, but they were getting nowhere and would soon run out of ammunition. "Okay, Kevin, we'll go with your plan. You ready?"

Kevin nodded and clutched his gun. He looked over at David, silently praying that David would follow Greg's lead. He was the only one with experience that was relevant to this situation. David was a good guy but here, he was a serious liability.

Kevin stepped out from behind an overturned table and fired at one of the shooting holes in the wall. He kept the burst timed then swirled about and started shooting at the hole in the wall on the other side.

Greg got up and grabbed David by the arm and pulled him towards the doorway at the end of this room. At first, he sensed reluctance from David but, soon enough David was sprinting along after him.

Turning, Greg started firing shots at the holes in the wall the enemy was using for cover. "Come on, Kevin", he screamed, "I can lay down some cover fire, but I've only got a hand gun. I need for you to come over here."

Kevin looked at Greg who stood in the doorway firing one shot after another at the hole in the wall. The corner offered him some protection but, sooner or later, he'd run out of bullets, and then he'd have to make the run over without any supporting cover fire. Kevin said a small prayer and brought his cross to his lips. With a feral yell, Kevin burst from cover and began firing at the wall opposite to the one Greg was shooting at.

Bullets tore at the ground around him as he ran, but Kevin did not stop and made it around the corner without taking a hit. "Damn," he said, doubling over and trying to catch his breath, "I'm not in the shape I used to be. Let's try to avoid doing this in the future."

Greg looked at his friend with a wry grin. "Used to be?"

"Just shut it, wise ass."

"Come on, guys," David said, "Let's keep moving. I don't want to be around when whoever was shooting at us shows up."

The three men hurried down the tunnels. They passed several bodies of Viet Cong soldiers.

"Jesus..." Kevin muttered.

"What is it?"

Kevin pointed at the soldier closest to them. "Look at them, they were caught completely unaware. Notice how none of them was shot. See?"

Greg kneeled down next to the closest body. "You're right. His throat was cut."

"They all died the same way, Greg." Kevin turned over the other four bodies. "Look at their throats." Kevin motioned to the gaping wound on the soldier's neck. "The person or persons who killed them had to have been right behind them and then cut deeply from left to right."

"How do you know?" David asked.

"The entry is rougher and deeper on the left. It's then a smooth cut until it's pulled out on the right where the cut is still clean, but nowhere near as deep. Judging at how seamless the cut is, the person is very adept at using a knife."

"So where is all the blood?" Greg asked. "I've watched enough television to know that there should have been blood spatter everywhere."

Kevin walked around the bodies. "I don't know. Being killed the way they were would involve a huge spray and a lot of blood. There's none here. I'm guessing that they were killed elsewhere and dumped here."

David looked concerned. "Why go to all the trouble?"

"To make us hesitant and delay us," Greg said, "which is exactly what they've done. Come on, guys."

They rushed down the tunnel, which was dimly lit by single light bulbs hung intermittently from a running wire on the tunnel's ceiling. After a while, the tunnel came to a bend which seemed a lot more brightly lit. Kevin motioned for the men to crouch down and be quiet. He silently crawled forward and peered around the corner.

Kevin motioned for Greg to join him.

Greg peered around the corner and froze. His daughter was tied up and was hanging upside down over a large pit in the floor. She was clearly in distress, as she was thrashing about and screaming and crying. On each side of her stood a man with an AK-47 aimed in their direction. They were grinning and seemed to be enjoying Amy's fear, almost feeding off it. Without a doubt these had to be Anubis' men. They were clearly not Viet Cong, as both were easily six feet tall and Caucasian.

CHAPTER 35

In the House. Present day.

Paul stared in abject horror at the man holding his children. He seemed so unassuming, yet his very presence in the abduction of his children said otherwise. Tall and gangly, he didn't strike Paul as if he'd be a threat to anyone. Then he noticed his eyes. They were cold and almost reptilian and Paul realized that this man was a heartless and selfish individual who cared only about himself. The lives of others did not matter to him and for that he had to be extremely careful in his approach. He looked at his children who were screaming for help and felt his legs tremble and threaten to give out under him. He knew he had to stay strong. His children's lives depended on it.

"Come on, friend," Ari said slowly while aiming his Eagle at the man, "this doesn't have to go down this way. We only want the kids. You can just walk away."

The man threw his head back and roared with laughter. "You think I can walk away? I have two options. I do as I'm told by the guy with the bird's head and get to live forever or I can be judged by the guy with the jackal's head and be destroyed. Want to guess which option I'll choose?"

Paul tensed. He wanted to rush the guy but knew he couldn't take a chance with his children's safety. "Look, I get it. We all want what's best for ourselves. So what do you want? I'll do anything."

"You don't seem to understand," Perry hissed. "I don't want anything. I'm to keep the kids away from you at all costs until I'm told otherwise. Then, they both belong to me."

"They're just children," Paul said. "Mike is only five years old,

Beth is two. They've never done anything to anyone. They don't deserve this. Please…let me have my children back."

Ari meanwhile had slowly moved to the wall at the far end of the room, allowing the smoke and dust to partially obscure him from the man holding the children. *Keep him talking*, he thought, praying that Paul was on the same wavelength. *Keep him talking, Paul, and focused on you.* He began inching his way towards the man, and closer to being able to help the two kids.

"Why should I care that they're kids," Perry screamed. "To me, they're my ticket to an eternity of doing whatever I like. And whoever I like. Children are not my usual preference, although I do like it when they beg."

Paul gritted his teeth. He reached into his pocket for his Beretta and aimed it at Perry. "Put the kids down," Paul growled. "I swear I'll put a bullet through your head."

"You won't," Perry replied. He held the kids even further over the edge. The kids screamed in terror. "Shoot me and they both die. It's as simple as that."

Paul felt his resolve weaken. His hand shook. That bastard was right. He wouldn't shoot. Not while his children's lives were at stake. Out of the corner of his eye, he saw Ari come out of the shadows and move within a few feet of Perry and his kids. Paul realized that he had to keep Perry's attention away from Ari. His kids' lives depended on it.

"Hey," Paul called out. "I've got a deal for you. Give me the kids and I'll get you out of the House. You can escape and not have to go through judgment."

Perry sneered. "Nice try, pal. But there isn't a way out of the House unless it's through the guy with the jackal's head. It's in my best interest to avoid that at all costs. A guy like me, let's put it bluntly, usually does not ride off happily into the sunset."

"Not true!" Paul yelled. "How do you think I got here? My brother and I, along with two friends, drove here. When this is all done, we intend to drive home as well."

"You lie." Perry screamed. "The only way in or out of this place is by way of a pine box. I should just dump the kids and to Hell with you all."

"I swear," Paul said, slowly softening his tone to appear non-threatening. "I drove here with my brother and two others. We came by a road that ran between worlds. It was called the Highway of Lost Souls. Our car is just outside. Once we get the kids, we intend to go back the way we came."

Perry appeared to contemplate this. He furrowed his brow and turned to Paul. "We can just drive out, you say?"

Paul felt a flood of relief. "Yes". He reached into his pocket and held up the car keys. "See? I have the keys right here. There is room for you if you just give me back the kids."

Ari, meanwhile, had slipped out of the smoke and shadows and was nearly upon Perry. He tensed, ready to tackle Perry when, from behind him, a spear shot out and pierced him through his shoulder. Ari screamed and turned to see a man who looked as if he had stepped out of a film set for Cleopatra. The man screamed something in a language which sounded a bit like Egyptian.

Perry's features darkened. "You tried to trick me," he screamed, the spittle flying from his lips. He turned and hurled Beth over the edge.

Paul screamed in horror as he watched his daughter thrown over the edge of the building, disappearing into the smoky emptiness outside. Paul started firing blindly, fueled by rage and despair. One bullet struck Perry in the leg and another punched a hole in his shoulder. He turned and, with a look of utter terror, lost his footing and fell back to the edge and slowly toppled over.

Ari, meanwhile, had turned and fired two shots at the Egyptian man. The first struck him square in the forehead and the second in the chest. He fell back dead.

"Save your son," Ari called to Paul. He grabbed the shaft of the spear, just below the tip, which protruded from the front of his shoulder. He gritted his teeth and roared in agony as he slowly pulled the shaft through his shoulder.

Paul ran to the edge of the building and saw that Perry was holding on to a piece of rebar with his left hand and Mike by his ankle from the right. His face was ashen grey and he was sweating profusely. His eyes were glazed over and unseeing. He looked as if he were on the verge of passing out.

"Give me your hand," Paul called down to Perry, extending his hand.

Perry glanced up at Paul and then back down at Mike. He managed a dark and twisted grin. "I don't think so."

"Damn it!" Paul screamed. "You're stuck there. There isn't any way that you can climb back up. Take my hand and I'll pull you up."

Perry looked down and then back up at Paul. "I think I'll take the third option." He swung his body and landed on the floor below. He grabbed Mike by the collar, waved tauntingly at Paul, and then disappeared into the smoke and darkness.

CHAPTER 36

In the House. Present day.

Kevin grabbed Greg by the collar and pulled him back as hard as he could. He could feel Greg tensing, as if any moment he would try and break free.

"You have to take it easy," Kevin whispered. He motioned for David to join them. David inched along the wall to join his friends.

"What's going on?" David asked.

"My daughter's in there," Greg said, barely holding his voice above a whisper. "They have her trussed up, and hanging upside down like a slab of meat."

David paled. "Are you serious?"

Kevin sighed. "I'm afraid so. There are two of them, both armed with sub-machine guns. We can't go in for a direct assault because even if we weren't cut to ribbons in the process, there is a good chance a stray bullet will hit Amy."

Greg pulled forward once again and Kevin had to strain to pull him back. "Damn it, Greg, this isn't going to help your daughter. How will getting killed get her back? We need to be smart about this."

Greg stopped struggling. "You saw what those animals did to her. Right now I don't care if I live or die. I just want to know that she's safe and that I make sure that she's unharmed. Then, I swear to God, I'll make them pay dearly for what they've done."

"Okay, then," Kevin said, "here's what we should do. Greg, you and David walk in on the two men holding Amy. Your job is simple. Go in and be non-threatening and non-confrontational. Try and distract them from where we came in. Once it looks like they have their attention diverted elsewhere, I'll come in and put them down."

"There is no way I will allow that to happen, Kevin. What happens if your aim is off and one of your shots hits my daughter?"

"Look, Greg. I'm not going to lie to you. It could happen. But I'm a trained shot. I've been in the army as a reservist for over twenty years. I've fired weapons for more than half my life. If anyone can do this, it's me. Have you ever fired a gun?"

Greg thought for a moment. "I only touched a gun once before. When I was a teenager, this guy I knew had a gun and wanted to show it off. So we went to the high school at night and took turns shooting at the windows."

Kevin shook his head. He looked over at David.

"Sorry. Other than what we fired today, I've never used a gun."

Greg seemed to mull it over, and stopped struggling. "Okay, we'll do it your way. But leave them alive, if possible. I want to kill them myself."

"I'll do what I can."

"No, you will make damn sure she is not shot, do you understand? I'm putting my trust in you, Kevin. Her life is in your hands, so I want you to do everything in your power to ensure she stays safe."

Greg stood up and looked back at David. "I need you to follow my lead. We need to distract them, so I focus on the one on the left and you focus on the one on the right. Got it?"

David nodded.

Greg slipped his handgun into the back waistband of his jeans and then pulled out his shirt to cover it. He motioned for David to do the same.

They turned the corner and Greg slowly raised his arms. David followed a few paces behind. Greg slowly moved to the left of the room and David to the right, making sure to keep some distance between them.

A warning shot hit the ground in front of Greg. He stopped and raised his hands higher.

"Stop right there, asshole," the bigger of the two shouted. Greg took a moment to get a good look at the guy. He stood over six feet tall, and was of a stout build. His dirty blonde hair was cut short and he had a genial, frat-boy look about him. The only menacing thing the man was his eyes, which were ice cold and hard.

The other man was a bit shorter, and of a slim build. His dark hair was log and brushed back, almost in a mullet. His lean face was unshaven and he sported deep bags under his eyes. He seemed twitchy, shifting back and forth from one foot to another, as if to contain a lot of nervous energy. He had the look of someone who tended towards drug or alcohol abuse and was seriously in need of his next fix.

Tense moments passed and neither man said another word.

"Who are you guys?" Greg asked.

"None of your business, pal," the smaller of the two men replied. "Why don't we start with you telling me who the fuck you are. You certainly ain't one of the gooks."

Amy, meanwhile, began thrashing even more furiously against her bonds. She was screaming and tears were streaming down her face. In the midst of all that, she managed to cry out 'Daddy'.

The bigger of the two men, who looked surprisingly like a cross between Kevin James and Landfill from the Beerfest movie, threw his head back and laughed. "So this is the girl's father, eh? You hear that, Nicky? We've got the little girl's daddy." He turned and aimed his AK-47 at Greg. "You've got balls coming here, you know that?"

Greg lowered his hands and tried to look as non-threatening as possible. "Please. I don't know you and, honestly, I don't care who you are. I just want my little girl back."

The one called Nicky walked up to Greg and gave him a huge smile. "Come on, Brett. He just wants to know his little girl is safe. I can relate, mister. I'm a dad, too. Maybe we can work something out?"

"Are you serious?" Greg asked, a bit surprised at the sudden turn of events.

Nicky spun his weapon around and swung the stock of the gun, clipping Greg hard under the chin and sending him sprawling backwards. "No, you dumb shit. We have our marching orders. We're to watch the girl until we get word that we're to bring her back."

Greg got slowly to his feet. He wiped his hand across his mouth and saw that it came away covered with blood. He spit some blood onto the tunnel floor. "Why are you listening to Horus?" He turned to Nicky, "What did he promise you if you'd help?"

"Immortality," Nicky replied. "We help him, we never die. It sure seems as good an incentive as any. Do you know what happens to me if I refuse? Horus laid it all out for me. I get to go before Anubis and, after being judged, my soul gets torn apart. I know what I did in life. This is the only offer that makes any sense."

Greg looked over at David who had slowly moved closer to the bigger one, Brett. "Okay, Brett. It is Brett, right? What makes you think he can give you even an extra day, let alone everlasting life?"

"It's like this," Brett replied, "Horus is taking over as the Lord of the Dead. He needs the girl to do so. By asking for our help, he has promised that we'd never have to die. To me, being able to live forever, to do anything I want without any fear of repercussion, is simply too much to ignore."

"Let her go, Brett," Greg implored, "she's just a little girl. Look, I don't know about Horus, but I do know that Anubis can offer you immortality. Let the girl go, come back with us, and have Anubis grant you what Horus only pretended to be able to offer."

"Sorry, pal. We're not that stupid," Brett replied. He pointed to where Amy was hanging. "See that? The girl is hanging upside down over a pit. Inside the pit are dozens of venomous snakes, largely cobras and vipers. It's how the Viet Cong used to get information from their prisoners. Hang someone over a pit filled with venomous snakes, slowly lower them down, and even the toughest men will crack. That is our insurance. If you come any closer, I cut the rope and she falls down into the pit of snakes. Then it's good-bye little girl."

Greg looked defeated. "Okay, Brett. You're holding all the cards. What do you want from me?"

Brett grinned and looked over at Nicky. "What do we want from our new friend? Do you have any ideas?"

"How about we put a bullet in each of them and then go back to waiting on Horus."

Greg looked over at David who had been silent during the exchange. He had gotten a bit closer to Nicky, but not near enough to alleviate the situation. David was looking at Greg for guidance, but Greg didn't have any to give. If Brett and Nicky opened up with their AK-47s, they would be cut down and that would be that.

Suddenly, Kevin burst into the room, screaming at the top of his lungs and firing rapid bursts from his own AK-47. He shot at Brett initially and Greg saw him go down in a hail of bullets. Nicky turned towards Kevin and opened fire on him.

He hit Kevin point blank in the chest and Kevin went down, hard.

"Kevin!" Greg screamed and began running towards his fallen friend.

Nicky turned and tried to get Greg in his sights. He began firing, the bullets whizzing dangerously close to him as he ran.

A single shot rang out and Nicky fell forward, the front of his forehead completely blown out.

Greg turned and saw David standing directly behind Nicky, his handgun smoking in his shaking hands.

"I," David began, and then turned forward and threw up.

Greg ran over to Kevin who was lying face down on the floor. He turned him over and saw the seriousness of his friend's wound. Kevin looked up at Greg, his pupils starting to dilate. Blood welled up in his mouth as he tried to speak.

Greg held his friend and watched his life drain out of him, knowing that there was nothing that he could do. Kevin reached up and grabbed Greg by the arm, motioning for him to lean in closer.

"I did good, right?" Kevin asked, spitting blood as he did. "We saved your daughter. Make sure that you get her back to Anubis and stop Horus. I need to know that my family will be safe after this."

"I will, old friend. I promise."

Kevin smiled weakly and coughed more blood. His pupils dilated fully and then he was still.

"Oh God, Kevin," David cried out as he ran forward to join his friends.

Greg looked over to David. "He's gone. He gave his life for Amy's. He knew that saving the children was critical if the world was to be saved. Let's go get her and get back to Anubis. Then we can decide on our next steps."

Amy began screaming. They turned and saw Brett sawing away at the ropes. He was bleeding freely from several wounds, yet he sawed at the ropes like a man possessed. Amy screamed for her father who could only watch in horror as Brett fully severed the rope and Amy fell headfirst into the pit.

CHAPTER 37

In the House. Present day.

Paul lay down on his stomach and tried to peer over the edge. Just moments before, Perry had disappeared into the darkness of the floor below, taking Paul's son with him after callously hurling his daughter Beth to her death. Paul felt broken inside. He wanted to curl up and die. He had failed to save his sweet little girl. She was dead because of his actions.

Paul felt a hand on his shoulder. He turned to see Ari standing over him. "We need to find him, Paul," Ari said gently. "He still has your son and he's wounded. He will be even more dangerous now because he's hurt, perhaps dying, and he won't think twice about taking your son out with him."

Paul stood up and brushed the tears from his eyes. "If he touches a single hair on the boy's head…"

Ari nodded solemnly. His shoulder throbbed where he had been impaled with the spear. He glanced at it, propped up against a table, still slick with his blood. "Don't worry, Paul. We'll get him. There's nowhere he can run. We'll catch him and get your son back."

"And then he's mine," Paul snarled.

Ari smiled, "I wouldn't have it any other way. Come on, let's head downstairs and find the son of a bitch." He grimaced against the pain. He knew that Paul was barely holding it together and was on the verge of a complete breakdown. Ari's right arm was numb and he could barely move it. He was sure there was substantial nerve and muscle damage and, with the dust and dirt in the air, it would surely get infected. That was a worry for another time. Right now, his plan was to salvage what was left of their mission, save Paul's son and get back to Anubis in time for the Ascension. He knew the longer they lingered in the judgment, the lower their odds of getting out were.

Ari helped Paul reload his gun. He checked his as well, making sure that he had a full clip. His right arm might be useless, but he was ambidextrous and could fire a weapon as effectively with his left as he could with his right. They started out, and Ari then doubled back to grab the Egyptian's spear. He might still have use of it.

The two men left the office and made their way out to the hallway. The sound of the rushing wind from outside was quite loud. The building shuddered and shook, causing pieces of the ceiling and walls to crack and break off. Fires were burning everywhere and the air was filled with smoke and dust. They had to cover their mouths with their shirts in order to breathe. The air stung their eyes and made it difficult to see. More than once, they had to stop and wipe the grit from their eyes with their grimy hands. Off in the distance they heard screams and cries for help. Paul stopped and looked to Ari for guidance. Ari merely shook his head, and reminded Paul that these people weren't real, but rather a reanimated memory for the purpose of someone else's judgment. They had one target, the guy who had taken his son and nothing should distract them from that path.

They found the staircase and slowly descended. The stairs seemed mostly undamaged. There were large fissures in the walls and the lights were off, replaced by the dim flickering provided by back-up generators, many clearly out of commission.

They encountered no problems as they made their way down to the next floor. Even more surprising was the complete absence of people.

"Why is no one around?" Paul asked softly.

Ari shrugged. "The only thing that I can think of is that whoever's judgment this is did not extend to this floor and, hence, there was no reason to populate it."

"That makes sense. Still pretty creepy, though. It's like a set from a movie, but without actors."

The men carefully tried the door that exited the staircase to the floor. Ari touched the handle and pulled his hand back quickly. "The handle is hot. There might be fire beyond the door."

"I don't care, Ari. My son might be there. Let's just kick it open and step back in case of flames."

Ari nodded motioned for Paul to stand clear before he kicked the door open. A blast of searing heat shot out at them. Ari jumped back and leaped up the stairs. The flames shot out, eagerly reaching the new oxygen from the staircase, then just as quickly, seemed to pull back.

Ari grabbed Paul and then quickly pulled him through and into the hallway past the flames. They stopped once well past the fires to catch their breath.

"Jesus," Paul said, gasping for air. He winced as the heated air hit his lungs. "I don't see how Perry in his weakened condition, while dragging a five year old, could have made it through that door. My poor boy must be terrified."

Ari looked thoughtful. "No, I don't think he would have made it past the door, which means that he's still here on this floor. But we'd better find him quickly as we are rapidly running out of time." He put a reassuring hand on Paul's shoulder. "Be strong, Paul. We'll get him back."

They got up and began checking office space by office space. Both Ari and Paul were very cognizant that time was rapidly running out. They did not want to make any noise and alert Perry but, in moving quietly, it also meant moving slowly, and time was working against them right now. The tower was destined to fall, and if they didn't find Perry and Mike, they would all die as the tower came down.

After the third set of offices, they heard the sound of a child crying. Paul snapped to attention. "Do you hear that?" he hissed.

Ari nodded, and motioned for Paul to keep quiet and follow him. They quickly worked their way through the hallway and came upon another set of doors. The doors were wide open and let into a large open area with countless cubicles. The ruins of a large conference room stood in the back behind the cubicles. The glass to the conference room had long since shattered and, the back wall, which had once majestically looked over the New York skyline, was gone, replaced by the flames and smoke which filled the cool September air.

Ari motioned for Paul to go right while he would go left. He indicated for Paul to stay low and be less visible. They both crouched down low and entered the office. Paul moved quietly and quickly to the door of the conference room. He peered inside and saw Perry slumped against the far wall, breathing laboriously. His son was huddled in the corner, softly weeping.

Paul inched his way in and positioned himself behind a chair so he'd be in Mike's line of sight. He hoped that Perry, who clearly was close to death, would be more focused on his own injuries. He cautiously waved his arm, trying to get his son's attention. Mike sat there sobbing, oblivious to his father's presence.

Paul looked around for Ari and couldn't see him. He cursed softly under his breath. "Mike," he hissed.

Mike looked up and yelled, "Daddy!" He got to his feet and ran over to Paul who gave him a big hug. Perry, meanwhile, had gotten up and grabbed his knife. He bellowed with rage and threw himself at Paul and his son. He stabbed at Paul and grazed his shoulder. Paul grabbed Perry around the neck and started squeezing as hard as he could. Perry flailed wildly with the knife, slicing Paul on two more occasions.

A thunderous crack filled the air and Perry collapsed on the ground before Paul and his son, the top of his head blown off. Pieces of his skull and brain matter were sprayed all over Paul's face and chest. Paul looked up to see Ari standing there holding his gun.

"Sorry, Paul," Ari said, "I know that you wanted justice for what this animal did to your daughter but I couldn't risk him hurting you or the boy." He looked at Paul with a haunted expression. "Also, once you take a life, even one as rotten as this one, you start down a dark road from which you can never go back."

Paul hugged his son even tighter, shielding him from the ruined mess that was Perry Christopher. His son cried into his shoulder and Paul did his best to soothe him. Eventually he stood, still holding Mike and looked over at Ari who stood patiently waiting. "Here, take Mike for a second."

Paul handed Mike to Ari and grabbed Perry's body by the collar of his shirt. He pulled him to the gaping hole in the wall and then, with a howl of rage, pushed him over the edge.

He walked over to Ari, his features set and grim. "Okay, Ari. Let's go."

They hurried through the hall. At the door to the stairway, Paul wrapped his arms around Mike and rushed through the flames into the staircase. Ari followed quickly behind. They checked themselves and seemed unharmed. Rushing up the stairs, they exited on the floor where that they had initially arrived when they first had entered the judgment.

"Where's the doorway?" Paul called out.

Ari pointed down the hallway. "We came in down there, around the corner. Come on."

Ari started down the hallway, hurrying as fast as he could with the searing pain shooting down the left side of his body and ensuring that Paul did not fall behind. They were coming to the corner when the building shook once more, a huge aftershock. Ceiling tiles rained down on them and sections of the floor started falling away. Mike was screaming in terror and Paul had to shield the boy from falling ceiling tiles.

"We don't have much time!" Ari yelled. "This building will collapse any time now."

They rounded the corner and came to a dead stop. The hallway ended shortly after turning the corner. The side of the building had collapsed upon itself and had disappeared along with several dozen floors below it.

"Oh my God, where is the doorway," Paul cried out. "What do we do now?" He turned to Ari who looked deathly pale. Ari pointed out into the smoky sky. Hanging there in the sky, about ten feet away, with the city of New York sprawling out behind it, was the doorway back to the House. It was glowing faintly and starting to blink in and out of existence.

"Paul," Ari said, "the doorway is fading out. We have minutes before the building completely collapses. If we don't make it to the door, we'll die alongside the thousands of others who perished on nine-eleven."

CHAPTER 38

In the House. Present day.

Greg and David watched in horror as Amy fell headfirst into the snake-filled pit. Greg pulled out his gun and began firing wildly in Brett's direction. Brett, through badly wounded and limping, managed to escape through a tunnel at the other end of the room near the pit.

"Come on," Greg screamed, "I won't let Amy die, especially after Kevin gave his life to save her."

Greg and David ran towards the pit. They peered down but it was too dark too see anything. No matter how hard they tried, they couldn't see where Amy fell or if she was even still alive. All they heard was the hissing of what must have been dozens of snakes.

Greg pointed to the rope which hung from a wooden beam overhead. "Try and pull the rope down. I've got an idea."

David started pulling on the rope while Greg ran to one of the walls and grabbed a lit torch. He ran back to where David was still working on getting the rope.

"How are you doing, David?"

David looked at Greg, his face red from exertion. "I think it's loosening."

"I'm counting on you succeeding," Greg said grimly, "because if you don't, my daughter and I will die."

Greg turned and, with the torch in one hand and his gun in the other, he leaped into the pit.

The fall took only a few seconds, but to Greg it felt like an eternity. Conflicting emotions were rolling around in his head and he fought to keep himself in check. He landed hard and he felt a small twinge in his ankle. He prayed that he didn't hurt himself. He needed to be at one hundred percent if they were going to make it out of this nightmare judgment. He gauged that his fall was about fifteen feet. The rope that David was getting would have to be at least half that if he had any hopes of reaching it and pulling him and his daughter out. He was able to see the top from where he stood but was unable to see his friend.

Greg lifted the torch to get a good look of his surroundings. He saw that he was in a circular pit, with hundreds of snakes hissing and spitting around him. He aimed the torch at the snakes by his feet and they recoiled from the open flame. Sweeping the torch in a semi-circular arc, Greg was able to clear some space around him.

A few feet in front of him he saw his daughter. She was lying on the ground, unmoving, while dozens of snakes slithered all over her prone form.

"Amy," Greg said softly, "Are you okay, honey?"

Amy didn't stir. Greg couldn't tell if she was even still breathing. The fall could have easily broken her neck. If the fall didn't kill her, then any of the hundreds of poisonous snakes could have. It didn't matter, Greg realized. He'd have to know one way or the other and wouldn't leave her here, even in death.

Greg thrust the torch in front of him as he slowly moved towards his daughter. A snake struck out at him and he managed to kick it away. A smaller, green snake spit at him and then bit down on his shoe. Greg instinctively reached down to pull it off when a larger snake with mottled coloring shot out and clamped down on his arm. Greg pushed the torch down on the snake and took a small pleasure when it started to burn. The snake released its hold on his arm and fell sizzling to the ground.

Greg used the torch to force back the snakes that slithered over his daughter. Fighting back revulsion, he brushed off the remaining snakes and threw her over his shoulder.

"David, are you there?" Greg called out. "I really need the rope"

David lowered the rope down as far as he was able. Greg grabbed it with both hands and slowly began pulling him and his daughter up. The added weight of his daughter over his shoulder began taking its toll and he struggled to keep climbing. At the top, David leaned back and with everything he had, pulled the rope back until he saw Greg getting to the top of the pit. He extended his hand and pulled them both up. Amy fell soundlessly to the ground. Greg crawled over and put his ear to her mouth.

"I don't think she's breathing," Greg cried out.

David rushed over. "She is, although it's a bit faint. The fall must have knocked her out."

Greg carefully began checking his daughter for bites. He carefully checked every inch of her body. He was mostly done when he saw the tiny bite mark on her ankle.

"Oh shit," David said barely above a whisper.

"I read that if you cut an 'x' where the snake bite is, you can suck the poison out."

"Does that even work?" David asked. "Besides, where are we going to get a knife?"

Greg looked about the room. "I don't know. I – wait. The VC we saw at the start. He had a knife in his belt. He certainly won't be using it anymore. David, can you run back and get it? I'll stay here with Amy."

Without another word, David turned and ran back the way they had come.

Greg cradled his daughter in his arms, gently stroking her hair and whispering in her ear that she would be all right and that he would get her home, no matter what. He was starting to feel lightheaded and was slipping into sleep when David returned.

"Did you get it?" Greg asked.

David nodded. He looked Greg's way with concern. "You don't look so good."

"I don't feel so good, either," Greg said grimly. "I've been bitten a few times as well and I can feel the venom working its way in."

"Let me have a look," David said.

"Later. Let's tend to Amy first."

"We don't have time for martyrs, Greg."

"Just give me the knife," Greg said.

David held the knife back. "Let me do it, Greg. You're worn out and have snake venom coursing through your body. My hand is steadier."

"David, give me the goddamn knife," Greg growled. "She's my daughter and her life is in the balance. This is on me and me alone. After I'm done with my daughter, then you can help me. I've been bitten in a few places and I won't be able to cut and suck the venom from my own body."

David reluctantly handed Greg the knife. "I hope you know what you're doing."

Greg used the knife to cut away Amy's jeans from her ankle, which was now swollen and a purplish-black. Greg touched the skin gingerly and it felt hot and spongy to the touch. He cut into the flesh, and then made a second cut, creating an 'x' in the skin. Greg leaned in and sucked out some blood and venom and then spit it to the side. He repeated this several more times.

"I think I got as much as I'm going to get."

Greg got up to stretch his legs and fell forward. David helped him to a sitting position. He handed David the knife.

"I think you need to work on me now," Greg said slowly, then passed out.

Greg came to with his daughter leaning over him, a look of concern etched on her features.

"Daddy!" she cried out and wrapped her arms around him.

"Hey pumpkin," Greg said weakly. He turned and saw David sitting nearby. "How long have I been out?"

"About two hours. Amy came to about twenty minutes ago. We got to you just in time. You were burning up."

"I still feel like shit," Greg said weakly. "Of course, it beats the alternative. After meeting Anubis and seeing what's in store for us when we die, I'm in no mood to come back here any time soon and face my own personal demons in some fucked up judgment."

"Daddy, your language," Amy said and giggled.

"Help me up," Greg said to David, and put his arm over David's shoulder so his friend could get him to his feet. "We're running out of time, and we can't sit around here feeling sorry for ourselves."

Greg leaned into David for support and the two men trudged back the way they had come, with Amy following close behind. They made their way back through the jungle without incident.

They arrived at the doorway which led back to the House and saw Brett slumped before the door. He had an AK-47 on his lap.

"Hey, boys," Brett called out. His skin was ashen grey and he was sweating profusely. "It seems your fat friend got me good. I'm glad Nicky took him out. I need to do one thing before I go back to the world. I have to kill the little girl so Anubis can't complete his ceremony. Maybe then Horus will patch me up and grant me immortality.

Brett raised the AK-47 and took aim.

CHAPTER 39

In the House. Present day.

Paul and Ari stood at the edge of the hallway where it had fallen away into nothingness and looked up at the glowing doorway which hung there in the sky.

"What are we going to do, Ari?" Paul asked. He cradled his son even tighter. "If we lose the door, we're all as good as dead."

Ari gritted his teeth and looked around for something to help them with their dilemma. The building shook and Paul had to step back to avoid falling over the edge. His son clutched him tightly, his eyes wide as he looked at the destruction around them. He was fighting back the tears, trying to be brave for his father.

"I've got an idea," Ari called out. He ran down the hallway and stopped at the firebox on the wall. He opened it up and grabbed the fire hose with his good arm. Ari ran back to Paul and pulled the hose until he had over two dozen feet of hose at his feet.

"What are you going to do?" Paul asked.

"Use the hose as a rope to help us get out of here."

Ari wrapped the hose around his waist and headed down the hallway. He put his head down and ran as hard as he could. At the end of the hallway, where the floor fell away, he jumped as hard as he could towards the door. For a moment, it looked as if he would fall short, but luck must have been on his side as he struck the door and quickly grabbed at the handle to avoid falling back.

Ari pulled himself up and turned the handle, swinging the door open slowly towards him. "Okay, I'm over. Do you think you can make it across?"

Paul stood at the building's edge and looked up at the floors above him then down to the ground so far below. He felt his knees weaken. "I don't know if I can. On my own, it will be close. With Mike in my arms…"

Ari frowned. He suspected this would be the case. He pulled the fire hose until it was stretched taut. Checking the door, he decided his best bet would be to wrap the hose around the door, circling the top and sides to ensure it didn't slip. Looking around, Ari realized that he'd have to jump back.

"Stand back, Paul. I'm coming back." Ari stepped back into the hallway. Not as long a lead as coming from the twin tower, but hopefully enough. Taking a deep breath, Ari ran as fast as he could and jumped back into the smoke-filled hallway. He barely cleared the edge and fell forward, landing hard on the industrial carpet on his bad arm. He howled in agony as searing pain shot through his whole body.

Paul rushed over and helped Ari to his feet. "Why did you come back?"

Brushing the dirt and debris from the front of his shirt, Ari looked sternly at Paul. "I came back to help you both cross over the gap. I'm not leaving you here to die."

Ari peeled off his shirt and tore it into strips. He tied the pieces of his shirt into knots and wrapped them around Mike's waist and then between his legs. He brought Mike over to the fire hose and then looped the makeshift rope over the hose and tied it back around Mike's body. Taking the fire hose in his hands, Ari gritted his teeth and lifted slowly, making Mike start sliding down the makeshift sling to the other side.

"Wait!" Paul cried out. "This is too risky. How will he get himself untied at the other end?"

"Want me to go back? You can pass Mike to me."

"No." Paul took a few steps back. "He's my son. I need to do this for him." Paul went as far back as Ari had and prepared to run. Another quake shook the building and part of the ceiling behind Paul came crashing down.

"You'd better hurry!" Ari called out. "The building is ready to come down."

Paul started running. The building was shaking even harder, with pieces of plaster coming down off the walls. Paul reached the edge where the floor fell away and jumped. He landed hard on the other side and quickly grabbed the hose. "Send him over, Ari and hurry."

Ari lifted the fire hose as high as he could. He was feeling weak from the blood loss and barely had any sensation in his left arm. Mike's harness slid easily down the hose and Mike quickly crossed the emptiness from the twin tower to his father who scooped him up and set about getting him out of the harness.

"Stand back," Ari yelled. "I'm going to come over."

Ari hurried back and steeled himself to run. The building shook even more and a piece of metal came crashing down from the ceiling and hit Ari hard on the back.

"Ari," Paul cried out. "Are you okay?"

Ari struggled to stand. He gave Paul a weak thumbs-up. He started to run towards the edge when the building shook once more. Paul watched in horror as the building started to collapse. Ari kept running, dodging falling debris. He was nearly at the edge when the floor fell away. He jumped as hard as he could. Paul saw him reach out, in a final desperate attempt to grab Paul's outstretched hand, but he was simply too far away. He fell into the billowing clouds of smoke and debris and disappeared without making a sound.

Paul grabbed his son and held him close. He closed the door behind him and stared at the silent, sterile hallway of the House. He knew that they had been in someone else's judgment, but it was real. His daughter and Ari would never be coming back. He didn't care about the damn Ascension. The price he had just paid was way too high. It was time to find Anubis and put this nightmare to rest once and for all.

CHAPTER 40

In the House. Present day.

Brett aimed the gun at Amy. His hands were shaking and he looked like he could barely keep his eyes open. Greg knew that from this distance Brett couldn't possibly miss and instinctively stepped in front of his daughter.

"Don't do it, Brett," Greg said weakly. "Let us through and we can have Anubis heal you and grant you immortality. You need to consider what we're saying here. You don't look so good. My guess is you're holding on by a thread. Do you really think Horus will heal you and allow you to live forever after screwing up the one task he gave you?"

"Not true," Brett said slowly, his features contorted in pain. "Horus said the kids would be used to help transition Anubis' power to him, but that he could manage as long as Anubis did not succeed in his Ascension."

"Go ahead and believe that. These Gods are selfish and want what's best for them. We are nothing to them. They couldn't care if we live or die. But we can help you. All we want is to get out of this nightmare and go home. Let us through and we'll let Anubis know you switched sides."

Brett coughed heavily and spit a wad of bloody phlegm on the ground. "Nice try, ace. You must think I'm pretty stupid. You know, you don't look so good yourself. What I think is that first I'll kill you, then the kid, then your buddy back there."

The jungle around them began to flicker and shimmer. Off in the distance, trees appeared to be dissolving. The ground shook and the sky paled to a washed out version of what it was.

"What's going on?" Brett asked.

Greg grinned. "This little pocket of time is shutting down. Clearly Horus never told you what these places are and why they are here. Like I said, he never expected you to come back. You are merely collateral damage to him."

Using the last of his strength, Brett managed to get into a standing position. "Guess time is running out." He aimed the gun at Greg. "Nothing personal, pal."

The sharp crack of gunfire was heard and Brett fell forward. David walked up behind him and fired another shot into the back of his head.

"I couldn't let him kill us all," David said and dropped the gun. "I'm sorry, Greg. I don't think I can do this anymore."

Greg took his friend by the arm. "That's twice now that you've saved our lives. I'll try not to make it a habit going forward. Come on, guys, let's get the Hell out of here."

They opened the door and quickly stepped through into the House. The door closed silently behind them.

The House was silent. A dim light illuminated the long hallway. Doors like the one they had just exited lined the hallway as far as they could see.

"Do you have any idea on how to get back to the hall?" David asked.

Greg looked right and then left. Both hallways seemed exactly the same. "I'm honestly not sure. We'd better hurry, though. I suspect that we're running out of time."

The three walked down the hallway, passing door after door. Greg felt himself faltering.

"Are you okay?" David asked.

Greg shook his head. "I think that there's still some venom in my system. I'm hurting pretty bad. Let's keep moving. If I stop to rest, I might not get back up."

They kept walking, following myriad twists and turns until they finally arrived at the doors to the Great Hall. Greg pulled the doors open and walked right in, followed by Amy and then David.

"Greg," a voice called from across the room. Greg looked up to see his brother, Paul coming towards him with his son.

"Thank God you're here," Greg said. He saw the look of sorrow on his brother's face. "Paul…where's Beth?"

Paul's lower lip trembled slightly and he wiped away a tear. "One of Horus' toadies killed her. The miserable prick threw her off a building."

"My God…Did you…"

Paul cut his brother off, his voice as cold as steel. "I got the miserable prick. He won't be coming back."

"There's been too much death, Paul. We should have walked away. We still can."

Paul sighed. "When I got here, that was the only thing on my mind. Wait for you, then get the fuck out of here and try and rebuild our lives. But then I realized that this is bigger than us. Would you want your daughter to have a child born soulless? What kind of a world would we be leaving to our kids?"

"I guess we're in this to the very end, then."

Paul looked around. "Where's Oakster?"

"He's dead. He was gunned down trying to save Amy."

"You know it's funny, Greg. He did not want to come along on this journey. It's like he knew that he wasn't coming back."

"I know. He sacrificed himself so that we could live…so our children could live. Let's hope all of this is worth it."

The doors to the Great Hall slammed open and Anubis came striding in. He was in his natural state, showing his tall, bronzed form and fearsome jackal head. He was followed by two large, terrifying creatures with glistening fur. They moved like undulating sacks of boneless meat. The sheer sight of them made the men recoil and immediately move their children behind them for protection.

"I am here," Anubis said, his voice amplified and echoing in the vastness of the Great Hall. "It is time for the Ascension to begin."

"What are those things?" David asked, keeping a careful eye on the two creatures.

"Those are Ammit," Anubis began. "They are the Soul Eaters. They are here to bear witness to the Ascension."

Anubis walked over to Paul and gently eased him aside. He got down on one knee and put his hand below Mike's chin. Mike trembled but did not say a word as Anubis took his index finger and ran it down his cheek, the nail making a small cut. A single drop of blood welled up which Anubis let fall on his fingertip. He watched as the blood got absorbed into his finger, leaving it as it was before.

"He is not the one," Anubis said. "I saw what happened to his sibling. Let us hope she wasn't the one."

Paul balled his hands into fists. "Her name was Beth, you bastard."

Anubis walked past him, ignoring Paul as if he were no longer there. He walked past Greg and stood before Amy. He kneeled down and looked her in the eye. Drawing his index finger down her cheek, he watched as the nail drew a drop of blood. He caught the blood on his fingertip and waited while it was absorbed. If he felt any anxiety, he didn't show it.

Anubis stared at his finger and watched as it began to glow with a rich golden hue. He smiled.

"She is the one," Anubis said. "Come with me, girl. The Ascension must begin immediately."

"Hold on one minute," Greg said. He knelt before his daughter. "The thing is, honey, no one actually asked you what you want. You were taken by Anubis, and then held hostage by the two bad men. The reason is that you are special. Your ancestors were those who made sure that the world ran as it was supposed to and that every person who died was properly judged and that every person born would receive a soul."

Amy looked nervous. "What does the man want me to do?"

"Well, what he wants, or more accurately needs, is for you to take his place. He wants you to become a God like him."

Amy seemed to ponder the idea. "What does becoming a God mean?"

"It means, honey, that you would live for many, many years. You'd never get sick and would never really die. Your mom and I will be here with you always. The thing is, though, you would not be able to leave here. You would never see any of your friends again. I suspect that you wouldn't miss them after a while, either."

"And what happens if I decide that I don't want to be a God?"

Greg gave his daughter a big hug. "Well, for one thing, no one would ever get a soul when they were born."

"What does that mean, dad?"

"It means that their lives would be empty and meaningless. They would be like the walking dead. They would be unable to show love, compassion, kindness, and so much more. Imagine a world where everyone was cold and unfeeling like a machine. And for those who die, there would not be any judgment, so the dead would walk the earth forever.

"This is your choice, honey. I think you should take on the role of Anubis. You'd be saving the world."

Amy started crying. "I'm scared, daddy."

Greg hugged his daughter again. "I'll be with you forever, sweetheart. So will your mom."

Amy sniffed and wiped away her tears. "Okay, daddy, if you think I should, I'll do it."

"Are you sure?"

Amy gave a weak smile. "I guess."

"I need the girl," Anubis bellowed. "Bring her to me."

"We'll come when we're ready," Greg growled, "and not before."

Anubis seemed to soften somewhat. "Please. We do not have the luxury of time."

Greg walked with his daughter over to where Anubis stood before a large altar.

"Have the girl lie down on the altar," Anubis said.

Amy looked at her father. "Will it hurt?"

Greg turned to Anubis. "Will it?"

Anubis smiled. "No. It will be quite painless."

Amy climbed up on the altar and lay down on her back. Anubis started to chant. His bronzed skin began to faintly glow. Amy began to glow as well and soon was fast asleep. Anubis' chanting grew louder and echoed off the walls of the cavernous hall.

The air around them crackled with energy. All eyes were on Anubis and Amy. The Ascension had begun.

CHAPTER 41

In the House. Time of the Ascension.

Grace awoke. She shook her head to get the cobwebs out. She couldn't understand why she felt so groggy. She realized, with growing horror that she did not know where she was or even how she got there.

She stood up and found that her body hurt. The pain seemed to emanate from all over. She hoped that she wasn't coming down with the flu.

She wondered where Greg and Amy were. She hadn't seen them since they had left. After that, her memory seemed a bit less reliable.

She walked around the darkened room. She couldn't see more than a foot in front of her. Grace reached out and kept walking until her fingertips brushed a wall. She felt the cold, rough stone and kept her fingers lightly touching the wall as she worked her way around the perimeter of the room.

Grace soon came to a huge double door which opened up to a long hallway with dozens of identical doors stretching as far as the eye could see on either side. She didn't know where to go and was pondering her decision when she felt a sharp stabbing pain through her skull.

Mommy… I need you.

Grace fell to the ground clutching her head. She had heard her daughter calling to her. She sounded scared and alone and Grace felt helpless that she wasn't with her little girl to protect her. She began walking, pulled towards where she felt her daughter's presence. As she walked, she felt searing red-hot pain in her chest and stomach.

What is wrong with me, Grace wondered as she doubled over in agony. It took several minutes for the torment in her body to subside and she felt strong enough to continue on.

She walked for a very long time and the pains in her body were getting progressively worse. She had no idea where she was going as each hallway looked the same. If it weren't for being drawn towards her daughter, she would have felt hopelessly lost.

Grace soon came upon a large set of doors. She didn't know why, but she somehow felt that her daughter was in there and needed her. She pushed the doors open and saw, with horror, the scene unfolding before her.

The room was a large hall, with polished stone floors and rough stone walls. On the walls, spaced at regular intervals were lit torches which cast a flickering light over the entire room.

In the middle of the room was a large throne on a raised dais. The throne was empty. Sitting near the throne was one of Greg's friends, David Burke. Just beyond David was her husband, Greg. His back was to her as he watched what was taking place deeper in the room.

Grace silently entered the Great Hall. Her head was pounding and her stomach and chest were hurting more than ever. At the far end of the room was a large stone altar. Grace saw a tall, muscular man with bronzed skin and the head of a jackal conducting some kind of a ceremony. Flanking him on either side were the most horrific creatures Grace had ever seen. They were about six feet tall and thickly built. Both were entirely covered from top to bottom with thick fur. They had rudimentary arms and legs, a small, misshapen lump for a head and no visible facial features. Their fur seemed to be charged with electricity and glistened wetly in the dim light cast by the torches. The two creatures were swaying rhythmically to Anubis' chanting.

Grace's attention was drawn to the altar. On it, lying on her back, still as if drugged or dead, was her daughter Amy. Grace tried to call out to Amy but no sound would escape her throat.

She decided that the only way that she could get Amy's attention would be to go to her directly. She didn't want to get anywhere near the two creatures flanking Anubis, but she knew that she had to if she wanted to be with her daughter.

CHAPTER 42

In the House. Time of the Ascension.

Anubis stood naked in front of the altar, arms extended out rigidly as if he were impaled upon a cross. His bronze skin glowed with a pulsating golden hue. Small cracks began to appear across his body and, where the skin split, a brilliant golden light emanated, nearly blinding those around him.

Anubis looked down at the young girl as she lay motionless atop the stone altar. Her breathing was shallow and barely perceptible. Aside from the occasional movement behind her eyelids, there was barely any indication that the girl was still alive. Her father stood off to the side, clearly uncomfortable, and Anubis was sure that the father was weighing his options. Certainly the man had to be wondering if his decision to allow his daughter to fulfil her role in the Ascendance was the right one. Anubis sensed that the man was weighing whether he should simply grab her and go. Of all those who Anubis had dealt with in order to ensure the Ascendancy would occur, the father was the most astute. He knew Anubis was weakened and likely could not offer any resistance should he choose to change history. Yet the man stood his ground, and Anubis breathed a sigh of relief. The man clearly knew the repercussions if the Ascension did not take place. A lot of people had made the supreme sacrifice so that events could progress. A few more minutes and things would be as they should for another millennium.

To either side of Anubis stood Ammit, the Soul Eaters. To Greg, they looked like featureless stuffed animals, yet there was nothing warm and fuzzy about them. Their fur glistened wetly as they stood there undulating and swaying to a pulse that only they could hear. They were there to bear witness to the ritual and, after, to guide Anubis to the next phase of existence. Greg wouldn't admit it to anyone, but they scared the shit out of him. He had feared them in his dreams, and here, up close and in person, they were much more horrifying. There was an ancient nature about the creatures, and he sensed that their power exceeded even that of Anubis.

A figure emerged from the shadows and slowly made its way towards the altar. Anubis saw the figure approach and frowned. He quickly weighed his options. Was the person coming to interfere with the ceremony? If he stopped the ritual, there wouldn't be enough time to start over. There was only one chance to ensure things went as they were supposed to. He saw, with grave concern, that it was the girl's mother, Grace. *How did she get here?*

Greg noticed his wife approaching the altar. He wanted to rush over to her, but something held him back. How in the world did Grace know where to find him, let alone make the journey here to the House? He had made the journey with Anubis' help channeled through his friends. He doubted Anubis would have brought his wife here as well. If he had, it made no sense why Greg was only finding out about this right now. Had Anubis brought her as a back-up in case Greg failed in his task? Greg doubted this and while he was very happy to see his wife, he sensed that something was very wrong with her. She moved slowly and stiffly, as if her will was no longer her own. *Was she dead? Is that why she's in the House?*

Greg took a cautious step towards his wife who seemed oblivious to his presence. He saw his brother Paul head towards her as well. Paul looked concerned and Greg realized that he must be thinking the same thing. Greg looked around the Great Hall. David stood back near one of the walls quietly observing the ritual. Aside from that, there was no one else in observance.

"Grace?" Greg said softly as he advanced towards his wife. She ignored him and kept walking to the altar, arms extending out towards her daughter. Paul decided that something was not right with his brother's wife and rushed forward, grabbing Grace by the shoulder. She spun around and glared at Paul, her eyes a mix of yellows and reds, threaded by veins of black. She grabbed him by the ears and opened her mouth wider than she had any right to open it.

It looked as if her jaw unhinged and split her face wide open. Large black beetles poured out of her mouth and began leaping onto Paul. He screamed as they found purchase on his skin and began burrowing deep into his flesh.

Paul thrashed about, trying to free himself from Grace's vice-like grip. He hit her repeatedly in the face, yet she would not let go. The beetles still poured out of her open mouth, an endless stream of glistening black. Some landed on Paul and immediately began digging into his flesh. Others fell to the polished stone floor and began making their way towards Greg and the altar.

"Greg, help me," Paul screamed while trying to dislodge the beetles from his body.

Greg ran over, carefully avoiding the beetles, and grabbed his wife. She turned to glare at him and he recoiled in fear when he saw her eyes. Her normally soft brown eyes were red and yellow and tinged with black. There wasn't a trace of his wife in those eyes. She hissed and spit a stream of beetles in his direction. *This can't be Grace,* he told himself as he dodged the beetles. It might look like her, but whatever stood in his wife's skin was not her. "Grace, honey, it's me. It's Greg."

Grace showed no sign that she recognized her husband. She then released Paul who quickly scurried away and grabbed Greg by the throat with her left hand. She lifted him two feet off the ground then casually tossed him aside as if he were nothing more than a toy. He hit a nearby wall and felt the jarring impact.

Grace moved awkwardly over to her husband and stood over him, snarling menacingly. She grabbed the buttons off her powder blue dress shirt, ripped it open and pulled it off. Greg was horrified to see dozens of places where the something moved below the surface of her skin. She threw her head back and screamed as large black beetles burst forth, splitting her chest wide open. Grace seemed to shrink as an endless stream of the large black beetles poured out of her chest cavity, mouth and eyes.

Paul raced over to the wall and grabbed a torch. He pushed the flame to his skin, causing the beetles to sear and drop to the floor, twitching. He kept this up until he was sure they were off his body and then ran to where Grace was standing over her husband. He swung the torch like a club and connected squarely with her head.

Her head seemed to deflate and then she fell to the ground and was still.

The ground was covered in hundreds of the giant beetles so Paul used the torch to set them all ablaze. Before long, they were all dead. The space around them was thick with the noxious and oily, black smoke of the burnt beetles.

Greg winced in pain as he forced himself to stand and slowly worked his way over to his wife. He tried hard to avoid looking at her twisted form as he felt for a pulse. He couldn't find one. Her skin was dry and warm, and was starting to feel a little waxy.

"I'm sorry, Greg," Paul said. "I had no choice. She was trying to kill you. Besides, whatever that was, it wasn't Grace. It certainly wasn't her any longer."

Greg forced himself to look down at the ruined mess of his wife's corpse. He felt a coldness grip his heart but knew there would be time for grieving later. "I know. Something is very wrong here. We were helped here by Anubis to ensure that the Ascension took place. If Anubis wanted her help, I doubt that she would have been brought here without our knowledge. The only way that it makes sense that Grace would be here is if Horus himself brought her. But, according to what Anubis said yesterday, his brother cannot come to his realm without repercussions. So, while I could see him sending someone, why Grace? She never would have willingly helped him."

"I don't know." Paul looked at the hundreds of dead charred beetles. "Who knows what these beings can do? What do you suppose happened to her?"

"If I had to guess, Horus tried one last attempt to stop the Ascension." Greg looked sadly at his wife's twisted body. "He used Grace to do his dirty work, hoping she'd get close enough to stop the ceremony." He balled his hands in fists and looked over at Anubis who was still performing the ritual. "When this is done, I swear that if it takes eternity, I'll find a way to make Horus pay."

They turned to the altar. Anubis had fully shed his near-human guise and stood over Amy's prone figure which now was bathed in a golden hue. Around her features, like a shimmering corona, was the form of Anubis, still ephemeral but slowly merging with her own features. Her eyes were now open and, where they were once a greyish green, they now were golden, just as Anubis' had been.

Amy slowly rose up from the altar. Still in a trance, her figure now hovered a full foot above the altar and was slowly rising. Anubis placed his long, taloned-hands on her forehead and threw his head back and began to chant.

Greg moved closer. He was still fighting mixed emotions. His daughter was set to become a God, his wife was dead and her body lay at his feet, and he was looking at a lifetime of being trapped in the House, never to leave. He could still stop this and force Anubis to choose someone else. He didn't have any proof that Anubis was even telling the truth about what would happen if the Ascension did not go through. How did he know Anubis wasn't being selfish and using them as his way out of being stuck for another millennium judging the dead?

Greg knew in his heart that he couldn't stop the ceremony. He didn't care much for Anubis, but in his heart he knew that if the Ascension did not go through, then Horus would usurp this realm. Having the God of War controlling death was a potential nightmare of epic proportions. What scared Greg more than anything else was what Anubis had said about the Ascension and if it failed, the number of human souls would quickly expire, never to be replenished. With only a finite number of souls remaining, and no one to judge the dead, then no more material to create souls would ever be available. Newborns would come into the world without a soul. He knew that, as much as it pained him, they were doing the right thing.

Paul put his hand on Greg's shoulder. "It's been a miserable journey getting here, Greg. We've lost so much." Greg saw the tears in his brother's eyes. His brother had just witnessed the loss of his son, whereas he had lost his wife and his daughter was to be tied to this House for the next millennia, and he'd need to be here to help guide her as long as he lived. It was hardly a win for either family. In addition, his friend Kevin had given his life to save theirs. So, there was plenty of grief to go around. The only one unscathed seemed to be David who stood quietly in the shadows watching the Ascension take place.

"I'm sorry about your daughter, Paul." Greg gently said to his brother. "This all sucks but, in the end, we saved the world. Surely that has to count for something."

Paul wiped his tears and smiled. "Sure. We're fucking heroes. The world will go on, but our role in saving it won't even be known. If I had to choose, I'd rather have my daughter back."

"We'll get Horus, Paul. We'll make him pay."

Paul was just about to speak when he felt something slam into his back. He looked down and saw the shaft of a torch sticking out from his belly. He coughed and tried to speak, the blood welling up in his mouth. Paul looked pleadingly at his brother and reached out to him, clawing at the air and then at the shaft of wood sticking out of his body. His eyes rolled back in his head and he fell forward, dead before he hit the ground.

Greg whirled around and stared at the tall, muscular bronzed man with the head of a falcon. "So," Horus said in a shrill and mocking tone, "I hear you will make me pay." He threw his head back and laughed. "After I stop this abomination and assume control of the dead, I'll let you try. If I were you, though, I'd run, because when I'm done with my brother, I will tear you to shreds."

CHAPTER 43

In the House. Time of the Ascension.

Anubis continued the ritual. He was so close. He could feel the essence of what made him the God of the dead being transferred to the young girl. She was a strong one. He sensed greatness in her. He understood why she had been hidden from him. With Horus trying to usurp his powers and elevate his own Godhood, it seemed as if Fate were trying to ensure that everything went according to plan.

He watched with growing concern as the girl's mother came towards the altar. Of greater concern was how she had changed. He knew the eldritch magic that had changed her and realized with utmost clarity that Horus was not going to give up. When the girl's uncle slew her mother, he hoped that the threat was at an end. He could not stop the ritual. At this point, to stop would be cataclysmic. He would cease to be and there would be no one to rule over the land of the dead. Horus would be able to absorb the realm into his own and create a future of endless war, with millions doomed to live forever as soulless beings waging eternal battles.

He then saw Horus enter the Great Hall, grab a torch and approach the brothers. He wanted to call out, but to do so would have disrupted the ritual and lead to the girl's death and his dissolution. He had to complete the ritual, no matter what. He was nearing completion when he saw Horus slay the younger of the brothers. Horus must be growing desperate to dare take a chance of setting foot in his realm. If caught, judgment would be swift and merciless. For him to risk so much was proof of the God of War's insanity.

With his brother dead, Greg lost it and rushed Horus, slamming him into the wall and punching him repeatedly in the head. He was screaming and kept hitting the God, oblivious to the pain in his hands. Anubis had to appreciate the man's spirit. He would not hurt Horus, and his brother, when he tired of the man's futile attempts to stop him, would crush him like an insect.

Horus stood and threw Greg off and into the wall as if he were nothing. "Enough," he bellowed, "My patience is at an end." He looked at Greg, his liquid black eyes blazing "You would be best to stay where you lie. If you even attempt to stand, I will rip you apart for the sheer fun of it."

Horus strode over to where Anubis was performing the Ascension. He saw that the girl had nearly taken the spirit of Anubis into her own soul. His accursed brother was becoming ethereal and devoid of substance. He roared with fury. The ritual was nearly complete. He had been forced to deal with his weak brother for countless millennia. Now, he would have to deal with this child until his own time to ascend took place. It. Would. Not. Do.

Horus pulled a spear from a sling and readied to slay the girl. He would not allow his brother to ascend. This realm would belong to him.

Anubis watched in terror as Horus readied to slay the girl. He was helpless to stop him. He knew his brother had been plotting to take his realm, but he never would have guessed the lengths that Horus would go to ensure he got as he wished.

"Stop!" a loud, booming voice filled the Great Hall. All except Anubis stopped and looked at the newcomer who had entered the Great Hall. The being stood at over twelve feet tall and had ebony black skin. His eyes were crimson and blazed with fury. He looked as one would imagine an Egyptian pharaoh would, having a long plaited beard. He wore an Atef crown with two large ostrich feathers at either side. In his hands he carried a crook and flail. His legs were wrapped as a mummy's and this made him seem to glide across the floor. "Horus, you dare?"

Horus turned to the newcomer. "Father, this doesn't concern you," he roared with fury. "This is meant to be my realm. I deserve it after the millennia I had to endure dealing with my wretched brother."

The newcomer turned to his son and bellowed in rage, "This does not concern me? You dare, Horus? You know the rules. You cannot simply enter another's realm without consequence."

"Who gives you the right to pass judgment, father?" Horus screamed. "Anubis is ascending and I, as blood, should have been offered this realm."

Osiris looked sadly at his son. "So many millennia and yet you've learned nothing. And now I must administer judgment on you, my son."

Horus threw his head back and laughed. "You are weak, father. You are viewed as a kind and forgiving God by the humans. That weakness does not make you fit to rule."

Osiris shook his head. "What you call weakness is seen as strength to most, as is wisdom and compassion. Sadly, as the one who rules, I am forced to make judgments that are most painful." Osiris raised both his arms and from the shadows Ammit came forth. They shuddered and undulated as they moved rapidly towards Horus.

Horus' eyes grew wide and he watched in horror as the creatures approached him. "Father, please. Have mercy on me. After all, I am your son."

Osiris looked sadly at Horus and then turned his back on him. "I no longer have a son," he replied and then glided off into the shadows.

Horus looked at Ammit who stood on either side of him. Their fur glistened and smelled of rotting meat. He threw his spear at Ammit on his right. It struck the creature and penetrated deeply. Horus turned and tried to run in the opposite direction. Ammit, who stood on his left, was faster and moved directly in front of Horus, blocking his escape. Ammit widened and wrapped around Horus' arm. Horus screamed at the touch of the creature. He tried to pull his arm free but it was held firmly in place. He pulled harder and managed to get free. His arm, where Ammit had touched, was gone. All that remained were a few melted tendrils of flesh and bone. He turned again, hoping to flee while Ammit was distracted, only to run directly into the other Ammit. The spear that was embedded in Ammit was now used as a weapon against him and impaled him clean through.

Horus looked at the spear impaled through his chest with shock. He tried to pull it free from Ammit, but to no avail. Ammit seemed to grow wider and then split down the middle, exposing a gaping chasm of nothingness.

"Please," Horus begged, "Do not do this." He looked into Ammit's gaping maw at the endless oblivion and knew that his existence was coming to an end. His eyes widened in fear. After a millennium of near prescience, the thought of oblivion terrified the God. He struggled but Ammit's grip was too strong. The creature pulled him towards the yawning void of nothingness. His leg went through first and he saw the leg begin to unravel as it entered the void. The pain was unlike anything he had ever felt, even with millennia of war under his belt. It felt as if he were being torn apart at the molecular level.

Horus looked over at his brother who was just finishing the ritual. The girl now completely bore the Anubis form and his accursed brother, barely an outline, looked upwards and smiled a truly beatific smile before he disappeared. Horus bowed his head. All his plans had been for naught. His brother ascended, a new Anubis was in place and he would be torn apart and banished to oblivion for eternity. His will was finally broken. He stopped fighting and allowed Ammit to pull him in and then the pain really began.

Greg watched in horror as Ammit devoured the God Horus. He wondered what would happen with the God of War out of the picture. Would another be chosen in his place or would the world be spared of war for a time. He suspected the former. He turned to his darling daughter, relieved that she was finally safe.

"Amy?" Greg asked, "Can you hear me?"

Amy climbed down off the altar and stood before her father. While she still looked like his daughter, he saw that she had a shadow around her in the form of Anubis. She smiled and took her father's hand. "I am fine, father," she said, in her innocent child's voice, although Greg did hear the underlying layer of something, an older, deeper voice that was eerily reminiscent of Anubis'.

Amy looked over at David who still stood in the corner. She smiled and then she placed her hand on his forehead. "I remember some of what my predecessor thought," she said. "You must return home. You must tell the families of those who passed on here what truly happened. Your accident, which left you with gaps in your memory, was planned far before your birth because that accident would allow you to retain in the missing pockets of memory what happened here in the House. Once you have then passed on this information to the others, your mind will begin to heal. With time, your journey to this House will pass from your memories and you will be whole.

Amy then turned to her father. "Let's go to our new home. We've had a trying day and tomorrow will bring a lot of change. She then smiled, her golden eyes twinkling and said, "I love you, daddy." Together they walked out of the Great Hall and into the House itself, a house that was now hers.

EPILOGUE

David stood in front of the duplex on Banantyne Street in Lasalle. He had been there before, only a short while back, yet it seemed a lifetime ago. He took a deep breath and climbed the steps. His hand shook, a slight discernible tremor, as he rang the bell. The door buzzed and, with a sigh, he grasped the knob and pushed open the door.

David stepped into the foyer and peered up the stairs at the woman who stood there. She was slim and of medium height with short brown hair. She looked down at David with suspicion and then her eyes grew wide. "I know you," she exclaimed. "I saw you in my dreams. You're a friend of Kevin's." She said the last line as though it were a question. David heard the tentative tremor in her voice and the gentle hint of a French accent.

David put on his best smile. "That's right, Mrs. Oakster. My name is David Burke. May I come in?"

Leanne Oakster stepped back from the door and David slowly climbed the steep stairs to Kevin's second floor unit. He nodded at Leanne who motioned for him to sit on a couch in a small room directly across from the door.

"Can I get you something to drink? Would you like some coffee, perhaps?"

David smiled, but shook his head. He'd have loved a cup, but he honestly didn't want to be there and was hoping to say his piece and go. He was about to speak, but Leanne beat him to it.

"I saw Kevin in my dreams." Leanne stood and hugged herself. "The day after he left, I started having the dreams. He was with you, his old friend Greg, and Greg's brother Paul. It's funny, you know. You look just like I imagined you did in my dreams. Kevin always laughed when I said I was psychic, but the truth is, I've always been able to see things."

David leaned forward in his seat. He felt very awkward as Leanne kept staring at him intently. "Mrs. Oakster," David began, "what exactly did you dream?"

"Please. Call me Leanne. I've always thought of myself that way. Mrs. Oakster is way too formal." She stood and straightened her slacks. "I'm getting a coffee. I could really use one. You sure you don't want one?"

"Well," David paused. It had been a long day, after all. "I suppose one cup wouldn't hurt. And please, call me David."

Leanne turned and disappeared down the hallway. David heard her getting the coffees in the kitchen. He looked around the den and noted the pictures on the walls and on the furniture. Most were of Kevin, Leanne and their two daughters. In each picture, Kevin beamed as if he were the proudest man in the world. The pictures of Kevin so happy and so alive made David begin to regret his coming here. He had a role to play. It had been destined from before Greg had shown up at his door. He now understood that he was but a pawn in a much broader plan. How his TIA and subsequent memory loss was critical, allowing room for the memories of what happened in the House to be retained, so he could chronicle what had happened and be able to bring solace to those left behind.

Leanne returned carrying a small metal tray with two steaming cups of coffee on it. She handed one to David and placed the other on a coaster on the coffee table in front of her. David did likewise.

Leanne added a few spoonfuls of sugar into her cup and stirred it wistfully. David waited patiently for her to begin.

"I dreamed of Kevin the day he left," Leanne began. "He was with you in a dark house and you were with a man whose head was that of a dog or wolf." She paused to blow across the steaming liquid and then take a long sip. "The man with the dog's head in my dream needed something from you all. That's right. He needed you to find some children. They belonged to Greg and his brother. You know, David. I had that same dream every night that Kevin was away."

David shifted uncomfortably in his seat. He had found himself outside of Kevin's house immediately following the events in the House. He honestly had no idea how that had happened, yet he knew that he had one final task before he could go home, and that was to reach out to the families of those who were not coming back.

"I know that this sounds like an odd question, Leanne, but how long was that?"

"I dreamt of Kevin every night for two weeks. Last night's dream was different, though. I saw Kevin fighting some men in a kind of tunnel and then it all went black." Leanne paused and then looked David in the eye. "Kevin is dead, isn't he?"

The question caught David by surprise. He hadn't expected to be asked so bluntly. "Yes," he finally replied.

Leanne sat very rigidly. Her lower lip trembled slightly. "Were you there when Kevin died?"

"Yes, I was," David replied. He fidgeted in his seat. He hoped that he didn't look as uncomfortable as he felt.

Leanne grew silent. She stood up and walked from one length of the room to the other. "Did Kevin's death have meaning?" she asked, her voice clearly wavering.

"Leanne, let me say that Kevin went out as a hero. Not only did he save a child's life but, thanks to him, events that had been set in motion, events that would have destroyed everything we hold dear were stopped so things could return to normal."

Leanne turned to David and he saw the tears in her eyes. "Return to normal? While I am proud of my husband, how will things be normal for me? He had a family to take care of. Our lives won't ever be normal again, now will they? His daughters, though older, still need their father. I need my husband. Why did it have to be him who was taken? And why is it you who shows up at my door? Where is Kevin's friend Greg?"

David shook his head. He couldn't look her in the eyes. She was right. Sure, they had saved the world, but it was small solace to his family. There was so much he wanted to tell her, but some things were best never spoken of again. "I'm so sorry," David said softly. "For what it's worth, we all owe a debt of gratitude for the sacrifice Kevin and the others made. I know it doesn't bring him back, but if you ever need anything, please don't hesitate to reach out to me. I owe him my life, as well, and I'll always be grateful. Please understand, Greg is never coming home again and his brother is dead. I know it doesn't help any, but we all paid a huge price."

Leanne wiped a tear away. "Please leave, David. You've delivered your news, and it's time for you to go." She turned and walked back to the kitchen, leaving David standing there by himself. He wanted to call after her, to offer words of solace, but none came. He turned and walked down the steps, leaving Kevin's house behind him. He had one more stop in Vaughan, at Paul's house, and then he could go home. First, he had to find a place to rent a car. He missed his family and he was thankful he had one he could still return to.

Greg looked at his daughter on the throne. She really had acclimated to the position in such a short time. He supposed it was for the best. His role as advisor was hardly necessary, but it did allow him to be with his daughter, and there were some perks to the role, as well. Near immortality was one, he supposed. Plus, while she was more than just a nine year old girl now, she still could use guidance from her parents. Seeing as how her mother was dead, he was all she had in the world.

Greg left the throne room and walked out into the House. He turned left and came to a wall that seemed to waver before him. He extended his hand and a glowing door appeared. He grasped the golden door knob and felt it tingle beneath his fingers. The door swung easily inward, revealing a hallway that was very different from the other hallways in the House. This one was less austere, and felt more like home. In fact, for all intents and purposes, it was home. He made his residence in this area of the house. He had his own home virtually duplicated here, with a den and kitchen and bedroom that were exact copies of his own home in Windham, New Hampshire. Of course, he would never see his old home again so, while it left him with some sense of familiarity, he knew this reality was but an illusion.

There were many days that he sat alone in the den watching television that he really missed his family. He understood the price they had all paid, but he wondered if Amy wouldn't have been better with him being dead and his mother whiling her time away in a mockery of the life that had once been real. It was easy to become maudlin in the House. Of course, the refrigerator was always full with whatever he wished, so getting beer wasn't an issue. There was a time where he might have wondered about how the food was replenished, or even how there was television in the House, but no longer. He went through the motions each day until the days blurred together.

There were some extra rooms, though, in this special wing of the House. He passed through his own personal living space and came to the extended hallway. He walked to the first door and paused. It always took a piece out of his soul coming here yet, he knew that for all the pain it brought, it also brought a measure of peace as well.

Greg opened the door and peered inside. He saw his brother, Paul playing in the yard of his home in Vaughan, Ontario with his two children, throwing a ball and running and laughing as they played. His wife was on the deck, tending to some steaks on the grill. The sun was shining, the sky overhead was a bright blue and the temperature was in the low eighties.

Greg smiled. He knew that his daughter would eventually have to offer judgment on Paul but, until she did, he could certainly spend millennia enjoying a perfect time in his life with his family where he was at his happiest. He didn't know that his wife and son were back in the world living their lives, missing him each day. Hi daughter, of course, was lost, killed in a vicious gesture that Greg would never forget. While he was thankful he didn't have to witness that heinous act, his brother had and it was with him until the moment he died. Thankfully, here, in his extended judgment, he would have no memories of the horrors that he had endured in his last days of life.

One day in the future, when it became his wife's time to pass through the House, he would ask his daughter to ensure that she joined Paul in his judgment until their son could join them years later. Then, she could have them all go through judgment together so they could pass on as a family. It was a small price to pay for his role in helping to save the world.

Greg smiled and closed the door. He walked down the hall and stood before another door. He opened it and peered inside. He saw Kevin at his desk on his computer watching a movie. His daughters ran into his room and crowded him, asking for money and whether they could have time on the computer, too. He shooed them away and secretly smiled. His kids were his pride and joy and, while he always pretended that they bothered him, he knew that nothing was further from the truth.

He called out to his wife to bring him a beer. Leanne came in with a cold Molson Export, handing him the frosty bottle, and patted her husband on his back before heading back out. Kevin returned to his movie, a big grin etched across his features.

Like Paul, Greg ensured that Kevin would get special treatment in the House and that his judgment would be put off until his family could join him and that they could move on together. In the interim, he'd be undergoing his own special extended judgment like Paul, and relive pleasant moments from his life.

He walked back to his own personal residence. He saw Grace sitting at the kitchen table. She was sitting there quietly and Greg suspected that she was just having another bad day. Amy had been able to summon a mix of magic and draw energies from herself to bring Grace back to life. It might have been the extent of the damage done by Horus or simply a matter of her own inexperience, but while Amy was able to bring Grace back to life, she wasn't fully able to undo the damage done by the scarabs. Some days, she showed perfect lucidity whereas, others, she wasn't even aware of her own name. Greg hoped that one day she would regain full use of her faculties. Until then, she was kept safe and cared for. He sighed. It was a rough route to take, but he knew that at least he could sleep easy knowing that they had saved the world from Horus' twisted scheme.

The man stood in the shadows beneath the balcony of an aging duplex. He saw the people milling about on the crowded street, yet he dared not move. The heat emanating from their bodies nearly drove him to action, but some inner will kept him restrained. It was more than a hunger. It was a primal need and was growing stronger. The man had lost sentience long ago, and was now driven on by pure instinct. He knew that there were too many out there to be able to safely move about, but if he only waited, the opportunity would surely come.

Earlier, he and the girl had sought refuge from the crowds. As she was rapidly becoming less lucid, she helped them find a place where they would be safe when their ability to reason failed. There, they could rest and be safe until it got dark and they would be able to escape. At the place, they found two others who glowed with brilliant light and heat. The man and girl could not contain their need and attacked and ferociously tore the older couple apart to get their still beating hearts. As they took their essence and absorbed their souls, the world around them came back into clarity and began to make sense. The girl howled in grief as she remembered what they had done to her parents and was sickened to look at their mutilated bodies after the feed.

There is so much blood in the body, the girl thought.

The man knew that the hearts only gave them their memories and humanity for a short while. The souls of the living provided only momentary respite against the cold emptiness of their soulless existence, but the temptation was too strong to resist. And while the souls burned bright in the living, it got used up fast in the soulless dead.

"I'm so sorry," Claudius said softly to the girl Mary who sat by her dead parents, silently weeping. His chest itched where the skin had closed over the father's heart. He knew that Mary had taken the mother's.

Claudius estimated that they had perhaps an hour or so before their bodies burned out the souls they had stolen from Mary's parents. He knew it hardly seemed fair, stealing the rest of their lives for an hour of humanity, but it was beyond his control. Their need was so powerful that he couldn't stop it even if he had the will to do so.

There were times that Claudius prayed to be caught and simply wished he could take his own life, but it wasn't to be. The need for the warmth of the living, to absorb the soul of another was too strong, too powerful, that it was all that drove them.

After about an hour, Mary and Claudius felt themselves start to lose their cognitive abilities.

Claudius put his hand on Mary's shoulder. "We can still find our way to the road between life and death before we do any more damage to the people of your town."

Mary looked au at Claudius, her eyes slowly glazing over. "No. The heat from the living is too strong a pull. Knowing we can have it, even for a short while, makes it too hard to give up. Besides," she said with a sneer, "there were many people who made my life a living hell. I intend to get payback on them all. You owe me, Claudius. You made me like this. This is all your fault."

From the corner of the room, Mary's parents began to stir.

With her intellect rapidly fading, along with the heat from the soul she had stolen from her mother, Mary turned to Claudius and said, "The folks are up and I'm getting hungry. Let's go get some."

Claudius nodded, not sure why. He looked at Mary and her parents and realized that while they looked familiar, he did not know them. It was clear that neither of them knew him either.

They all turned as one and left the house, moving out to the street to find more souls so that they could stave off the darkness and bask in the welcome light of life.

ABOUT THE AUTHOR

GORDON ANTHONY BEAN was born in Laval, Quebec but now lives and works in New England. He is married with one daughter. He has published the short stories 'From a Whisper to a Dream' in the *Sinister Landscapes* anthology, 'Out of the Corner of His Eye' in the *From Beyond the Grave* anthology and 'Knob Lake' in the *Forgotten Places* anthology. His debut novel, *Dawn of Broken Glass*, was released in 2013 by Guardian of Forever Publishing. *Bloodlines* is his second novel. He is also releasing the short story collection *Down the Dark Path*, also by Guardian of Forever Publishing, in late 2015. He is hard at work on his third novel, *Shadowspawn,* due out in 2016. He is also a member of the New England Horror Writers Association.